TRUTH IN HIDING

Also by M. M. Frick

OPEN SOURCE
THE COMPLICITY DOCTRINE

TRUTH IN HIDING

M. M. FRICK

MATTHEW M. FRICK

ST. JOHNS, FLORIDA

Truth in Hiding
M. M. Frick

This book is a work of fiction. The names, characters, places, and incidents are the product of the author's imagination or are used fictitiously. Any resemblance to actual events, locales, or persons, living or dead, is coincidental.

Library of Congress Control Number: 2016908687
CreateSpace Independent Publishing Platform, North Charleston, SC

ISBN-10 153336026X
ISBN-13 978-1533360267

Published by CreateSpace Independent Publishing Platform
Printed in the United States of America

*For Janelle, Jade, and Gavin
(and Juno)*

TRUTH IN HIDING

I am a firm believer in the people. If given the truth, they can be depended upon to meet any national crisis. The great point is to bring them the real facts.

-Abraham Lincoln

Chapter 1

Dasht-e Kavir, Semnan Province, Iran

A solitary bird darted among the wilting shrubs, its nimble legs a blur as it navigated the arid terrain. It was January, and the dark-stemmed mugwort that pocked this portion of the Great Salt Desert were not yet in bloom, leaving little to mask the bird's movements. Despite the ground jay's nervous flitting, it was anything but nervous. The only living things around bigger than the bird were two stationary figures five hundred meters from the lone dirt road that dissected the north and south horizons, but the bird discounted them as predators. They had been there for two days, and the bird was still alive.

The bird was right to ignore the men. They were not interested in the desert's sparse indigenous wildlife. They were interested in something entirely different.

Babak Abed checked his watch for the tenth time in seven minutes. He scanned the open desert in front of him and turned to the man crouched low beside him. "Is it ready?" he asked.

Hafez Madani verified the power indicator was still lit, and the sampling syringes were still secure. "It is ready," he said. Hafez wiped the sweat from his forehead with a dirty rag, thankful it was not August, and the temperature was only 22° Celsius. "How will we know when it happens?" he asked.

"We will know," Babak assured him. He looked at his watch again. Babak Abed's outward confidence masked his internal anxiety. He wasn't lying to Hafez when he said they would know. He'd been briefed on as much many times before he and his fellow MeK fighter took the long drive from Kashan. But he was nervous about what would happen after.

At first, the mission Babak was given sounded easy enough—take a portable atmospheric sampler to the Dasht-e Kavir on a specified date and wait. After he was told what the machine was for, he began to have his doubts. Babak and Hafez were recruited to collect radiation samples during Iran's first underground nuclear weapons test. Babak wasn't sure if intentionally exposing himself to radiation was such a good idea, but his Mujahideen-e Khalq commander insisted the data he would collect was vital to proving to the world that the Islamic Republic of Iran had finally crossed the line. Just as MeK was the first to break the news to the international community about Iran's nuclear program in 2002, MeK would be the first to inform them their economic sanctions, soft-handed reprimands, and endless negotiations, did nothing to keep the mullahs from building the bomb.

Babak checked his watch again. *Any minute now*, he thought. *If our source is right, that is.* He stared across the road, wondering if there would be any visible sign of detonation. In any case, they would be packing up and starting the twenty-kilometer hike back to their "abandoned" vehicle as soon as the sun went down.

"Babak, look," Hafez said, pointing toward the brush just south of their position.

Babak followed Hafez's outstretched hand and saw a small bird batting its wings furiously as it flew low to the ground. "Soose' le'ng," he said, amused that his young comrade was biding his time bird-watching, especially because the Pleske's ground jay was the only bird they'd seen in two days.

"I know," Hafez said. "But they don't fly, they run."

Babak Abed only had two seconds to process the statement when the earth rumbled violently beneath them. He and Hafez both grabbed the radionuclide sampler to keep it steady. They looked directly at each other, and Babak allowed a nervous grin to form, hoping the gesture would calm his companion. But the grin slowly disappeared as the gravity of what they just witnessed set in. *The game just changed.*

Chapter 2

Doha, Qatar

"This is a great day for Iran, and one the world will not soon forget."

Around the table, all heads nodded in agreement as hushed thanks to Allah and praise for the Supreme Leader filled the room. Dr. Fereydoon Abbasi-Davani, head of the Atomic Energy Organization of Iran stepped away from the table, exchanging handshakes and kisses as he made his way to the door.

The news he brought was no surprise to the men and women in the room—each had played a part in funding it—but the success of Iran's first nuclear weapons test was still comforting to hear. Coming from Abbasi, one of the main architects of Iran's nuclear weapons program, made the words that much sweeter. If things had gone differently just four years earlier, Abbasi would not have been able to relay the test's success to the group of Iranian business elite. He would not have been able to do much of anything at all, because he would have been dead.

The visit that night was brief by design. Abbasi had planned to address the group during a break in the hectic schedule of the World Economic Forum, and he was not able to enjoy the Indian cuisine of Souq Waqif's famous "Royal Tandoor"—though the smell of taza kadai khumb and kheema mutter made him wish he had more time. For reasons everyone in the room understood, Abbasi's assigned escorts were keeping him on the move until he flew back to Tehran in the morning. The fifty-six-year-old scientist didn't argue, following the men to the two black BMWs waiting outside.

"How long to the hotel?" Abbasi asked when his driver pulled onto the northbound road that followed the corniche around Doha Bay.

The driver quickly glanced at Abbasi's shadowed reflection in the rearview mirror. "Twenty minutes," he said.

Two kilometers away, a pair of motorcycles headed east on Mohammed bin Thani Street, past the fire station. The black-clad riders ignored the traffic to and from the Ministry of Defence buildings on their right. They were on a time schedule

Abbasi peered listlessly out the window at the black waters of Doha Bay. The lights from Old Palm Trees Island and the sparse boat traffic did little to break the darkness, the waxing quarter moon having disappeared below the horizon almost half an hour earlier.

He couldn't wait to get home. His trip to Qatar was not part of his normal duties as one of Iran's twelve vice presidents. For all he was concerned, the people in that room could have heard the news of the successful nuclear test on Al Jazeera or BBC, like the rest of the world. But he did it as a favor to Ayatollah Khamenei—as if he had a choice to refuse the Supreme Leader's *request*. Apparently one of the men at the Indian restaurant was a cousin, or something.

Abbasi sighed as the car slowed in response to the bright red tail lights ahead that flooded the cabin of his own car with their annoying glow. "Was this factored into your twenty minutes?" Abbasi asked the driver. He saw the driver's eyes glance briefly at him in the mirror. "Never mind," he added. "Don't answer that."

At least my flight is not until morning, he thought and closed his eyes.

The motorcycles turned onto the corniche road in single file, moving deftly between the lanes of traffic. The rear rider opened the distance between them to twenty meters before matching speeds again. The cars around them began braking, but the riders moved on.

The slam of a car door and horns from irritated drivers startled Abbasi, and he sat upright. *Where in the hell is he going?* Abbasi thought with more than a little worry as he watched his driver on the street beside the car. His worry grew exponentially when he saw the man leveling a rifle and aiming behind them.

Abbasi rolled onto the floor of the car at the first rifle crack. The first was followed by another and another. The sound of each shot seemed farther away as the rifleman-driver made his way into the traffic behind the car.

The rear motorcyclist squeezed the hand brake hard when the front rider went down—too hard it turned out. The bike flipped, and its rider landed on the hood of a beige Toyota pick-up. He continued the slide onto the street and subconsciously felt for the messenger bag over his shoulder. Crouching low, he made his way between the other two lanes of traffic, still heading for the target, but out of the line of fire.

Ten meters into his foot pursuit, a bullet struck the rear window of a car to the motorcycle-less rider's left. *How the fuck?* he thought as a second round pierced his back just between the shoulder blades.

He was dead before he hit the ground.

"Are you okay?" a voice asked after the car door opened.

Abbasi looked up and saw the familiar face of his driver. "Yes, yes, I'm not hurt," he said as the driver helped him out of the car. Two other men approached the pair from behind the car. Abbasi recognized them as his government-assigned escorts. *They must have been following us*, he thought. He watched the escorts while he asked his driver, "What the hell just happened?"

"*This* happened," one of the escorts said, holding up two identical satchels. "Mossad," he added. "Motorcycles and magnet bombs."

Abbasi shuddered, remembering that day in Tehran four years ago when the Zionist terrorists blew apart his parked car only seconds after he shoved his wife out the passenger door. A man on a motorcycle sped by that November morning, and only his earlier training in the Islamic Revolutionary Guard Corps taught him to recognize the sound of a heavy magnet on the side of the car, giving him just enough time.

"You are certain it was Mossad?" Abbasi asked, looking past his own men to try and see his failed attackers.

"We knew they would be coming," the man with the unused bombs said. "We just didn't know how many."

Abbasi's jaw tightened. "You *knew* they were coming? And you didn't think that might be something I should know?" he yelled above the horns of increasingly frustrated drivers. The sound of approaching sirens added to the noise and reminded the men they were on foreign soil. Trying to explain away the two dead bodies in the middle of the corniche road would not be easy, if it was possible at all.

"We should leave," Abbasi's driver said. No other words were spoken as the four men returned to their vehicles and continued down the road as if nothing had happened.

Chapter 3

New York City

Casey gently touched the monument and looked up to the top of the black marble obelisk twenty feet above. Inscribed in the tiered base below were sixty-three names. Names of the innocent victims of the Manhattan bombings that ripped through the city less than four years earlier. Located in the south courtyard of the massive 9/11 Memorial, finished in earnest after the July 2011 attacks, the lesser bombing monument stood in silent contrast to the perpetual waterfalls commemorating the loss of nearly three thousand people when a group of committed radicals led by Osama bin Laden brought down the towering symbols of America's economic might with two passenger jets on the morning of September 11, 2001.

The official blame for the 2011 bombings was pinned on Houthi rebels from Yemen, but Casey knew that was a lie. His hand found the name of Mariam Fahda, and the scenes from that morning at Soren's Deli came flooding back into his consciousness. It wasn't that he tried to repress those memories, but what followed as a result of the bombing altered his own perception of the world around him, and his life changed course because of it. Casey Shenk, the vending machine stocker-turned geopolitical analyst, was less sure about the line between good and evil. He was more cynical of people's true intentions, while at the same time more cogizant of others' feelings. And while Casey's name was not on the monument in front of him, it could have been—more and more he thought it should have been and wondered why it wasn't.

Casey rounded the stone memorial and pulled short, almost knocking down a twelve-year-old boy. "Geez, you startled me," Casey said, purposely keeping his usual, salty vernacular in check in the presence of the minor. "I thought I was the only one here this early." Casey did a quick look around, but there was no sign of an adult to whom the kid belonged.

"It's okay," the boy said. "Spies are quiet. I wouldn't expect you to hear me coming."

Casey smiled. "Spy, huh?" He looked at the boy—green winter coat, blue jeans, and an Avengers backpack. *Probably on his way to school,* he thought. "So who are you spying on?"

The boy never once looked at Casey. He focused, instead, on the folded newspaper in his left hand. "I'm not spying on anyone," the boy said. "It's a dead drop."

"A dead drop."

This time the kid looked up. "A dead drop," he repeated. "It's tradecraft." He turned back to his paper.

Casey laughed, amused by the boy's vocabulary and stone cold seriousness. "I know what it is," he said. He looked closer at the newspaper the boy was busy marking up with a ballpoint pen. "You leaving a coded message for another spy?"

The boy ignored Casey and worked faster. He underlined whole words, single letters, and random numbers. At least, they seemed random to Casey. The boy's concentration belied that assumption and indicated a definite purpose to his actions.

"Stephen!"

Now Casey understood the boy's urgency.

"You can't just wander off like that," a woman scolded as she rapidly approached from Casey's right.

"It's Wednesday," Stephen told the woman. "I had to get the message to him."

"But you need to let me know where you're going before you just take off like that."

"I'm sorry, Mom."

Stephen's mom relaxed and ran her fingers through her hair. "I know it's Wednesday, and I'm sorry for being so frantic. But next time, please wait for me." She put her hand on her son's shoulder and said softly, "You're all I've got left." Stephen continued his work as his mother looked over at Casey, noticing him standing there for the first time.

"Howdy," Casey said with a half-grin in response to the woman's glare. He felt as if *he'd* just been reprimanded. The woman looked back to her son, and Casey turned to leave.

"His father."

Casey halted his retreat and turned back around. The woman was looking over Stephen's head at the monument, and Casey wasn't sure if she was talking to him or not. "Excuse me?"

"He's leaving a message for his father." The woman turned her head to look at Casey. "He was at St. Pat's that morning. When the bomb... when the explosion happened."

Casey looked at Stephen, then back at Stephen's mother. "I'm sorry," he said.

"He wasn't even supposed to be there," the woman continued. "He stopped in on his way to work to light a candle for his mother. She lost her fight with cancer a week later. Stephen's father used to write coded messages for Stephen and leave them on the breakfast table every Wednesday morning. It was their secret game, and ever since the bombing, Stephen's been leaving these messages for his father. Every Wednesday. When they built this memorial, Stephen insisted that he leave the messages here. It's a lot closer than the cemetery."

"I see," Casey said. He didn't ask to hear the story. But for some reason, people always felt comfortable telling Casey everything about their lives. He didn't know why, and many times, like just then, he wasn't sure he wanted to hear them. But Casey was too polite by nature to push people away—so he listened.

"Okay, Mom," Stephen said bringing both his mother and Casey back to the present. "We don't want to be late for school."

Stephen's mom smiled and mussed the boy's hair. "Alright honey, let's go." She smiled at Casey as mother and son made their way out of the park.

No good bye. Casey was glad for that. He looked back at the monument and shook his head, smiling. The folded newspaper with the underlined "codes" sat at the base of the marble structure. A message from son to father, that only they could decipher. He looked back to the top one more time before leaving.

Casey wondered if the message got through.

Chapter 4

Hump day. Casey hated that phrase. The idea was that if you got past the middle of the work week, Thursday and Friday would be smooth sailing—an easy slide into the weekend. *Bullshit*, he thought. Ever since Casey entered the ranks of the full-time employed, first as an Engineman in the United States Navy, then as a vending route driver in Savannah, Georgia, Wednesday was generally a day to reflect on what he failed to accomplish during the first two days of the week and a chance to stress himself out about what he still had to get done before Saturday.

Now that he was an analyst for the private geopolitical consulting firm Intelligence Watch Group, Wednesday also meant he owed his boss a mid-week progress report on whatever assignment he was currently working on. Others in the Middle East/Southwest Asia cell dreaded these meetings, but Casey looked at them as a chance to get help from others in the room without actually asking for help. He wasn't above asking for assistance when he needed it, but if he wasn't aware that he needed help, he couldn't ask. The meetings offered his co-workers the chance to voice their own opinions about where he was going on a project and possibly offer a little course correction or constructive criticism. At least, most of the criticism was constructive.

"That's the stupidest thing I've ever heard."

Casey leaned back and took a deep breath, turning his pen over in his hand as he shot a menacing look at the man across the table. "Then tell me what *you* think it means, Oscar."

Heads turned to Oscar Horstein, IWG's Israel analyst, waiting for an answer—some were actually curious, others just wanted the meeting to end. "I think it means they don't have any more money to throw around," Oscar said. "The economic sanctions imposed by the U.S. and UN are choking Iran."

"That's the easy answer," Casey said.

"Because it's the right one."

"Look, Oscar," Casey said, "I'm not saying the sanctions aren't hurting Iran, I'm just saying they're not hurting Iran that bad. And they're damn sure not tough enough to keep Iran from building the bomb."

"That's not even the same argument." Oscar pointed his index finger accusatorily. "You said Iran stopped overtly supporting Assad because they've made enough progress on a nuclear weapon that they don't need Syria anymore." Oscar retracted his hand and sat back. "Where's your evidence, Casey? Do you have any?"

Casey was silent and didn't take his eyes off Oscar. After a silent five-count for effect, he said, "No."

"Amateur," Oscar said under his breath but loud enough for everyone listening to hear.

"Columbus wasn't a hundred percent sure the Earth was round, either," Casey said, "yet, here you are." That brought cautious laughter from many and a more vocal response from George Smithfield.

"Here you are," George repeated from the seat to Oscar's left. He added a playful shove and got an irritated glare in return.

The verbal jousting came to a sudden halt as Susan Williams

entered the room, followed by Jim Shelton, the head of IWG's Middle East/Southwest Asia cell. Susan sat down in the empty chair next to Casey while Jim closed the door. "I apologize for making you all wait," Jim said as he sat down, "but we just learned some news that will affect everything we're doing. Susan," he said, nodding to his lead Iran analyst.

Susan looked briefly at her co-workers and announced, "Yesterday, the Islamic Republic of Iran conducted an underground nuclear test that our sources estimate was somewhere in the range of seven kilotons."

There was a brief moment of silence around the table—not out of respect for anyone, but because people didn't know what to make of the news. Casey was the first one to say anything when he smiled at Oscar Horstein and said, "Told ya."

Oscar tried his best to ignore the comment. He looked directly at Susan and asked, "How could that happen? I mean, how could the U.S. let that happen?"

"I don't think anyone *let* it happen, Oscar," Susan said.

Oscar shook his head and tugged his nicktie loose as if preparing for a long night at the office, though it was only nine-thirty in the morning. "What about that Stuxnet worm? Wasn't that thing in place to strike again when we needed it to?" Oscar asked.

"That was just to slow them down," George Smithfield, the company's other Iran analyst, commented.

"And it was deployed at Natanz," Casey added. "As far as anyone knows, there wasn't any cyberattack on Fordow, so in reality, Olympic Games didn't do shit to stop them from moving forward." He turned to his left to give Susan a chance to talk.

When she saw Casey was done, Susan said, "Look, guys, it's not our job to be pointing fingers and wondering who knew what and when. I'm sure Congress will be doing that soon enough. All we know right now is that a test occurred somewhere in the Dasht-e Kavir, also called Kavir-e Namak or 'Great Salt Desert,' about 250 miles east of Tehran based on GSN readings reported from Albuquerque."

"G-S-N?" the India analyst, Leslie Meyers, asked.

"The Global Seismic Network," Jim Shelton answered. "U.S. and international stations all around the globe feed into a network to monitor earthquakes, or in this case, underground nuclear detonations."

"But how do we know it was nuclear?" Oscar asked. "Maybe it *was* just an earthquake."

Susan and Jim exchanged looks before Jim said, "One of our sources reported PMOI was able to obtain atmospheric readings from the site that indicated signature levels of xenon isotopes consistent with a nuclear detonation."

Casey smirked at the mention of the People's Mujahideen of Iran. Almost four years earlier he argued, with varying degrees of success, that the United States was involved in a clandestine proxy war with Iran. Casey opined that congressional efforts to have PMOI removed from the State Department's list of Foreign Terrorist Organizations was evidence the U.S. was maneuvering to provide funding and support to groups like PMOI's militant arm, the Mujahideen e-Khalq, and by association, the Iranian Baloch resistance group Jondallah. More tenuous, but potentially more damning, Casey also accused members of Washington's power structure of orchestrating the Manhattan bombings that killed scores of people, including Susan's college roommate, Mariam Fahda, as part of the most despicable element of what Casey termed "The Complicity Doctrine." Conspiracy theory or not, PMOI's de-listing and subsequent intelligence gathering activity seemed to back up Casey's ideas—some of them at least.

"What does that mean?" George asked Jim.

"It means the end of Israel," Oscar answered quickly, blankly staring at the center of the conference room table.

"No it doesn't," Susan said.

"Not if they don't do anything stupid," Casey added.

"Okay, everyone. Let's just slow down for a minute," Jim said, trying to take control of the conversation early and turn it into a meaningful discussion before it reverted to a shouting match. He looked at Oscar and said, "This one test doesn't mean Iran's busy mounting a warhead to a Shahab-3 right now. But it does change the calculus quite a bit." He broadened his attention to the other people around the table and said, "Our job is to figure out just how much this changes things, so I want to hear your ideas." Questioning looks were exchanged around the table, but no one jumped at the chance to be the first to speak. "We're just brainstorming here, people," Jim added.

Oscar finally looked up from the table and said, "I think this changes everything."

"How so?" Jim asked.

"Well, for one, it shows the West's response to Iranian threats didn't work," Oscar said. "As much as I hate to say it, Casey was right."

"But how does that change things?" Jim pressed.

"All options are on the table," Oscar said, echoing the president of the United States' own words.

"That's just political hot air," Susan said. "There's no way our country is sending troops into Iran."

"What about bombing them?" George asked.

"Israel already tried that, remember?" Susan said.

"Not *nuclear* bombs," Casey said. There was silence in the room

as people let Casey's words sink in. Casey saw the looks on his colleagues' faces and said, "C'mon, man, everybody knows Israel has
nuclear weapons. A few tactical nukes on the right targets just might
get the job done—not that I'm advocating that course of action. The
question is, would they actually go that far?"

"I don't know, would they?" Jim asked, putting the question back
on Casey.

"With Likud in power?" Casey asked. "I'd say there's a good chance
Netanyahu gives the order."

Jim Shelton looked at his Israel expert and prodded him for a
response. "Oscar?"

Oscar shook his head. "No, I don't think they'd go that far. But
I think the threat from Iran is now real enough that Israel may go
public about their own capabilities—maybe try to bring back a little
bit of the Cold War?"

"It's not the same," Bill Meyers, the Pakistan analyst and husband
of Leslie chimed in. "One test doesn't exactly make *mutual assured
destruction* a sound reason for an arms race like we saw between the
Soviet Union and the United States."

"It's not even on the same level as the perpetual stand-off between
India and Pakistan," Mrs. Meyers added. "Both of those countries have
warheads mounted and ready to launch. And it took them years after
initial testing to get to that point."

"Oscar makes a good point, though," Casey said. "If Israel comes
out and tells the world they have their own nuclear missiles, and they're
not afraid to use them, just watch the number of rocket, suicide, and
IED attacks go through the roof. An announcement like that will
threaten all kinds of folks—even if it's only meant for Iran."

"So not really a *cold* war, then," Bill Meyers said.

"Not in the MAD sense," Casey agreed, "but the threats and proxy wars will definitely be kicked up a notch."

"Alright, but how is that any different than if Israel doesn't admit what the world already believes is true?" Leslie asked.

"Because much of the Arab world doesn't believe it, that's why," Susan said. "They are so used to being lied to by their own governments that they question anything they hear from the state-run media. So unless they see Netanyahu making a declaration of Israel's nuclear capability on CNN, BBC, or some other illegally-obtained Western news source, they're going to ignore it."

"Let me frame the question in a different way," Jim said, drawing everyone's attention. "What are the short-term impacts of Iran's nuclear test, and what are the long-term effects? Casey, you said that we'll most likely see an increase in violence around the region if Israel publicly announces their own capabilities, and I have to agree with you there. But Leslie brought up a good counter-point, whether she meant to or not. What if Israel keeps quiet about their own nuclear arsenal? We still have Iran's newly emerging nuclear capabilities to deal with. How is this going to affect our clients in the next few weeks or months?"

The room was quiet as everyone contemplated how to answer the question. IWG's clients included international businesses, the U.S. government, and private individuals—each one with a different stake in the game of world geopolitics.

"Economically, I don't think there's gonna be a big impact," Casey said. "Well, maybe the stock markets might take a hit, the way those folks freak out about stuff. But Iran's so damn isolated as it is, because of the sanctions," Casey added, glancing at Oscar, "there really shouldn't be a big change from business as usual."

"What business?" Oscar asked.

"Exactly," Casey said.

"What about militarily?" Jim asked, looking around the table and hoping one of his other analysts might decide to join the conversation.

"Nothing from the West," George obliged. "If we've already counted out the U.S. or Israel doing anything, I think the best chance for a military reaction is going to come from Saudi Arabia, or maybe Egypt."

"But only if it's part of a larger GCC response," Susan said. "And the likelihood of the Gulf Cooperation Council mustering the forces to attack Iran on any scale is next to nil. They didn't do anything to upset the Iranians before the nuclear test, and they for sure won't do anything now."

"Fair enough, but what if the Pentagon does decide to do something about it?" Jim asked. "What will be Iran's response?"

"Mine the Strait of Hormuz," Bill said. "Stop the shipping of 40% of the world's oil."

"Won't happen," Susan said. "Iran can't afford to leave that mess when this hypothetical conflict we're talking about ends, as it eventually would. They ship oil too, remember?"

"I don't see how we can come up with a plausible answer to what Iran may or may not do in response to an American attack until we know what that attack looks like," Oscar said.

"Then that's your homework assignment," Jim said. "Think about what military options America has against Iran, and then assess the probability of success or failure for each of those options." Groans resonated around the table. "Enough, people," Jim warned. "This is what you get paid for." Casey was the only one smiling. He looked forward to the challenge of a military planning exercise.

"I want you all to work together on this one," Jim said. "And George, go see if you can find Dan Hillman over in the Southeast

Asia cell. He's an ex-Marine who can give you people a quick lesson in operational planning. That should help jump-start your efforts."

"What's the deadline?" Bill asked.

"Next Friday," Jim answered. "I would want it sooner, but as Leslie pointed out, the timeline from initial testing to warhead deployment isn't an overnight affair, and we all have our regular workloads we can't just push to the side." Jim looked around the table. Some people jotted notes, while others just sat with dejected looks on their faces. "Are there any questions?" Jim waited for a moment, and when no one spoke up he said, "Then let's get to it."

There was none of the normal end-of-meeting-chatter as everyone got up from the table and headed to their respective cubicles to take stock of just how much more work their boss just signed them up for. As Casey exited the room, a vibration in his front pants pocket alerted him he had a new text message. He'd only given in six months earlier to the idea that technology's progression wasn't such a bad thing, and he bought his first cell phone.

It only took Casey a month and three embarrassing episodes to learn how to silence the thing—a requirement, he found out, for bringing cell phones into the IWG offices in the first place. There were some rooms where electronic devices of *any* kind were prohibited, but the ninth-floor conference room was not one of them.

Casey read the message and turned back around, almost knocking Jim Shelton down as the man headed back to his own office. Casey collected himself and asked his boss, "Sir, could I take my half-hour for lunch right now?"

Jim was puzzled, since it wasn't even ten o'clock. But then, Casey seemed to operate on his own schedule when he was chasing something down that he felt was more important than published working hours. "Sure, I guess," Jim said. "Is something wrong?"

"No, sir," Casey said. "I mean, not that I know of. I just have to go meet someone."

"What about?" Jim pressed.

Casey shrugged his shoulders. "I just know he wouldn't have asked me to meet him ASAP unless it was important."

Jim's eyes narrowed. "Who?"

Casey knew he was taking a risk of being on the receiving end of another stern talking to from Jim Shelton if he answered, but it would probably be worse if he didn't. "Paul Giordano."

Jim closed his eyes and opened them slowly. "Detective Giordano," he said, more to himself than to Casey. "This wouldn't happen to be about The Council, would it?"

Casey's internal temperature rose, and he hoped it wasn't visible on his face. "I don't know, sir. I doubt it. We've both been too busy to keep going down that road," Casey said, not lying, but not being completely honest, either.

"But you still talk to him," Jim said.

"Yes, but not regularly," Casey said. He was beginning to think he should have just gone without asking for permission first. "Like I said, we're both busy."

Jim decided not to push the issue. "All right," he said. "Thirty minutes. And then I need you back here."

"Yes, sir."

"You thought you were busy before?" Jim asked, not expecting an answer. "I was serious about that deadline."

Casey nodded and made a beeline for the exit.

Chapter 5

"I can't stay long, so I'll make this quick," Detective Paul Giordano of the New York Police Department said when Casey approached. He chose the meeting place for both convenience and security. The subway station wasn't far from his office at the Joint Terrorism Task Force headquarters, and movement was constant through the station, making it easier to identify anyone loitering who might be listening.

Casey moved to the side to make room for the other people coming off the subway. "What is it?" he asked.

"Greg Clawson's dead," Giordano said.

"What? How?" Casey asked.

"Suicide," Giordano said. "At least that's the official story. Guard found him this morning on the floor of his cell. He hanged himself from the cell bars with his own socks...just tied 'em together around his neck and sat down 'til it was done."

Casey shivered slightly at the mental image. Greg Clawson, Casey's former neighbor in the run-down apartment building by the East River, was in prison for attempting to assassinate Senator William Cogburn. Casey was able to stop him before he succeeded, and Clawson was given a speedy trial and a sixty-year sentence with no parole

25

for his efforts. Clawson's partner, Anthony Ward, was not so lucky. Arguably the brains of the pair, Ward was killed by a rifle shot from Giordano, saving him from having to face any judge but Saint Peter.

Casey never got to know Greg Clawson very well, but he never suspected Clawson would take his own life. He thought Clawson would fit right in at the United States Penitentiary in Allenwood, Pennsylvania—maybe make some friends among the other white supremacists who were no doubt part of the population. "You said, 'official story.' Does that mean you don't think it was suicide?" Casey asked.

"No, I don't."

"Why not?"

Giordano looked around to verify that no one else was listening before he answered. "Clawson never stopped blaming Keith Swanson for Jared Prince's death. He said it at the trial, and he never said different after. But over the past few months, maybe because he'd had time to think about it, he started pinning the bombings on Swanson, too. Only thing is, no one listened to him. Because Clawson had been whining for so long, they wrote it off to just more ranting from a guy who knew he wasn't going anywhere soon and just needed something new to add to his conspiracy story."

Casey thought for a minute and said, "Nobody cared what he said about Swanson killing Prince, because Prince was cremated and gone before anyone could say anything about it."

"Right, but there's plenty of physical evidence left from the three bombs," Giordano said. "If the right person was interested enough, all that shit is on file, and maybe they could start making connections to back up Clawson's accusations."

"But *you* couldn't get access to anything, and you work at the JTTF," Casey said.

"Only for six more months when my rotation ends," Giordano said. "And anyway, I'm not the right person."

"Then who is?"

"Hell if I know," Giordano said. "But the point is, someone was afraid the wrong people might start listening to Clawson, so they shut him up. Permanently."

"And you think Swanson might have something to do with that?" Casey asked.

"Or The Council," Giordano said, going exactly where Casey thought he was going. "And that's the other reason I wanted to talk to you. Has your professor friend found out any more information about The Council? A name we could investigate, even?"

Casey didn't expect that question. He hadn't talked to Dr. Davood Raad in over two years. Ever since Raad first told him about The Council, things had not gone well—meaning Casey was witness to one guy getting smeared across a New York street by a dump truck, the aforementioned assassination attempt, and he and Susan Williams were held at gunpoint before a hidden sniper's bullet punched a hole in the would-be executioner's head through the window of Casey's apartment. That was all within about a week. Through all of it, Casey was only able to confirm the existence of The Council through innuendo and hearsay. And everyone Casey suspected of being a member of The Council, or at least having firsthand knowledge of it, were either dead or out of Casey's reach.

"I haven't talked to the guy since I told him about Keith Swanson and Mitchell Evans," Casey said. "Truthfully, I thought The Council dialed back their activity after the bombing. Especially since they spent so much effort to clean up the mess."

"Well, we still haven't proved that," Giordano said.

"Nothing else on Evans?" Casey asked.

"Just the body in your apartment," Giordano said. "In fact, the Evans murder was moved to the 'unsolved' case file eighteen months ago. Problem is, we can't find shit on who the guy was to begin with, and nobody cares enough about him to keep the case open."

"So we've had nothing new on The Council since Clawson's trial," Casey said.

"Not until this morning," Giordano said. He could tell Casey was interested, but he needed him to be a hundred percent onboard, or they ran the risk of letting The Council slip through their fingers again— maybe for good. "Look, man. You sold me on this *Council* business after the bombing, and I haven't stopped trying to finger the assholes who were responsible. You know what I'm up against. I've been shut down at every level from pursuing this angle, but the dust has settled. I think this may be our chance to bring the whole fucking thing down."

Casey looked at his watch, and confirmed he was already five minutes beyond the thirty-minute pass Jim gave him—reminding him of Jim's warning. But Giordano was right. There hadn't been anything either of them could find that smelled of The Council's involvement until Greg Clawson's death. "What do you need me to do?" Casey asked.

"*That's* what I'm talking about," Giordano beamed—as much as a man dedicated to finding those responsible for injuring his wife and killing his unborn son could beam. "I just need you to find your professor friend and try to get me some names that are tied to The Council. If I can make a connection between any of those names and the people being questioned in the investigation of Clawson's death, we might get that break we've been looking for."

"Will they let you do that?" Casey asked. "I mean, start digging around the Clawson investigation?"

"I'm just a cop interested in the death of someone I helped put away," Giordano said. "Nobody's gonna question that....If we do this fast, anyway."

Casey agreed to help, and he descended the stairs back to the train.

Casey finished jotting the address down and hung up the phone, stuffing the paper in his wallet for safekeeping. As soon as he returned to the office, Casey called the Jennings Institute where Dr. Davood Raad, noted author and critic of the Iranian government, was working as a visiting scholar and advisor to the prestigious think tank. When the receptionist at the institute informed him that Dr. Raad was no longer with them, Casey asked to speak to Dr. Eitan Brackmann. Dr. Brackmann had been the link, through Oscar Horstein, that led to Raad and Casey's introduction—when Casey first learned of The Council. Brackmann told Casey that Raad was still working for the Jennings Institute, but that he was in D.C., working from the institute's office there and giving lectures at some of the local universities.

As soon as Casey heard of Dr. Raad's absence, a knot formed in his stomach. Paul Giordano had stressed the need to get information as quickly as possible if he was going to be able to look for something connected to Greg Clawson's death without raising suspicion. Raad would only discuss the The Council in person, and that wasn't going to happen as long as Casey was in New York and Raad was in D.C. The drive was easy enough....

"There you are."

...but Casey had other issues to address first.

"I've been looking everywhere for you," Susan said as she walked into Casey's cubicle. "Dan said he'll give us a thirty-minute crash course in planning at one thirty, but I figured we can at least get together and brainstorm first. Maybe if we already have some ideas on paper, things will go a little quicker." She sat down in the other chair in Casey's cubicle and put the end of a pen cap in her mouth.

Casey stared at Susan without saying a word. He watched her write a heading on the steno pad in her lap, underlining it to separate it from the notes she planned on taking once the brainstorming started. His eyes were repeatedly drawn to the very large, very shiny diamond on her left hand. Casey couldn't recall ever seeing it before. In fact, Susan never wore jewelry. He knew that much about her after four and a half years and two failed attempts at an intimate relationship. No, he definitely hadn't seen it before, and a diamond ring like that only meant one thing.

"Dylan asked me to marry him last night," Susan said after she surmised the reason for Casey's prolonged silence.

Casey refocused with Susan's declaration, and he sat down. He wasn't even aware that he'd been standing ever since Susan walked in. "Congratulations," he said. It sounded as insincere out loud as it did in his head.

The smile on Susan's face that grew from her memory of the night before faded with Casey's statement. "Come on, Casey," she said. "Don't be like that."

"Like what? I'm happy for you. Really."

Susan put the cap back on her pen and closed her notepad. "Casey, I'm sorry things didn't work out between us, but it didn't, all right? We've been through this before," she said. "And don't tell me you didn't know this day was coming."

Casey felt Susan's admonishing glare before he looked at her eyes and confirmed it. "I know," he admitted. "It's just...it's just *that*," he said, waving towards Susan's hand. "I mean, that's for real. It's not talk anymore."

"Talk?" Susan asked. "Dylan and I have been dating for two years, Casey. We decided we wanted this six months ago. We were just waiting for the right time. When he knew he wouldn't have to deploy anytime soon."

Casey's eyes dropped to Susan's midsection. "Six months?"

"I'm not pregnant!"

Casey jumped slightly at Susan's exclamation. His face reddened. "I didn't mean...."

"But that's what you were thinking," Susan interjected. "Look, Casey, I'm sorry things didn't work out between us that way, but it just wasn't meant to be. It's different with Dylan. It was different from the first time I met him."

Casey knew Susan was right. The times when he and Susan "dated" were born out of life-threatening circumstances. They became comforts to each other—someone the other could talk to about their shared experiences. But each time, the natural healing process overcame any amorous feelings they had for each other, and their relationship drifted back to platonic. Casey was glad their friendship endured, but after Susan became involved with Dylan Lawrence, "The Man with Two First Names," Casey's own lonliness and lack of romantic companionship needled at his psyche—a feeling he hadn't experienced since Jennifer left Savannah. *Decades ago*, he thought. Though since he was only thirty-five years old, he knew it was a bit of an exaggeration.

"I'm sorry," Casey said. "I didn't mean to imply that I hoped we could've got back together. I knew that wasn't going to happen."

"Then what is it?" Susan asked.

Casey looked at the floor and said, "I guess I'm just jealous, that's all."

"But that's..."

"Not jealous of Dylan," Casey interrupted. "Jealous of both of you. Together."

Susan's eyes showed her confusion.

Casey sighed. He looked around the cubicle and at the flourescent lights above. "I still have this," he said, leveling his eyes on Susan and smiling to try and lighten the mood.

Susan leaned forward, understanding. "Casey, you're not losing me. You're still one of the best friends I've got, and I still need you. Being married doesn't mean I'm shutting the door on everyone else in my life."

"Including me," Casey said, embarrassed by his adolescent anxiety.

"Especially you." Susan patted Casey's knee and stood to leave.

Casey looked up at Susan. "Since y'all will be moving in together and consolidating the stuff you both have, can I have your silverware?"

Susan laughed and shook her head. "We're going to use that silverware." She started walking away and paused at the cubicle entrance. "So, one thirty? Will you be able to make it?"

"What? Oh, Dan's thing," Casey said. "Sure. I'll be there."

Susan tapped the cubicle wall and headed for her own space.

"Can I have *Dylan's* silverware?" Casey yelled.

"One thirty!" came the distant reply from somewhere out in cubeville.

Casey shrugged and stared at the map of Iran pinned to the cubicle wall Susan had just been standing beside. Circles of different colors surrounded the names of various cities—Bushehr, Natanz, Isfahan, Parchin, and others. Each city had some role in Iran's nuclear program ranging from research to uranium enrichment to the heavy water reactor at Arak. Casey found a pencil on his desk and put a light oval around the area labeled "Dasht-e Kavir."

He stood back and looked at the map. *At least I have this*, he thought. Susan's visit just made Casey's decision that much easier.

Chapter 6

Washington, D.C.

The secretary of Defense removed his reading glasses and looked to the general seated next to him for affirmation. With all eyes on him, the chairman of the Joint Chiefs of Staff nodded. No one in the White House situation room said anything. Each person knew the importance of the early morning meeting, and they waited for their boss to respond first.

The president of the United States sat up straight and put his elbows on the table. He continued to look down at the briefing notes in front of him and addressed the defense secretary directly, though his words were meant for everyone. "A direct assault is out of the question," he said. "We're trying to get our folks out of the region, not sign them up for another decade of fighting."

The Thursday morning gathering of the president's closest advisors was just the latest of a series of emergency sessions since they learned of Iran's nuclear test just forty-eight hours earlier. Along with the SecDef and CJCS, the vice president, secretary of State, national security advisor, White House chief of staff, and deputy national security advisor were all in attendance. They were tasked with bringing the president options for dealing with Iran and the redline set by the U.S. which the world knew had now been crossed—all options.

The initial presentation came from SecState, who backed harder sanctions on Iran, along with unfettered use of drones within Iranian airspace for intelligence gathering, and if needed, "surgical" strikes against some of the soft targets identified as cruicial to the Iranian nuclear program. When asked what those targets might be, the secretary was unprepared to answer, and he suggested that the director of National Intelligence should have probably been in attendance to give his assessment.

The president dismissed SecState's semi-diplomatic solution as a "kick the can down the road" option, and he asked the SecDef for his opinion. What the secretary laid out were updated versions of operational plans from the Cold War that had been dusted off in a frantic attempt to come up with a viable campaign against arguably the Middle East's most powerful military. The numbers he gave the president were not pleasant—too many casualties, too much money, and too much time. Despite all options being on the table, as the administration repeatedly claimed, a conventional fight with carrier-borne airstrikes, an amphibious assault, long-range bombers, and tens of thousands of U.S. troops on the ground was commiting political suicide for anyone who backed it and would break the country's slowly recovering economy in just a few short years.

"Out of the question," the president repeated. "So what other options do we have?" He looked around the table for any takers. "Anyone?"

"We could do nothing," came from the end of the table farthest away. Everyone turned to get a better look at Scott Parker, the deputy national security advisor.

"Nothing?" the president asked with wrinkles of incredulity simultaneously appearing on his foreheaded.

"Condemn them publicly, sure, but let somone else do the dirty work. Like Israel," Parker said. "Maybe our best play is just to back them up in private while they attack Iran. We only come in when Israel needs our help—which is what everyone expects, anyway."

"Leo?" the president asked, wanting to hear what Leo Ambrosi, the national security advisor and Scott Parker's immediate supervisor, had to say.

"Sir, Scott just mentioned an option that's been bandied about around here for months," Ambrosi said, "but it's not something I would recommend."

"Why not?" the president asked.

Ambrosi purposely avoided turning to his left where he could feel Parker's damning gaze boring into the back of his head. "Well, for one, sir, if we give Israel the green light on this one, the corallary that Scott mentioned is inevitable. We *will* be in a full-blown military confrontation with Iran before the end of the year, guaranteed. If you want to avoid getting us into another war over there, keep Israel out of it."

The president looked at Parker and said, "I appreciate your input, Scott, but Leo's right. We need to do everything we can to keep Israel's leash tight right now."

"I'm meeting the Israeli ambassador on Sunday, Mr. President," the White House chief of staff, Kurt Vanek, said. "I'll be sure to relay that message."

"Well, wait 'til you hear from me for talking points," the president said. "I'm calling Netanyahu in a couple of hours, and I want to make sure we're conveying the same message."

"And that message is?" SecState prodded.

The president glanced at Scott Parker before turning to his right. "We do nothing."

*   *   *

"Shut the door," Ambrosi said as Scott Parker followed him into his office in the West Wing.

Parker sat down in one of the antique chairs in front of Ambrosi's desk. "What is it?"

Ambrosi sat and stared at his deputy. "What were you thinking? 'Do nothing.' What kind of advice is that?" he asked.

Parker didn't answer.

"You are the deputy assistant to the president for national security affairs," Ambrosi said. "When the president asks for options, you don't just tell him to sit on his hands. We are here at his leisure. If you want to stay in this job for long, give him advice he can use."

Parker returned Ambrosi's stare with an equally stern countenance. "I told the president what I thought he should do in this situation, and in case you didn't notice, he took that advice."

"Some of it," Ambrosi said.

"Okay, so he's not going to unleash the hounds. But he's not going to commit the U.S. to any kind of violent response, either. And isn't that the part you're bitching about?" Parker asked.

Ambrosi gave in, dropping his gaze. He pulled a paper from under the pile on the center of his desk, moving it to the top and said, "Fair enough. Look, you told him what you think. I'm only saying that you need to work on your delivery. Don't forget that you're talking to the most powerful man on earth when you're in there. And like him or not, he deserves our respect."

Parker smiled. "I like the man fine," he said. "President or not, he still puts his socks on one foot at a time. And I'm sorry I don't have the polished Ivy League delivery you're used to, but he also deserves to hear things straight. That's respect."

"I don't mean to imply that you should hide anything or throw softballs," Ambrosi said, "but a little less candor next time, all right? You've got a lot you can offer this administration and this country, and I don't want to see you get canned after only two months on the job."

Parker raised his hands. "Okay. I give up," he said. "I'll work on it."

"Thank you."

"Can I go now?" Parker asked.

"Please," Ambrosi said, motioning to the door. "I need you to get in touch with someone from Bill Cogburn's staff and make sure the senator's not thinking of jumping the gun on this one and committing us to anything before the president does," he added, primarily because he needed Parker to do just that, but also because he wanted to remind Parker that he was the *deputy* national security advisor, and Ambrosi was still in charge.

"No problem," Parker said as he left the room. In a parting act of petty defiance, he left the door open.

Chapter 7

New York City

On Thursday, Casey knocked on Jim Shelton's door as he opened it. Jim was hunched over his desk carefully reading through one of the many reports he received each day, but he looked up at the interruption. "Sir, could I bother you for a minute?" Casey asked.

"Since you're already bothering me, why not?" Jim said. "What is it?" he asked as he sat up in his high-back leather chair.

"I want to go to D.C." Casey said.

"Okay," Jim said. "When?"

"Tomorrow."

"Tomorrow?"

"Yes, sir," Casey said. He sensed Jim's reluctance, and he had planned for that inevitability. "I want to consult someone with their pulse on the Iranian street to find out what public reaction to the nuclear test is really like there," he explained before Jim could say anything. "He used to work for the regime, and I can also get his assessment of how Iran might try to leverage their nuclear capability in the region."

"What about the project I assigned all of you yesterday?" Jim asked.

"This trip is *for* that project," Casey said. "Plus, I front-loaded the rest of the group with my input yesterday to help get things started."

"And to clear the way for your research trip," Jim said, voicing what he suspected was the ulterior motive for Casey's apparently proactive input to the operational planning exercise.

Casey didn't deny it. "Sir, look, if he was here in New York, I wouldn't be asking to go," he said. "I'll even take leave. You can call it a vacation. But if we want his assessment of the situation, I have to go meet him in person."

"Because he won't talk to you over the phone or through email," Jim said.

Casey nodded.

Jim sighed audibly. "You're going to see Dr. Raad, aren't you?" he asked.

Most likely, Jim had no idea Davood Raad had even left New York, let alone set up shop in D.C. But Jim was a smart guy, and Casey knew it wouldn't take him long to surmise that Raad was Casey's Iran connection. And Jim didn't like Raad.

"You're not planning to go there on a Council hunt, are you?" Jim asked. Before Casey could answer, Jim added, "I know what Raad asked you to do, but don't forget you almost took a bullet because of your digging."

Two bullets, Casey thought. "I know, sir," he said. "I was lucky."

"But you don't deny that you intend to talk to Raad about The Council," Jim said.

"No, Your Honor," Casey said.

Jim smiled and shook his head. "Alright, point taken," he said. "But I'm serious about The Council, Casey. I warned you off of them before, and I'm saying it again. You don't want to keep sticking your nose in their business—especially in D.C. That's like walking into the lion's den, and the only thing that'll come from you asking too many questions is your picture on the evening news when they drag your body out of the Potomac."

This time, Casey smiled. "I'll be careful, sir. I promise, I'm *really* going to ask Dr. Raad about the Iran nuke thing. If The Council comes up, there's nothing else I can give him," Casey said. "My only lead was through the bombings, and now Greg Clawson's dead, Simpson's dead, Evans is dead, Prince and Ward are dead....It's a dead end."

Jim thought for a minute, contemplating Casey's sincerity. He finally looked down at the open calendar on his desk. "How long do you plan on being gone?"

Yes! Casey thought. He wasn't sure Jim would agree to let him go when he walked in the room, but it was starting to look good. "Five days," Casey said. "That's only three working days."

"Five days to talk to Raad?" Jim asked.

"I'm gonna go visit my grandfather when I'm there," Casey said.

"I didn't know your grandfather lived in D.C."

"Arlington," Casey said softly. "He's buried there."

Jim nodded his head. That was how he always seemed to learn a little more about Casey's background—when he least expected it. He waited until Casey made eye contact again. "You'll be back on Wednesday?"

"Yes, sir," Casey said. "Well, I'll be back in New York on Tuesday, but I was going to come back to work on Wednesday." He watched Jim anxiously, noting that his boss hadn't agreed to let him go yet.

Jim jotted down the dates in his calendar. "And the group's okay with you leaving?"

Casey felt victory slipping from his grasp. "I haven't told them yet," he said.

Jim put down his pen. "Were you going to?"

"I was going to see Susan right after this," Casey said. "I mean, if you approved it."

Jim glanced at the clock on his desk to confirm that he still had time to get more coffee before he had to meet Doc Borglund for the weekly data dump he gave the IWG CEO. "I'll approve it," Jim said, "but it's gotta be charged as PTO."

"No problem, sir," Casey said. He had a year's worth of personal time off that he had to use before October, anyway, or he'd lose it—like usual.

"I can't justify letting you go on company time...even to visit your grandfather's grave," Jim said.

"Sir, that's just a side trip," Casey said. "I told you, I'm...."

"...going to see Raad," Jim said, finishing Casey's sentence. "I know. But if there's an off-chance that you go sniffing around The Council outside of a conversation in Raad's office, IWG's not paying for that, either."

Casey got the message. Jim wasn't buying his story of dropping his extracurricular investigation. Not completely, anyway. But Casey had been telling Jim the truth. He had no intention of talking to anyone about The Council besides Davood Raad. And in that case, it was only to get a name or two that Paul Giordano might be able to use. *Giordano* was the detective, after all, not Casey—a fact Jim had reminded him of repeatedly.

"Don't worry, sir," Casey said. He stood up and thanked Jim, adding on his way out, "I won't go looking for any trouble down there, I swear."

Jim watched as Casey left the office. *But trouble always seems to find you, Mr. Shenk.*

* * *

Casey stopped outside of Susan's cubicle, halted by the ear-splitting cackling unimpeded by the six-foot "walls" that separated one IWG employee's workspace from another. Casey eavesdropped, but it only took him a second before he learned what the ruckus was all about.

"Honey, that is beautiful," Sharon from the records division said.

"It must have cost a fortune," Deb from the policy office observed.

"You did good, girlfriend," added Wanda from finance.

Casey could only take so much, and he broke up the coven. "Mornin', ladies," he said as he walked in. All heads turned to identify the interloper. Casey dismissed their stares and looked directly at Susan. "Could I talk to you for a second?" he asked.

"Sure," Susan said. The other women took the hint and said their goodbyes, commenting on the various work they still had to do before lunch as they left, whether or not it was true.

After quiet had returned to that corner of the building, Casey sat down. His eyes involuntarily drifted to the engagement ring on Susan's hand that had been the cause of the commotion. He caught himself, embarassed, when Susan pulled the sleeve of her sweater further down her arm. She couldn't hide the ring, but Casey understood the gesture—*we're not talking about this anymore.*

"What is it?" Susan asked.

"I'm going to D.C. tomorrow," Casey said. He saw a look of concern on Susan's face, and he added, "Just for five days."

Susan relaxed. "What for?" she asked. Before Casey could answer, she tensed up again. "Wait a minute. We still need your help on the Iran reactions project."

"I know," Casey said. "That's part of the reason I'm going."

"The Pentagon?" she asked, thinking maybe Casey had a connection there from his time in the Navy.

Casey knew Susan wouldn't like the answer, but he didn't have a good reason for keeping it a secret—not from her. "No, I'm going there to see Dr. Raad," he said.

Susan put her forehead in the palm of her hand and closed her eyes. "How is *he* going to help us?"

Casey gave Susan the same explanation he gave Jim a few minutes earlier. He hoped her reaction would be different, but in reality, he suspected it would be worse.

"Why the fuck are you still messing with The Council?" she asked. "How many people have to die before you throw in the towel, Casey?"

He was right. Susan's reaction was worse. Casey's hobby of analyzing obscure or underreported news items and posting his theories on the *true* story behind larger world events based on the connections he made had put not only his life in danger, but Susan's as well—on more than one occasion. Shortly after he wrote *The Complicity Doctrine* theory on his "Middle-Truths" blog, Casey was introduced to Dr. Davood Raad. Raad had been an advisor to Prime Minister Mousavi of Iran in the Eighties when he first learned of The Council, and after hearing Casey's theory following the Manhattan bombings, Raad told him everything he knew about the group.

Shrouded in secrecy, The Council lived in the realm of conspiracy theorists worldwide. After World War II, a group of businessmen, academics, politicians, and military leaders in the United States came together to map out a plan for a new world that would be shaped by American ideals. With no intention of trying to commit their country to ruling an American *empire*, they focused on ways to influence countries around the globe to accept the United States as the undisputed world leader. They envisioned a world of willful followers who would choose America's example as the one to emulate. The method preferred by The Council to achieve its goal was manipulation, both political and economic—recognition of the inseparable nature of the two.

When The Council decided to add military manipulation to that list, things began to change. The Iran-Contra hearings brought to light The Council's first foray into the world of providing arms to groups fighting wars whose outcome they wanted to dictate. History and congressional records provide evidence to how well that went. The Council escaped discovery and public incrimination, but the conspiracies were bolstered, and mere Cold War rumor began to gain more traction in Washington and elsewhere, forcing the group to downsize and reassess its tactics. Things changed yet again on September 11, 2001.

The effect al Qa'ida's attack had on The Council was two-fold. First, the group became committed to the use of violence as a tool to achieving the manipulation required to attain their goals. And second, they had the top cover to do it. While certainly not the intent, the passing of laws such as the Patriot Act, and the invasions of Afghanistan and Iraq made it easier for The Council to push its agenda using the material support of the United States without showing its hand. It was at this point where Casey's *Complicity Doctrine* caught the attention of Davood Raad, and he elicited Casey's help to identify members of the group with the intent of ultimately taking down the clandestine organization.

It was Casey's acquiesence that placed him and Susan in front of a loaded gun before Mitchell Evans' life was ended by an unknown assassin. The close call was enough to illicit Susan's vehement insistence that Casey drop any and all investigations into The Council, but Casey wasn't as easily deterred. "I haven't even touched The Council since Greg Clawson was sentenced," he said. "But his suicide is just too convenient to ignore. Besides, I'm only passing the information to Raad. What he does with it is his business."

"That's all?" Susan asked with a tilt of her head.

"You don't believe me?"

"No, I don't."

"Why not?"

Susan's eyes narrowed and she shook her head. "Exposing The Council isn't your job," she said. "Ever since you met Raad, you've been obsessed with it, Casey."

"Bullshit."

"Don't tell me you haven't been," Susan said. "You may have pushed it to the background, behind your other work at IWG, but you can't deny you've tried to tie everything you could to The Council every chance you got. Hell, you're not even sure they exist."

"Of course they exist," Casey said loudly. "The Council almost killed you, too. Remember?"

"It was one guy, Casey," Susan said. "And yes, I remember. He was shot right in front of me. But he's dead. Just like you and I were almost dead." Her voice got progressively louder. "Is that what want? You want these guys to kill you just to prove they exist?"

"That's not..."

"I'm not finished," Susan barked. "Is it worth it, Casey? So what if The Council exists. If they're as connected as you say they are, what does it matter if you find out who they are? If they're that big, they'll just keep doing what they're doing, and you'll be dead." She leaned forward and said, "You don't always have to be right, you know."

"It's not about me being right," Casey said as he stood up to leave. "It's about finding the truth."

Chapter 8

Washington, D.C.

Howard C. Shenk, MSG, US Army, World War II. Casey ran his hand over the top of his grandfather's gravestone. Now more gray than white, the marker seemed on the verge of being overtaken by the newer marble additions to Arlington National Cemetery—the final resting places of those killed in action during the wars in Iraq and Afghanistan. He stood up and looked east through the trees with a view of the Pentagon below. Casey had never been to Arlington before, and it was the first time he had a chance to talk to the man who died when Casey was just six years old but who had nevertheless been a strong influence on him growing up.

Most of what Casey knew about Master Sergeant Shenk came from stories his father and grandmother told. Fearless, kind, and smart-as-a-whip was how his grandmother described him. Casey's father painted the picture of a stern disciplinarian who would do anything for his children, but would not hesitate to let them face the consequences if they ran afoul of the authorities, be it the law, school, or otherwise. The one intolerable crime in the Shenk household was lying. Howard Shenk believed the measure of a man's character was in his ability to tell the truth without regard for the potential consequences, and Casey's father continued that teaching in his own family.

Casey tried to live up to the expectations of his father and grandfather, though his realist view of life sometimes got in the way. On a higher level, though, his reverence for the truth translated into a vehement loathing of sinsiter falsehood. At first it was limited to lies that affected him personally, but it wasn't long before Casey learned deception and misdirection could be just as bad, if not worse than outright lies. It angered him more when those deceptions were perpetrated by people in positions of trust, whose decisions and actions affected those who put them there in the first place, and even those who had no say in the matter.

On the drive down from New York, Casey thought a lot about what Susan said. In one sense, she was right. Casey *was* trying to find any angle he could that would help expose The Council. But he wasn't obsessed with it. While Susan refused to acknowledge The Council's existence despite what she'd seen with her own eyes, Casey had no doubts, and he began to see The Council as the product of an even larger culture of corruption that had taken root in the halls of American leadership. It was that moral corruption Casey wanted to call out, and The Council represented its manifestation. He believed that once this group's actions were brought to light, the good people in Washington—and there were some—would demand a stop to their activity, and America's ship could be righted.

Casey looked back at the headstone and said, "I don't know if I can do it, sir, but I'm gonna try." He peered down the row one last time and began the long walk to the cemetery gate.

"How've you been?" Andie asked as she took a seat across the table. Even sitting down, Andrea Jackson was noticeably taller than Casey.

It was her looks more than her height, however, that drew stares of admiration, some less discreet than others. Andie was used to the attention her nearly six-foot frame and visibly unblemished African skin got her, and ignoring that attention was second nature.

"I'm good," Casey said. "How 'bout you? You happy to be back in the thick of stuff down here?"

Andie smiled. "Yeah, I am," she said. "I mean, don't get me wrong, it was fun working with y'all in New York, but the reporter in me wasn't ready to let go. I don't think being chained to a cubicle was what I was really looking for. No offense."

Casey laughed. "None taken. And I hear what you're saying. That's why I try to stay out of the office as much as I can. Like this field trip I'm on now," Casey said. "Thanks for meeting me, by the way."

"I didn't have a choice," Andie said. "My momma taught me to never turn a friend away when they ask for help. Unless they're from Alabama." Andie and Casey both laughed at one of the deep-seated predjudices they learned growing up in Georgia. Based more on university football affiliation than anything else, the good-spirited discrimination was acceptable, in contrast to the racial and religious issues that divided the South for so long, and in some ways still did.

"Hi, I'm Penny. I'll be your waitress today," a young woman said as she came to the table and handed out menus. Andie and Casey halted their conversation until the woman left with their orders.

Andie resumed it. "Raad is giving a lecture tonight at Georgetown," she said. "It's open to the public, so you can go hear him speak and then catch up with him after that if you don't want to wait until tomorrow."

"That's great," Casey said. "What's he talking about?"

"The rise of Iranian oppression since 2007," she said. "It's part of a seminar course in Iranian democracy he's teaching there, and also the subtitle of his new book, *Withering on the Vine.*"

"Have you read it?" Casey asked.

"No, my calendar's full just reporting on *American* politics. Hell, I hadn't even thought of Raad since I left New York until you called and asked me to find out what he's been up to since he got here," Andie said. "Why, is it any good?"

"I don't know," Casey said with a grin. "I haven't read it either. I read slow as shit, and when you throw in *Foreign Affairs, Political Science Quarterly*, and the forty-or-so email reports I get everyday, I'm lucky to get through three books a year. Plus the Braves and Falcons eat up a lot of my free time."

Andie nodded her head. "I know what you mean."

"Well, after tonight I won't have to read it anyway," Casey said, getting back on topic. "I'll just listen to Raad give the audience the highlights."

"You're right," Andie said. "That's probably all it's going to be." She studied Casey's face for a moment and said, "Besides, you didn't come down here to just sit in a class, did you?"

"Not exactly," Casey said. Andie had been an employee at IWG for a total of one day when bombs ripped through Manhattan in 2011. As far as Casey's involvement with The Council, she was there from the start. Casey had used her help then, and he was using her again now. But in this case, he planned on keeping her as far away as possible—just in case things went sideways. "I'm just going to give Raad some information," he said. "Which isn't much, to tell the truth. But *he's* the one who's really invested in this. I'm just the part-time help."

Chapter 9

"And it will only increase, the further Iran moves from the guiding principles of its constitution." The auditorium filled with applause—most entusiastic, some merely polite—as Dr. Davood Raad gathered his notes and waved. He moved from behind the podium and shook hands with various university officials in attendance. Students and other guests began to file out of the building.

Casey left his seat and moved towards the stage, against the flow of bodies in the aisle. He was easy to pick out because he was the only one not headed for the door, but Raad didn't notice. The good doctor was too busy conversing with well-wishers and admirers who wouldn't let him leave. But someone in the back *did* take notice.

Casey stopped four rows from the front, and inquisitive voyeurism took over. The pause was triggered by a noticable change in Raad's demeanor from light-hearted chit-chat to aggrevation to worry—all in a span of seconds. Casey surmised that whatever the two men standing next to Raad said to him was not good news. The fact that Raad initially seemed angry at their mere presence made Casey focus his attention from Raad to the unwelcome pair instead. They were younger than Raad, maybe even younger than Casey. Definitely darker. Casey was sure the men were of Middle Eastern decent, Arab or otherwise, but in the melting pot of the United States, they could have just been students from Wisconsin who happened to be attending Georgetown University as undergrads. Because he couldn't hear the conversation, Casey couldn't get any more information beyond that, except for the observation that one of the men wore a black leather jacket that Casey wouldn't mind owning.

The trio parted ways, and Casey stepped out of the aisle to let leather jacket and his friend pass. Casey smiled politely as the men went by. He only received an angry glare in return from one of them, and he was completely ignored by the other. "Alright. Fuck you, then," Casey said under his breath. He looked back to the front of the room and saw Raad heading for a side exit. "Dr. Raad," Casey called loudly.

Raad turned upon hearing the familiar voice. "Casey, my friend," he beamed, extending a hand. "What brings you here? You are not a student here now, are you?"

Casey shook his head and Raad's hand. "No, sir. Still taking classes at BMCC." He smiled and added, "Slowly but surely."

"Certainly cheaper than here," Raad said with a sweeping gesture to indicate the campus where they were standing. "But the education is just as valuable—any education." Raad looked around the auditorium as the last few attendees made their way out. "So what *does* bring you here then?" he asked.

"Actually, I came to talk to you about Iran's nuclear test a few days ago," Casey said. "I wanted your opinion about the regional implications."

Raad clasped his hands in front of him. "Is that all?"

Casey did his own scan of the now-empty room and said, "And I have some news related to The Council. I didn't think you'd want to talk about it over the phone.

Raad raised an eyebrow and said, "You are right about that." He lowered his voice even more, gazing at the ceiling above. "They are always listening."

Casey knew Raad was right. Even a face-to-face discussion about The Council was risky in a semi-public venue. "Could we talk in your office? Back at Jennings?" he asked.

"An excellent idea. But I'm afraid I cannot spare the time this evening. Perhaps tomorrow?"

Casey agreed, and the two men decided to meet at the Jennings Institute office the following morning. They shook hands, and Casey walked back up the aisle toward the front exit.

The few trees that adorned Georgetown's Red Square provided minimal concealment, but the people leaving the Intercultural Center after the lecture made up for it. The exterior lighting exposed Casey well enough for a positive identification, and the man blended with the crowd of students heading to wherever it was American college coeds headed on Friday night. He put the thought to the side and focused on the job at hand. Following Mr. Shenk.

Chapter 10

Not far from Georgetown, Scott Parker set two drinks on an elevated table and returned to his seat. A steady rumble of conversation from the crowd of mostly government workers kicking off the weekend would have drowned out the background music if there were any. The atmosphere was light-hearted, rowdy, and private all at the same time. That was why Parker suggested he meet Adam Miller there.

Still in the navy blue suit he wore to work, minus the tie, Parker was a mirror image of most of the other patrons. His appearance was in stark contrast, however, to the dark-haired man in a polo shirt and pressed jeans who sat across from him. The two middle-aged men had been friends as undergrads at Northwestern University, but they had gone in different directions after graduation, and they hadn't communicated at all over the ensuing seventeen years. When Miller was able to reach him at his White House office, Parker was both surprised and curious.

"So how did you get my number anyway?" Parker asked.

"Through the chief of staff's office," Miller said.

"Okay. How'd you get *his* number?"

Miller laughed. "I was setting up a meeting with him."

Parker tilted his head. "You're meeting with the White House chief of staff," he said. "And your job is what, exactly?"

"I'm a diplomat," Miller said. "Well, sort of. I work for the Ministry of Foreign of Affairs."

"You mean the State Department?"

"No, the Israel Ministry of Foreign Affairs," Miller said. "I was born there, remember? So after I graduated, I went back. One thing lead to another, and I ended up staying."

"No shit," Parker said. "I always thought you were American. I'll be damned."

"I *am* American," Miller said, smiling. "My parents are American citizens, so that made me an American as soon as Mom squeezed me out. But since I was born there, I'm also Israeli. The best of both worlds," he said as he took a sip of his Heineken.

Parker shook his head and did the same. "Man, I guess I was too busy chasing girls around campus to pay attention."

"It probably never even came up," Miller said. "The dual-citizenship thing didn't even matter until I went back and decided to stay."

There was a brief silence before Parker asked, "What does a 'sort-of diplomat' from Israel need to speak to Kurt Vanek about, anyway?"

"New ambassador," Miller said. "Unlike most of the people who are assigned this post, Moshe Safran has never been to the United States. My job is to make sure he gets comfortable with his new surroundings as quickly as possible."

"And since you grew up here, you were nominated to babysit," Parker said.

"Something like that."

Parker smiled and raised his glass. "Well, it's good to have you back, Adam, even if you're leaving as quickly as possible."

Miller returned the gesture. "I'm not gone yet, but thanks."

Parker finished off his beer and asked, "When are you taking the ambassador to see Vanek?"

Miller put his glass down and wiped his mouth with the back of his hand. "Sunday," he said.

Parker gave Miller a quizzical look and asked, "Why not wait until Monday? Or next week? Is it that important the new guy makes the rounds before then?"

Miller shrugged his shoulders. "As quickly as possible, right?"

Parker contemplated that answer, while he made a vain attempt to get another drop of beer out of his empty glass. He was struck by a thought as soon as he set the glass back down. Parker's eyes narrowed, and he lowered his voice. "He wouldn't be going there to talk about Iran, would he?" he asked.

"I'm sure it'll come up, why?"

Parker grinned, and he leaned back a little. "Now it makes sense," he said. "A new ambassador just days after Iran conducts its first nuclear test. Coming to the White House on Sunday. Israel's planning something, aren't they?"

"I'm sure the Prime Minister's going to make a statement condemning the test, but I don't work for the Prime Minister, so I have no idea."

"Come on, Adam. You think we don't know what Israel's been up to? I mean, who do you think has been giving you guys the intel to...." Parker looked around to make sure no one was within earshot even with all the noise in the room. He lowered his voice and leaned closer to his college roommate. "We tell you guys where they are, and you go get 'em." He smirked and leaned back. "Right? You're like the junkyard dog, and we just let the chain out a little more when there's pickers inside the fence. 'Sick 'em!'" He laughed and picked up his empty beer glass, disappointed it was still empty.

"What are you implying?" Miller asked evenly.

"I'm not *implying* anything," Parker answered. "I just call 'em like I see 'em." He studied his friend's face for a reaction, waiting for a reply. He didn't get one—not the one he was looking for.

Miller stood up and pulled a ten-dollar bill from his pocket. He tossed it on the table and said, "Well, it was good to see you again, Scott." Parker stood up as Miller came around the table. The Israeli leaned close to Parker's ear and said quietly, "If I knew anything, I wouldn't tell you. And fuck you for asking." He turned and was gone, lost in the crowd of bodies.

Parker picked up his empty glass one more time, confirmed there was nothing left, and got up. He stopped after two steps, pocketed the bill Miller put down, and found the exit.

Chapter 11

One block off of Dupont Circle, the Jennings Institute Washington office was located in a non-descript building of dirty white stone and glass. The institute was sandwiched between the Embassy of Papua New Guinea on one side and an unassuming condominium complex on the other. The only indication Casey had that he was in the right place was a three-foot-high sign near the sidewalk. He checked his watch and confirmed the time, but decided Dr. Raad wouldn't mind if he was fifteen minutes early.

Casey pulled hard on the door, not expecting it to be as heavy as it was. He moved quickly to the security desk, acting like he'd been there before just to put the guard at ease. Casey suspected the Jennings Institute didn't have many visitors at 8:45 on a Saturday morning, and he hoped the annoyance at having to put his magazine down wouldn't prevent the guard from pointing him towards Raad's office. He was right, and the man gave him the room number and directed him to the elevator, returning to his reading without a second glance.

Casey got off on the fifth floor and moved down the hall where the arrow on the wall indicated 5204 should be. There were no other employees or visitors that Casey could see, and the building appeared to be deserted. When he turned the corner towards the back of the building, he was relieved to know that he wasn't alone. He still had not seen anyone, but at least he heard voices. From the sound of it, the voices were having a heated conversation about something, and as he approached his intended destination, he realized the sounds were coming from Raad's office. The door was shut, so Casey stopped outside and listened, trying to discern the subject of the mostly one-way conversation inside.

From what he could make out, the occupants of the room included Raad and at least one other person, but as far as what they were talking about, he had no clue. *Farsi*, Casey thought, not surprised. The analyst had been trying to learn Farsi in his spare time, but his commitment was not where it should have been, and his progress was stuck somewhere between slow and non-existent. The words he *could* understand didn't help decipher the conversation at all, and the best he could do was to try and remember a few phrases he heard and possibly translate them later. He made a mental note to call Susan when he left Raad's office and ask her. Maybe he would learn something new.

When the noise subsided, Casey decided it was safe to knock on the door and let himself in. He did have an appointment, after all. Casey stopped at the entranceway as Raad and his visitor quickly looked to identify the intruder. Casey was surprised to see the same man from the night before—same leather jacket, same annoyed expression. Raad made a short comment, and leather jacket nodded before leaving.

"Casey, so good to see you. Please, please, have a seat," Raad said, motioning to an empty chair. Raad took a seat on the other side of the small coffee table in the middle of the room. The two men stared at each other in silence for a moment before Raad smiled and asked, "When did you arrive in Washington?"

"I drove down yesterday," Casey said.

"You *drove*? From New York?" Raad asked.

Casey wasn't sure if Raad's astonishment was genuine or not, so he shrugged his shoulders and changed the subject. "How's your book sales?"

This time it was Raad who shrugged his shoulders. "I don't worry about those things," he said. "My publisher deposits money into my account every month, and that is all I care about. If my accountant ever tells me I need to watch my spending, then I suppose I will start to pay attention."

"Hell, I'm happy when I can pay my rent, buy a six pack, and still have money for pizza each month," Casey said. "I damn sure don't make enough to need an accountant."

"It wasn't always like this," Raad said pensively. "We had nothing growing up in Tabriz. Only each other. Family. But I got out," he added. "I was the lucky one."

"I didn't mean anything by that," Casey said.

"I know you didn't," Raad said. "Not to worry." His smile returned. "You wanted to ask me about the nuclear test," he said.

Casey was relieved that he hadn't upset the man. He didn't know Raad well enough to know which subjects were taboo, and he was glad to end the banter and get down to business. "Yes, sir," he said. "I thought you might be able to give me a better idea about what effects the test will have on the region than what the press is putting out."

"Yes," Raad said. "The American media's hyperventilation where Iran is concerned breeds nothing but fear in the public psyche and bellicose table-thumping from your politicians."

"You don't think it's warranted?" Casey asked.

"No, I don't," Raad said. "For one, what threat does Iran really pose to America? If they take this test to the next step and actually develop a warhead able to be placed on a ballistic missile, can it reach America?"

"They don't have any with that kind of range," Casey said. "But they're working on them."

"Without a doubt," Raad said. "But that does not mean they will be successful. It may be a decade before they are. And a lot can happen in ten years, my friend."

"You mean diplomacy?" Casey asked.

"Perhaps," Raad said. "The election in 2013 has already opened that door, but is America ready to walk through it? They have had the opportunity before and failed to act, because they always demanded that Iran stop its nuclear program as a pre-condition to talking. Now America must accept that Iran has this capability, and the two sides can move on to other topics—as equals."

"Equals?" Casey asked with raised eyebrows.

"Equal in that both are nuclear states," Raad said. "I'm only saying they may start *talking* to each other again—beyond just one phone call, I mean—which is more than they've done officially in over thirty years. It will take time before anything of substance is discussed, I imagine. And I wouldn't expect either country's embassies to re-open anytime soon. But eventually they will."

Casey pulled a folded piece of blank notebook paper and a pen from his back pocket and jotted down a few notes. When he finished, he looked back up and said, "Okay, that's one way this can play out in America. But what about locally? I mean, how does 'nuclear Iran' affect things around the region? Or even within Iran itself?"

"In Iran, it is a victory," Raad said. "And I don't care if you are a supporter of the regime or you hate them. Obtaining nuclear weapons has become a matter of national pride."

"What about Khamenei's fatwa?" Casey asked.

"Ah, yes. The 'no nukes' fatwa," Raad laughed. "A smokescreen, my friend. Just as your politicians said. But Khamenei, as weretched as he is, he's no idiot. By outlawing the use of nuclear weapons as something prohibited under Islamic law, the Supreme Leader not only tried to pull the wool over everyone's eyes, relying on the misperception that he truly is all-powerful, but he also brought in the support of the opposition who viewed the pursuit of these weapons as another chance for them to defy the Ayatollah. He removed a major platform of several protest groups this way. And let us not forget that Khamenei outlawed the *use* of nuclear weapons, not the *possession* of them. A subtle difference from his 1995 stance, no?"

"That wasn't just something that got lost in translation?"

Raad shook his head. "Not at all. As I said, Khamenei is a shrewd actor."

Casey took in everything Raad said and decided the project Jim Shelton had him and the others working on back at the office wasn't so academic anymore. He promised himself that when he returned to New York he'd push for excluding any options that didn't assume Iran had a fully-functioning nuclear arsenal. They might not have one now, but if Raad was right, they would have one soon enough. "Well that's good to know," Casey said. "I don't mean good that they're planning to go that far, but good to know there's no question. It kinda puts a little more urgency in coming up with a strategy for dealing with the whole situation."

"I suppose it does," Raad said.

"Even if that's just getting folks to the table sooner," Casey added.

"But who would come to that table?" Raad asked.

"You mean besides the United States?"

"Precisely," Raad said. "Or did you think both sides should jump right into bilateral discussions?"

"No," Casey said. "I hadn't thought about it at all. I guess I just assumed it would start with the P5+1 group, and after a few rounds, the presidents would join in."

"And that is the problem," Raad said. "This UN group has repeatedly failed to get anything done. If the United States wishes to have meaningful discussions, they should not invite the rest of the Security Council and Germany to tag along."

"And that's how Iran sees it?" Casey asked.

"It's the way they *should* see it," Raad said. "Perhaps in another year we will have an idea of what they are willing to do, but until then, we can only speculate."

Casey nodded, conceding the point. Neither man said anything to carry the conversation further, and before Casey could speak up, Raad broke the silence, reading the younger man's mind.

"So what news of The Council?" Raad asked, leaning forward to indicate the answer should not be spoken loudly lest others might hear.

"I think we hit a wall in New York," Casey said. "Greg Clawson died in prison last week, and there's no forward movement on finding out who Mitchell Evans was, let alone what connection he might have had to The Council's decision makers." Casey shook his head. "I don't see what else I can do."

Davood Raad smiled. "Not to worry," he said. "You have done quite enough already."

"What do you mean?" Casey asked.

Raad scratched his close-cropped beard and peered over his glasses. "My friend, the information you gave me about Keith Swanson's activities was the first break I've had in years investigating The

Council. Thanks to you, I was able to connect a high-level employee in the Department of Energy to that group."

"Who?" Casey asked.

Raad waved his hand in the air. "Do not worry about that," he said. "Just know that you have made this possible, and it is now starting to pay dividends. Things are already changing, Casey. And you were the one who made it happen."

Casey shook his head and said in a voice louder than Raad would have liked, "Nothing's changed. Swanson isn't in jail. Hell, he's still Cogburn's chief of staff. He's not even lying low after Tony Ward shot him in front of hundreds of people. And apparently it's easier to get facetime with the president than that guy."

Raad tried to calm the younger man down. "Listen, Casey, just because you do not see dark clouds, does not mean a storm is not on the horizon. The Council thrives on the secrecy of its activities, which is why it has taken me decades to peek behind the curtain. And why we must not let them know we can see. There will be a time when we can pull down that curtain and expose them for who they are, but that time is *not* now. We must have patience, or the curtain will close again, and The Council will disappear into the fog once more."

Casey was used to Raad's cryptic discourse. He figured it was accentuated on the lecture circuit, so he didn't ask him what the hell he was talking about, though he wanted to. Whatever insight Raad had gained into The Council's inner workings was something Casey knew he would have to find out later. But Casey was not so willing to just cut and run—not when he was the reason Raad had apparently made progress.

"Then tell me what I *can* do," Casey said. "I'm not going back to New York 'til Tuesday, so maybe I can be of some use while I'm here."

Raad stood up and brushed his hands on the front of his slacks. "Really, there is nothing more to do, Casey," he said. "Only waiting."

"Waiting," Casey repeated as he stood up. "Waiting for what?"

Raad smiled as he put his hand on Casey's shoulder and led him toward the door. "For the right moment."

Now Casey was tired of the puzzle-speak. He stopped abruptly and faced Raad. "And when is that?"

Raad let his hand slowly drop to his side. "Soon," he said. "Let us find out what The Council plans on doing about Iran first. Then we will have the chance to expose them *before* somthing happens." He removed his glasses and added, "That will the right moment. For the first time since its creation, The Council will be prevented from dictating the turn of world events. But we must have something to hang them with, or we may never get the chance again."

Casey nodded slowly. Raad made sense, and Casey chastised himself for choosing expediency over permanence. Giordano would not agree, but if they were going to bring down The Council for good, it would take patience and a little bit of self-control. Casey knew that, but it took Davood Raad to remind him.

"You're right," Casey said. "I'm sorry for the outburst."

"Don't worry, my friend," Raad said. "I know what The Council did to you, and I understand your eagerness to make someone pay. Justice is not an exclusively American concept, you know."

That drew a laugh from Casey. "No, it's not," he said as he moved towards the exit. He opened the door and stopped before leaving. "I meant to ask you...that guy who was in here before me...with the leather jacket?"

"Yes?"

"What did he do to piss you off so bad?" Casey asked.

Raad stared blankly at Casey. "I'm not sure I...."

"It sounded like you were tearing him a new asshole before I came in," Casey said. "It looked like you were giving it to him last night, too. After the lecture."

Raad smiled. "That was a student I was helping with a paper," he said. "His professor gave him a low score, and the young man blamed me for giving him faulty information." Raad shook his head. "I try to help the Iranian students succeed when I can, but sometimes this younger generation just wants things handed to them without having to do any work for themselves."

"I'm glad to see that isn't exclusively American either," Casey said. "Well, enjoy the rest of your weekend, sir."

"And you too, my friend. I will let you know of any progress should things begin to happen," Raad said, speaking cryptically again as they moved into the open passageway.

Casey made his way to the elevator and heard Dr. Raad's office door close. He felt slightly dejected, as if he had failed in his mission. The information Raad gave him would definitely help the group's project back at IWG, but the information Raad *didn't* give wouldn't help Paul Giordano in the least. He needed a name. Casey wasn't heading back to New York for three more days. Maybe by then he'd get Raad to throw him a bone.

The elevator signalled its arrival, and Casey stepped in. He pulled the sleeve of his jacket back and checked his watch. *I guess I can be early*, he thought.

Chapter 12

Despite being over 200 miles southwest of New York, Washington, D.C., in January was just as cold. As he left the Jennings Institute, Casey pulled his jacket collar higher on his neck to protect against the wind that wasn't there when he arrived. He was quick to note that none of the other pedestrians around Dupont Circle appeared to be as concerned about the possibility of frostbite. *Maybe they're used to it,* Casey thought. But he wasn't. After a lifetime in South Georgia, Casey's blood was too thin to ever be comfortable when the temperature dropped below fifty. At times he felt more akin to the gators of Folkston than the humans north of Chattanooga.

Casey tried to orient himself at the circle, looking for a sign that would point him toward the metro station. He looked at the hotel stationary where he had written down directions to Andie Jackson's apartment the night before and put any thoughts of The Council on the backburner. Casey hadn't forgotten that his primary reason for coming to D.C., at least the reason Jim Shelton agreed to let him go, was to find information to support IWG's analysis of possible ramifications of Iran's nuclear test. He hoped to exploit the two resources he had in the town. Dr. Raad was the first, providing the Iranian perspective. Andie was the second.

Andie offered to check with one of her colleagues in the White House press corps about any chatter coming from the Executive Office concerning initial reactions to the test. She thought the information would benefit Casey's project by giving him insight into the internal debates and not just the official statements. Andie reasoned that options were rarely discarded completely in Washington, and what the president and his team decided to do or not do in the first week, might not translate to policy shifts made a month down the road. In any case, the military was likely planning operations for every course of action, and if the Intelligence Watch Group was doing the same thing, Andie didn't see how a separate set of eyes on the problem could hurt—not when the U.S. government was one of IWG's biggest clients.

Casey found the sign he was looking for and made his way to the train.

Thankful for the relative warmth of the D.C. metro, Lev Cohen peered over the newspaper he was pretending to read in the back of the train car. He flipped the paper over to read the front page headlines below the fold—or that's what he wanted the people around him to think. The former Mossad assassin had boarded the train car a full four seconds before Casey Shenk, following from the front and using Mr. Shenk's focus on getting a seat to his advantage.

When Casey was situated in a forward-facing seat at the middle of the car, occupied with his cell phone, Cohen shifted his weight slightly. His back angled to the aisle, Cohen watched Casey through his reflection in the window. Cohen had been tailing the former vending route driver since Casey left the Georgetown lecture hall the night before, and the visit to the Jennings Institute only deepened the Israeli's suspicion. He began formulating a contingency plan. Unlike his last assignment that involved Mr. Casey Shenk of Savannah, Georgia, Lev Cohen was not there to kill him, but he was prepared to do just that.

Casey rang the buzzer to 3C when he arrived at the weathered brick two-story building in Arlington. A short walk from the metro station, the building was divided into five sections, each containing four apartments with a common door to the outside. The building was older, but it wasn't *old*, and judging from the Honda station wagon and rusting pickup truck out front, Casey surmised the rent probably wasn't that high—relative to other places around the District.

"Hello?" a voice answered from a box above the four buzzers.

"Andie, it's Casey," he said. "Could you let me in?"

"Hello?" Andie's voice repeated.

Casey huffed. It was too damn cold outside to be playing games. He leaned closer to the speaker and raised his voice. "Andie, it's me, Casey. Could you just open the door? I'm freezing my ass off." He pressed the buzzer again.

The box crackled. "Push the button on the speaker if you want to talk," Andie said.

Casey stepped back and reassessed the 1970s technological marvel and shook his head, smiling at his own stupidity. He did as Andie instructed. "Sorry about that," he said. "I hope I'm not too early, but you mind if I come up?"

"Top of the stairs to the left," Andie said as a loud click indicated the door was unlocked.

Casey pulled the door open and stepped into the building. Before the door swung shut, Casey was pushed forward and felt a stiff jab in his lower back. The sharp pain was quickly followed by a hand on his left shoulder and what felt like a pipe digging between his shoulder blades.

"No noise," a gruff voice whispered inches from his ear. "Keep moving."

"Who the fuck are...." Casey's question was cut short by another blow to his kidney. "All right. Shit. I'm going," Casey said between teeth clenched in pain. The two men moved up the creaking wooden stairs and stopped on the top landing. A gentle push of the pipe that Casey figured was more likely a pistol told Casey to stop stalling and knock on the door. He obliged, and five seconds later the door opened.

Before he could give a warning, a blinding flash filled Casey's vision as the butt of the pistol struck him hard behind the ear. The flash was replaced by darkness, and Casey collapsed at Andie's feet. Lev Cohen kicked Casey's feet out of the way and shut the door, turning the deadbolt while keeping his eyes and Glock G30S fixed on the speechless woman in bare feet and sweatpants in front of him.

"Sit," Cohen said with a down motion of his gun. Andie did as she was told, and when Lev was satisfied he wouldn't get any resistance from this stranger he kicked Casey in the gut to wake him up.

Casey groaned and slowly rolled onto his elbow, sliding to the closest wall for support. He looked over to Andie and, seeing that she was apparently unharmed, up at his assailant. A hint of recognition tapped on his memory bank, but he couldn't come up with an identity for the man in front of him. "What do you want?" Casey asked.

"The first thing I want is for the two of you to move over to the couch," Cohen said. Andie and Casey stood up cautiously and walked further into the apartment to the worn leather sofa. When both were seated, Cohen moved in front of them, keeping his pistol trained on

Andie as she was the unknown quantity in his calculations. The last thing he needed was an overzealous martial arts expert disarming him—a possibility Cohen wasn't willing to risk. "It seems I misjudged you, Mr. Shenk," Cohen said, still standing to project an image of power over his seated hostages. "Perhaps I shouldn't have let you off so easily last time."

Casey's face betrayed his confusion.

"I had other wolves to deal with five years ago," Cohen said. "And while it appeared you did your part back then, things have certainly changed, haven't they?"

Casey quickly thought back to what he was doing in 2010 and where he may have run into the man with the gun before. Five years earlier, Casey was driving a vending truck in Savannah—until he heard the story of the MV *Baltic Venture*. It was that event that landed him at IWG in New York. And it also nearly got him killed, claiming the life of Mike Tunney, instead. Casey's eyes widened, and the recognition he sought was unmistakable. "Cohen?" he asked, knowing but not believing.

"So you remember," Cohen said.

"Yeah, last time we met you nearly broke my hand with a rifle stock," Casey said. He rubbed the back of his head. "I'd say *nothing's* changed since then."

Now that he and Casey were re-introduced, Cohen opened his jacket and holstered the pistol. Before he removed his hand from the grip, though, he looked at Andie and asked, "Is there going to be any trouble?"

Andie shook her head, still having no idea what was happening.

"Good," Cohen said, focusing again on Casey. "So, Mr. Shenk, would you mind telling me when you decided to betray your country and start selling secrets to the enemy?"

"What?"

"Was it before or after Eli Gedide sent me to kill you?" Cohen asked.

"Hold on a minute," Casey said. "What the fuck are you talking about?"

"Davood Raad," Cohen said. "You're helping him. Or do you deny that? Despite meeting with him last night at Georgetown and then again this morning at his downtown office?" He watched as Casey exchanged looks with the woman next to him. "So it *is* true."

Casey remained silent.

"That makes you an accessory," Cohen said. "So please, give me one good reason why I shouldn't put a bullet in your head right now."

"Because I didn't do anything," Casey said.

"Nothing?" Cohen barked. "You think the deaths of almost a dozen Mossad agents in six months is *nothing*?"

"Whoa, wait a second," Casey said. "What Mossad agents? Look, I'm helping Raad bring down The Council so they don't have free rein to manipulate world events as they see fit. If they're involved in... whatever you're talking about, you should be thanking me. Maybe we can stop them before any more people die."

Cohen's eyes shifted between Casey and Andie, both of whom sat eagerly awaiting a response.

"The Council?" Cohen asked.

"Isn't that what this is about?"

"This is about you working with a known operative for Iran's Ministry of Intelligence and Security," Cohen said. "That's what this is about. And if you're providing information to Raad on planned covert operations, I'm here to make sure you never get that chance again."

"Okay, first of all, I don't have access to any covert operations plans even if I wanted them," Casey said. "And second, I would never sell out my country, so fuck you, sir."

"And Davood Raad is a scholar, not a spy," Andie said, speaking for the first time since Cohen and Casey made their violent entrance.

"A scholar," Cohen said with a grunt. "Davood Raad has been working for the Iranian government longer than you've been out of diapers, I'm afraid." He turned his attention back to Casey. "I suppose you're going to tell me you were unaware of Raad's regime service?"

Casey winced as he shifted his weight on the seat. He took a deep breath and exhaled audibly, sinking gingerly into the cushions. "I know Raad worked for Mir Hossein Mousavi in the '80s, if that's what you mean. But he left when Khomeini died and Mousavi wasn't prime minister anymore."

Cohen shook his head. "He never left," he said. "Raad was a spy during the revolution in '79, and he's been a spy ever since."

"What about his anti-government publications?" Andie asked. "He's pretty much known around the world as one of the regime's most vocal critics."

"And because of that, he has the ability to travel anywhere he wants," Cohen said. "Western governments welcome him with open arms because his arguments reinforce the views they already have. Who better to garner international opposition to Iran than an Iranian who once worked for the Islamic Republic's prime minister?" He looked directly at Casey and said, "*You* trusted him. As have many others. It's that trust which Raad takes advantage of, manipulating people into handing over their countries' secrets or those of their allies. For years, Raad's activities have been of no great concern, but recently things have changed."

"I hear what you're saying, but why should I believe you?" Casey asked.

"Because you would never sell out your country," Cohen said. "And if you meant that when you said it, you can't take the chance of not believing me."

Cohen's reasoning made sense, and if Raad *was* working for the Iranian government, Casey could understand why Cohen was suspicious of his meetings with the man. Given the circumstances in which Casey and Cohen met the first time, he could even understand the Israeli's erroneous assumption that Casey had access to classified information Raad might be looking for. What he couldn't understand, however, was what Cohen hoped to gain by holding him and Andie hostage. "I told you, man, I don't have access to any secrets," Casey said. "I haven't had a security clearance for years. And if Davood Raad is the spymaster you say he is, why don't you just take him out? Or better yet, turn him in to the FBI?"

"Because I can't take down Raad until I find out who's providing him the information that is getting my people killed," Cohen said.

"So you're going to kick the shit outta anybody you think might be giving Raad secrets until you find the right one?" Casey asked. "That's outstanding."

"Not everyone who meets with Raad has had Russian hitmen and Kidon assassins trying to kill him," Cohen said. "So when I saw you show up at Raad's lecture last night, you quickly became a person of interest. And why the secretive meeting so early on a Saturday? I don't believe in coincidence, Mr. Shenk, and your entry into my operation was too convenient to ignore."

"Then let the Israeli prime minister ask our president for assistance," Casey said. "The FBI doesn't have to arrest Raad, but they can have a hundred agents working on the case this afternoon if they're given the order. No offense, but these guys are the best cops on the planet, and they'll probably find Raad's source faster than a lone Mossad assassin on foreign soil."

"I no longer work for Mossad," Cohen said. "But I am still sworn to protect the citizens of Israel, no matter whose soil I happen to be on." Cohen's aging knees popped as he sat down in a matching chair close to Andie's couch, thankful for the respite from standing. Despite the drama, Cohen never truly believed that Casey was the one passing operational plans to Davood Raad, but he had to be sure, and their conversation in the unknown woman's apartment did much to dispel any suspicion he had. "So you really had no idea that Raad was a spy? Or that he was still working for the Iranian government?"

"Not a clue," Casey said. "The thought never even crossed my mind until you brought it up. And even now, I still don't see it."

"That's because you weren't looking for it," Andie said.

"Or because you didn't want to see it," Cohen added.

"Either way, my business with Raad doesn't have anything to do with Iran's government," Casey said. "The Council's more of an American problem."

"That's the second time you've mentioned 'The Council,'" Cohen said.

Casey was surprised that Lev Cohen had apparently never heard of the group, and he was uncertain whether an explanation would help his case or not. The shroud of secrecy surrounding The Council was precisely what caused its very existence to occupy the realms of conspiracy theory and urban myth. Even Susan's firsthand encounter with The Council was not enough to convince her of the truth. Casey doubted his *word* was good enough for Cohen, but perhaps Casey's willingness to trust the Israeli would be reciprocated if he told him all he knew about the group and Raad's interest in it. He leaned forward with his elbows on his knees and said, "Raad was the one who first told me about The Council after the Manhattan bombings."

Cohen listened intently while Casey outlined the history of Davood Raad's investigations into The Council as relayed by the Iranian. He wanted Cohen to understand that Raad had been interested in The Council's activities long before Casey was enlisted to help, and Casey was only interested in exposing the group for its involvement in the 2011 terrorist bombings in New York City. "I came to D.C. to find out if Dr. Raad had any names I could give to the NYPD that might tie The Council to a prison death a few days ago."

"Prison death?" Cohen asked.

"One of the bombers...well, he was never charged with that," Casey said. "He was in prison for trying to assassinate a U.S. senator, but I think he was trying to kill Keith Swanson, the senator's chief of staff—who's also a member of The Council. Problem is, Detective Giordano of the NYPD is the only other person who believes that."

"So *you* were trying to get information from *Raad*," Cohen said.

"Exactly," Casey said. He watched Cohen working through the scenario and added, "The only thing I ever did for Raad was identify Swanson as someone he should look into. Raad said that helped him find an insider with the group, but other than that, he told me all we could do was wait for the right moment to expose them."

"Who?" Cohen asked.

"*Who* what?" Casey asked.

"Who is the insider Raad mentioned?"

Casey shrugged his shoulders and sat back in the couch. "He didn't give a name, just that the guy worked for the Department of Energy."

"Do you think he might be the one giving Raad those plans you were talking about?" Andie asked Cohen, reminding the two men that she was still in the room.

"That depends," Cohen said. "Would this Council have access to joint American and Israeli covert action plans?"

"Possibly," Casey said. "According to Raad, there's active duty military officers and politicians in The Council who might know that stuff." As soon as he finished the sentence, Casey realized how bad it sounded. First, because he was relying on an Iranian spy—according to Lev Cohen—to support his argument for the pedigree of The Council's membership. And second, except for Raad's declarations, Casey had nothing to back up the assertion. He had personally witnessed the reach and power of The Council, but aside from Keith Swanson and the late Mitchell Evans, Casey didn't know the name of a single person in The Council.

Cohen contemplated the information he'd just been given and asked Casey, "Has Raad ever given you a reason for his interest in The Council?"

Casey shook his head, mentally kicking himself for never asking. "It never came up," he said. "I was so focused on exposing whoever was responsible for the New York bombings that I was just glad to find out there really was something behind the guy I saw outside the deli that morning and the cover-up and U.S. reaction that followed."

"Well, let's assume this group has access to operational plans," Cohen said. "That would certainly explain Raad's interest in them."

"What exactly are the covert plans you're talking about?" Andie asked. "You said your people were getting killed because the Iranians, I mean, Raad was finding out about them, but we can't help you unless we know what we're dealing with."

Cohen stared blankly in response to the question.

"You do want our help, don't you?" Andie asked.

"Lady, I don't even know your name," Cohen said.

"Andie Jackson," she said.

"And what is it you do, Ms. Jackson?" Cohen asked.

"I'm a reporter."

"Then how can I be sure you won't 'report' anything I tell you?" Cohen asked.

Andie blinked deliberately. "You're the one with the gun."

"Somehow I don't think that matters to you." He looked at Casey and asked, "Can I trust her?"

Casey looked at Andie and nodded. "She's been involved with this as long as I have."

Cohen stood up and went to each window in the room, closing blinds and drapes one by one. He went through the process less as a precaution against surveillance than as a means to impress upon Casey and Andie that what he was about to tell them could not be repeated. Cohen knew he shouldn't be telling them anything at all, but time was not on his side. When he was finished, he sat back down on the edge of the chair.

"For the past twelve years, Israel has been targeting elements of Iran's nuclear program to hinder its progress," Cohen said. "A direct attack on their facilities was never our first choice, and we felt that focusing on the development side would be more effective."

"What about the Natanz airstrike?" Casey asked. "That was a direct attack."

"Again, not our first choice," Cohen said. "We obviously haven't ruled out that option, but you can see how ineffective it was, though it did let the world know we were serious. So in the background, we have been tracking the leadership and academic circles to find critical drivers that can be disrupted clandestinely."

"You mean assassination," Andie said.

"Yes," Cohen said. "Only our methods are a bit more discriminate than your drone strikes."

"I'm not judging," Andie said.

Cohen continued. "Until recently, we've been successful in targeting those individuals responsible for the progression of Iran's nuclear weapons program—those who hold considerable influence with the Ayatollah and the Majlis to keep the program a national priority despite the international pressure. But there's a leak, and now our operations are compromised."

"Raad," Casey said.

"No," Cohen said. "Raad runs agents. If the leak is here in America, Raad is receiving the information from an agent he recruited and is passing it back to Tehran. I'm here to plug that leak."

"What if the leak is on your side?" Andie asked.

"Not likely," Cohen said.

"Why not?"

"Because there are very few people in Israel who know the operational details of each hit, and ten percent of them are dead."

"So you deduced the leak is coming from America," Casey said.

"Not just me," Cohen said.

Casey rolled his eyes. "Okay. You and the people you work for. But if there's already a leak on this side of the pond, why risk telling us about it?" he asked.

Cohen looked at Andie and back at Casey. "Because I need your help."

Chapter 13

In a nondescript, six-story office building just across the Potomac River from the governing center of the world's sole superpower, a bi-weekly gathering was taking shape. At first glance, the only thing the men and women taking seats around the massive oak table in the middle of the room or along the walls on either side seemed to have in common was the executive business attire of corporate or government officials, with a few military uniforms thrown in. The occupants of the room ranged in age from 25 to 75, and any outsider eavesdropping on the simultaneous conversations combining to make each individual exchange harder and harder to hear would notice that the majority of races and ethnic groups in America were more or less represented. Attendance varied meeting-to-meeting as schedules permitted, but the importance of that day's discussion brought more people than usual.

Scott Parker was one of the last to arrive. He spotted an open seat against the far wall of the conference room that occupied a good portion of the building's third floor, and he waded through the sea of bodies who would likely only quiet down two minutes after the meeting began. Parker sat down and nodded to his right.

"Packed house," he said to Walter Korzen, a perpetually grumpy State Department officer.

"Yep," the man replied without turning his head or his eyes from the long center table. He coughed into his fist and kicked the briefcase under his chair a few inches further away from Parker.

Parker knew from experience it was a wasted effort to try and engage Walt in small talk. The man was never in the mood. Balding, shorter than average, and a little overweight, Walt Korzen was not what you would call a ladies' man. Parker tended to think of him as the human version of the internet meme sensation, "Grumpy Cat."

Walt had been with State for over ten years. A watch officer at the Bureau of Diplomatic Security's command center in Rosslyn, Virginia, he had applied and been turned down for transition to the Foreign Service Officer program no less than seven times. He hated the odd rotational hours that came with manning the 24/7 watch center that monitored the security of America's diplomats overseas. His personal social life suffered for it. Not married, with no current prospects that Parker knew of, Korzen lived alone in a pricey but run-down townhouse in Alexandria.

But it wasn't his social status that earned him a seat on The Council, it was the connectivity he had as a watch officer and his ability to warn of coming problems in current and future global hotspots that made him valuable. If the watch officer promotion potential was minimal, at least The Council offered him the opportunity to voice his opinions to some of the most powerful people in the country. That, as it turned out, was precisely why many of the people were in the room.

Detecting that Walter Korzen was grumpier than usual—if that was possible—Parker gave up on the small talk and scanned the room to see who else was there. He counted two army generals, six congressmen, three senators, two former senators, a bank CEO, an undersecretary of State, a deputy undersecretary of Defense, an assistant secretary of Treasury, and a secretary. His eyes moved down the slender length of the secretary and paused at her toned calves, unaided by the high heels so many women with less-shapely curves relied on to achieve the same effect.

"If everyone could take their seats, we'll get started," a voice boomed in deep baritone over the noise. Parker's attention shifted from oggling the legs of General Maxwell's personal assistant to the end of the table where Judge Calvin Westbrooke threw menacing stares at anyone who didn't immediately halt their conversations. There were not many. With a voice that was equal parts God and Darth Vader, Judge Westbrooke had the ability to make even the president of the United States snap to attention.

"In a moment, we're going to hear from Cyrus Shirazi on his thoughts for getting Greece back on track before it drags all of Europe down with it," Westbrooke announced. "But before we tackle that issue, we need to discuss the Iran nuclear test. I've asked Simon Wexler from the Brookings Doha Center to give us a verbal primer."

"Thank you, Judge." Wexler moved from his seat in the back corner and stood to Westbrooke's left. "As we all know, Iran has continued to advance its nuclear weapons program despite the economic sanctions levied against it. This week's underground testing is evidence of just how much progress Iran has made. The initial assessments of how long before Iran would reach the breakout level required for a test was five years. That was two years ago."

Wexler paused as a few muted whispers and shifting of weight in chairs indicated that people were listening, and they were concerned. "As we also know," he continued, "there is a lag time between success-ful testing and weaponization. Historically, this has taken countries anywhere from five to ten years—if they ever got that far. But given our faulty estimates of Iran's technical ability to reach the first step in the development cycle, I believe the Islamic Republic will have an operational weapon that could strike Israel or Saudi Arabia by next summer."

The noise instantly grew louder as Wexler's prognosis drew comments from nearly everyone in the room—either to themselves or their neighbor. Judge Westbrooke allowed the commotion to continue for half a minute before slapping his open palm on the table, improvising his daily courtroom gesture sans gavel. It only took three raps before people quieted down and turned their attention back to The Council's forward contact in Qatar.

"Thank you, Judge," Wexler said. "I expected that this estimate might cause some unease," he said, addressing the audience again, "but I don't want to seem like an alarmist. On the contrary, I think eighteen months is more than enough time for us to address the problem."

"How do you figure that?" someone asked from one of the wall seats.

"Because now there is no doubt about Iran's intentions," Wexler said. "Now the president no longer has to tiptoe around the issue, worrying about provoking Iran with accusations during negotiations. For all intents and purposes, Iran has shut the door on the nuke talks and dared the U.S. to make the next move."

"And what *is* that move?"

"That's the question we're all here to answer, isn't it?" Wexler answered.

"Thank you, Dr. Wexler," Westbrooke said as Wexler took his seat. Westbrooke finished jotting down a note and looked up from the yellow legal pad in front of him. "So how should the president respond?" he asked the group.

"We send in saboteurs to shut down their operations, like we should have ten years ago," Cole Dumfries, the leather-faced former naval officer-turned-former director of operations at the Central Intelligence Agency said. "If not their people, then ours. I don't care if it's DoD or CIA, but we need people on the ground to put a hard stop on their development."

"That wasn't a viable option in 2005, Admiral, and it's even less so today," Wexler said from the corner of the table. "Iran's operations are too dispersed, and frankly, we don't even know the locations of all their facilities."

"I'm just saying that our little Stuxnet computer games didn't work, so if we're serious about stopping the sons-o'-bitches for good, we need a kinetic response that will set them back a quarter century."

"What about recruiting some martyrdom-seekers for the job?" Kelly Hunt from the U.S. Agency for International Development, or USAID, chimed in. She was new to the group, brought in for her overseas connections, and because she was the granddaughter of the late Ambassador Adolphus L. Hunt, III, one of The Council's founding members. "Maybe some people from al Nusrah or the Khorasan Group that we've helped arm in Syria."

"It's unlikely any of them would abandon their fight against Assad. At least there they have a chance at victory," Wexler said. "Even jihadis do a cost-benefit analysis before agreeing to blow themselves up."

"And trying to find takers among the Iranian population is even more of a stretch than recruiting Syrian jihadis," Cyrus Shirazi, the four-time Democratic congressman from California's 42nd District added. "An Iranian bomb is a source of nationalistic pride that will likely strengthen popular support for the Khamenei regime. Even the moderates want to see Iran as the regional hegemon and a leader on the world stage. Let's face it, having a nuclear arsenal will make people pay attention, and right now, Iran sees this as its best bet for stopping the bully-tactics it feels the West—in particular the U.S.—has been using for decades. By and large, the Iranian people support that view."

"But we can't just do nothing," Dumfries said. "That would almost guarantee Dr. Wexler's timeline holds true."

There was about a minute of silence as people searched for an alternative. Finally, Westbrooke posed the only option he could think of. "Then we continue the Mossad operations. Maybe expand the target list to include members of the Majlis or any of those IRGC bastards. Somebody the Iranians wouldn't expect us to hit."

More muted talking.

"Mossad isn't having an easy time of it right now, in case nobody noticed," Air Force General Christopher Maxwell of U.S. Strategic Command said. "Hitting their parliament members or Guard Corps commanders will mean more security barriers, not less. I like Cole's option. We should dump the Israelis, send in a bunch of snake-eaters, and take care of this ourselves."

"Maybe they're just having a run of bad luck," Westbrooke offered.

"Yes and no."

Heads turned to the back of the room where Colonel Tim Jankowski was seated. Though dressed in a navy blue blazer and pressed khaki pants, there was no mistaking his affiliation. The high-and-tight gave that away. Jankowski was one of the rising stars of The Council, if not the United States Marine Corps. A member of the Joint Chiefs of Staff Intelligence Directorate, commonly referred to as the J2, Jankowski had distinguished himself in both Iraq and Afghanistan. But his unapologetic brashness that made him a popular and effective field commander was viewed by much of the JCS brass as borderline insubordination. He was not afraid to speak his mind and call out his superiors—civilian or military—if he felt their actions would harm his beloved Corps or the country he was awarded a Navy Cross and three Purple Hearts defending.

"The Israelis think there might be a leak," Jankowski said.

"A leak?" Westbrooke asked.

"Of the operational details of the assassinations. Israel doesn't know how much the Iranians are getting, but it's at least the target names and locations of the planned attacks."

"And the leaks are coming from the Israeli side?"

"They don't know that either," Jankowski said.

"Christ," Maxwell muttered. "So we really are out of options." He turned in his chair to face Jankowski. "What about *Turnstile*? Is that still on?"

Jankowski slowly nodded. "*Turnstile* is still on."

"But how do we know that program isn't compromised, too?" Maxwell asked.

"We don't."

Maxwell shook his head and grinned disgustedly. "You fuckers in J2 don't know much, do you, son?"

"We know what we don't know, General," Jankowski said. He looked at Maxwell's personal assistant, making it obvious enough for the general to notice. "We even know things *you* don't know we know...*sir.*"

Westbrooke noticed Maxwell's face flush red, and he stepped in before things quickly got out of control. "Alright, gentlemen." He focused on Jankowski. "The first *Turnstile* operation is set for Tuesday, correct?"

"Yes, sir."

"Well, assuming all goes as planned, I guess we'll find out one way or another if *Turnstile* is compromised. In the meantime, we need to check our own people—anyone outside of this room who has anything to do with the intel-sharing or logistics support, or anyone who's even heard of *Quick Note* or Mossad's involvement in it. If the leak is on our side, we need to stop it now. We are out of time, ladies and gentlemen."

The buzzing of conversation picked up again as people stood to leave. Parker leaned over as he stood. "What is *Turnstile*?"

"Hell if I know," Walter Korzen said while he buttoned his coat. "Those fucking ops guys love to keep everyone else guessing. Even here." Walt picked up his briefcase and was gone.

Parker looked around the room, wondering who else was in the dark about *Turnstile*. He also wondered if anyone there was leaking information about *Quick Note* to the Iranians. His eyes stopped on Cyrus Shirazi. *I wonder if Westbrooke's Golden Boy knows what* Turnstile *is.*

The thought quickly vanished as Maxwell's assistant walked into view. She said something to Shirazi, and both of them laughed. After a kiss on the congressman's cheek, she deftly moved through the crowd to catch the general as he departed. Parker watched Shirazi shake his head, still smiling.

Parker scowled. *Golden Boy.*

Chapter 14

Casey passed through the large rounded portico of the Holocaust Memorial Museum a block from the green expanse of the National Mall. It was late morning on Sunday, and a slow trickle of tourists came and went, though nowhere near the number that would flock to the area in six months as parents hauled their kids on summer vacation to the nation's capital. Casey shook off the cold as he entered the building, grateful for the modern convenience of central heating in January. He looked up at the monstrous skylight and then to the red brick "buildings" on either side of the large open area that was nothing like what he expected after seeing the ubiquitous D.C.-gray facade that was the front of the museum on 14th Street SW. There was a somberness to the room that made what few patrons there were speak in whispers as they made their way to the long staircases at the far end or to any of the other exhibit entrances.

"Follow me."

Casey jumped, startled as Lev Cohen passed briskly to Casey's left and headed for an exit halfway down the room's right side. Cohen was a full four strides ahead of Casey before the younger man stepped in that direction and had to jog to catch the door. Casey caught his breath as the two men made their way to what Casey figured was the second basement level, though he didn't see any signs to back up that assessment.

They entered into a long hallway with doors on each side. Casey tried to determine which direction they were headed relative to the museum entrance, but he gave up when Cohen entered a door two-thirds of the way down. *At least* he *knows where we're going*, Casey thought. Two more turns and they were in a darkened part of the larger room, only a small telescoping table lamp providing any light beyond what bled in through the open doorway. A small man with sporadic wisps of white hair hunched over the illuminated table and motioned with an outstetched hand for the two intruders to wait until he was finished. Casey almost laughed at the scene he was sure he'd seen in dozens of B-grade action and mystery movies on Netflix.

The old man put down his pencil and moved a book to a curling corner of the parchment he was laboring over. He looked up and pivoted the table lamp to get a better look at the two men who interrupted his work. His face went from tired inspection to bright cordiality. "Levi. It is good to see you my friend," he beamed with outstretched arms. He and Cohen embraced briefly, and he looked at Casey. "And who did you bring with you?" he asked, still smiling but with a narrowing of eyes behind thick glasses.

"This is Casey Shenk. He has agreed to help us."

"Help *us*?" Casey asked.

Cohen motioned to the old man. "Josef Kronfeld is an old family friend."

"Not that old," Josef said with a wink as he shook Casey's hand. Casey's eyes moved to the blurred tattoo on Josef's forearm—numbers indicating the man had been in one of the Nazi death camps in World War II.

Josef noticed Casey's gaze. "I was six years old when the Americans liberated Buchenwald," he said. "My mother took me to America after the war, and I have been here ever since." He inhaled deeply. "My father was not so lucky. He was killed when a group of the prisoners resisted our Nazi captors as they tried to exterminate as many of us as they could before evacuating."

"I'm sorry," Casey almost whispered.

"Do not be sorry, Mr. Shenk. I am alive, you are alive, Levi here is alive. Life is a gift we must celebrate every day. We should never forget the courage and sacrifice of those who came before us and who stood up to evil and allowed us to live. Our celebration is a tribute to them."

Casey nodded, humbled by Josef's optimism. He looked at Cohen, then back at Josef. "So you are a curator here?"

"Among other things," he said, winking again. "Please. Follow me."

Josef gathered his cane from a stool by the table and switched off the lamp. Cohen and Casey followed him to a smaller adjacent room. Josef turned on an overhead light and sat in an oversized leather armchair in front of a gray metal desk piled high with papers. The contrast of luxury and utility seemed perfectly normal to Josef and Cohen, so Casey kept the observation to himself.

Josef produced a key from his pants pocket and unlocked a large file drawer at the bottom of the desk. He flipped through a few visible tabs and removed a worn, brown leather portfolio secured with a dirty rubber band. He handed it to Cohen.

"Davood Raad is slippery outside of his public speaking engagements," Josef said as Cohen leafed through the papers in the portfolio. "He rarely keeps to any discernible office hours, either."

Casey began to understand. Cohen was using Josef Kronfeld to watch Raad. Or rather, to find out who Raad was getting information from. He didn't see how a 76-year-old man, by Casey's estimation, could be expected to trail someone alone, so he assumed there must be others doing the surveillance work.

Cohen held up a tri-fold pamphlet printed on pale green paper. "Significance?" he asked.

Josef looked closer. "Ah, yes. The Islamic Community Center in Manassas. One of the suburbs in Virginia. Very nice people, the Manassas Muslim Association. I cannot say the same for some of the other groups here in America. You see, the attitude is very different away from New York or Minneapolis."

"That's nice, Josef, but why is this in with the other papers you handed me?"

"You asked us to follow Raad. We followed him," Josef said. "He went there to sign books two weeks ago. He has not been there since."

"Any other book signings?" Cohen asked.

"Two, aside from his lectures. It is all in there," Josef said, sounding slightly irritated. "If we had been given more time, perhaps we could have found more useful information."

Cohen straightened the papers in the portfolio and replaced the rubber band. He put his hand on the old man's shoulder. "Thank you, Josef. I will take this information and see what I can come up with. Your help on such short notice is a testament to your dedication to the protection of Israel."

"Not just Israel, my friend. The world. If Iran develops a nuclear weapon, it is not only Israel or the Jewish people who will be in danger, but all of mankind. Because if Iran launches one, there will be retaliation, and events will cascade such that the loss of life will make this...," Josef motioned to the museum above them and by inference the holocaust itself, "...merely a shadow of the horrors that will follow."

"Let's hope it doesn't come to that," Cohen said. He shook Josef's hand. "The next time I see you, old friend, I pray it is under less somber circumstances."

"You think he's right?" Casey asked as they ascended the staircase from the basement. "I mean, about armageddon if Iran gets the bomb."

Cohen stopped, almost sending Casey tumbling down a flight. "Josef Kronfeld has seen evil firsthand," Cohen said. "Not the sort of evil you, or even I, have seen, but pure, unfeeling, burning evil where children and innocent people were herded like cattle into sealed rooms, where their last breaths were of blistering, choking poison. Their bodies were bulldozed into open pits they dug themseves just hours earlier, their corpses covered in lime to mask the stench of decaying flesh as newly arrived trucks offloaded their passengers, some knowing what fate ultimately awaited them—others with no idea.

"That same evil is back again. In Syria. In Iraq. In Sudan. Only this time the victims are hacked to death, beheaded, drowned, or burned alive. So if you ask me do I think Josef Kronfeld is right, that armageddon is coming...I say it is. Will it be a total nuclear war as Josef sees it? No. I don't believe so. But you can believe this, Mr. Shenk, if Iran develops an operational nuclear weapon, it is only a matter of time before all of its proxies have one as well.

"The West thinks Hizballah and Hamas fighting the Islamic State of Iraq and al Sham is a good thing. But how much good are they doing? How will Baghdadi's legions be defeated? Not by Iran's terrorist puppets, and not by occasional American air stikes supporting the weak Iraqi military and security forces. And when Hizballah's forces are near depletion, and Lebanon is next to fall, do you think Iran will hesitate to save its most lethal and most loyal proxy by using a nuclear weapon?"

"No?"

"No. It will not," Cohen said. "The fight against ISIS will not end nicely. And the Middle East will be a different place for decades to come. But if Iran introduces a nuclear bomb into the equation, the region will be uninhabitable, and entire generations will be lost outright. That is why we must find Raad's agent. Unless we stop the leak, Iran will continue its progress toward a nuclear weapon unopposed, and that armageddon scenario will be more likely than you think."

Whatever doubts Casey had about helping Cohen were gone. Not once did Cohen mention the inevitable destruction of Israel or even a nuclear counterstrike by Israel should Iran strike first. Cohen was talking about the destuction of the entire Middle East—Arabs and Israelis; Christians, Muslims, and Jews. There were no selfish motives evident in Cohen's mission. He was there to save lives—by taking lives, to be sure—but to save them, nonetheless. His job was to ultimately protect the innocent who had no say in the matter by stopping those who did.

"So what's our next move?" Casey asked.

Cohen held up the portfolio. "Let's find out who's been talking to Raad."

Chapter 15

Scott Parker and Leo Ambrosi were already seated in the White House situation room when the president's chief of staff, Kurt Vanek, came in, followed by Adam Miller and a squat, slightly overweight man with brown hair, graying at the temples. Parker stood to shake hands with the new Israeli ambassador to the United States, Moshe Safran, after Ambrosi made the requisite introductions. Parker took Miller's hand and smiled. "Adam," he said, seeing a thinly veiled look of surprise and annoyance in Miller's eyes at Parker's presence in the meeting.

"Scott," Miller replied as everyone took a seat.

No one sat at the head of the table, customarily reserved for the president. It was *his* situation room, after all. Instead, the two Israeli officials sat across from the three Americans as if preparing for diplomatic negotiations rather than an orientation for the new ambassador. Despite the official schedule title, the meeting was exactly that—a negotiation.

"Thank you for agreeing to meet me on your sabbath, Mr. Vanek and Mr. Ambrosi," Ambassador Safran said with a slight British accent that left no doubt where he had learned to speak English. He nodded to Parker, nonverbally acknowledging his "sacrifice," as well.

"We all understand the gravity of this meeting, Mr. Ambassador," Vanek said. "It is important that our two countries maintain solidarity as we figure out how best to respond to the recent event in Iran."

"The State of Israel agrees it would be desirable for our two nations to act in concert on this matter, but my leadership feels the current U.S. administration is not taking the threat of a nuclear-armed Iran seriously," Safran said. "The support we have received from America for our current operations is appreciated and invaluable, yet as we all witnessed over the past week, it is not enough. Iran will continue to make progress towards developing a nuclear weapon at an ever-increasing pace unless more concrete measures are taken to stop it."

"You are talking about military intervention?"

"That is precisely what I am talking about, Mr. Vanek."

"And Israel believes airstrikes will accomplish this?" Vanek asked. "Or are you considering a full military invasion?"

"Israel cannot win a conventional ground war against Iran by itself," Safran said.

"So you want the United States to commit forces." Vanek shook his head. "That will not happen, Mr. Ambassador."

Safran leaned forward. "Then we will continue our current operations," he said. "But even if we are able to succeed, we can only slow the bleeding. Without a more direct and drastic response to Iran's advancing nuclear weapons development, the Middle East will hemorrhage, and America will have no choice but to get its hands dirty."

"The Middle East has been hemorrhaging for centuries," Vanek barked. "And how dare you imply the U.S. has been sitting on its hands while the whole region goes up in flames. We have lost thousands of American lives fighting two wars in Iraq and Afghanistan since 9/11 trying to stabilize that region."

"And it is those wars which caused the chaos that exists there now," Safran said, equally loud. "Perhaps if America had chosen the right enemy, we would never have witnessed the rise of ISIS, and Iran would not have conducted a nuclear test."

"Kurt, Mr. Safran, please calm down," Ambrosi pleaded. "This argument will get us nowhere, and we are losing focus on why we are here in the first place."

The two men quieted. "Thank you, Leo," Ambrosi said after sipping water from a glass pre-positioned on the table by the situation room staffers before the meeting began. He looked up at the Israeli ambassador across the table. "I'm sorry, Mr. Ambassador."

"No apology needed, Mr. Vanek. I know your son lost a leg in Afghanistan and your wife lost a brother in Iraq. It is I who should apologize for not being more sensitive to your feelings."

Safran said the right words, but there was a hint of insincerity in his voice. Unsure if Vanek made the same observation, Ambrosi spoke up before the shouting began again. "Mr. Ambassador, in the absence of putting boots on the ground in Iran, perhaps America could offer a more direct level of intelligence sharing that will help both of our countries better understand where Iran is in its efforts to weaponize its nuclear material. America would certainly benefit from a more solid read-out on any ballistic missile advancements that may have occurred in violation of the sanctions. And we could possibly provide Israel with whatever MASINT we collected on the detonation."

"Thank you, Mr. Ambrosi," Safran said. "This arrangement may be better discussed between our respective intelligence chiefs."

"Certainly," Ambrosi said.

"I would caution against an increase in intel-sharing right now," Parker said. "The world is going to be focused on what either of our countries do in response to the nuclear test, and if America is implicated in any way with unilateral Israeli actions, it could torpedo any chance at a diplomatic solution to this crisis." Parker looked around the table for any reactions. Safran and Vanek seemed to be considering Parker's statement, but Ambrosi gave his deputy an unmistakable evil eye before writing a note on the paper in front of him. Miller's eyes narrowed.

"I will bring up the intelligence sharing proposal with the president this afternoon," Vanek told Safran. "But I can tell you that he has already spoken with your prime minister, and we are looking into fast-tracking the delivery of improved Patriot missile batteries to complement your Iron Dome system. The U.S. is already preparing to announce more sanctions in an effort to bring Iran back to the negotiating table, though I would comment off the record that our negotiating position is considerably weaker right now."

"I'd say," Parker muttered under his breath, grinning. His grin slowly disappeared when he caught Miller's admonishing glare from across the table.

"The president has agreed to station additional tanker aircraft in Turkey for future joint use if those negotiations fail," Vanek said. "As always, the president is keeping all options open. Our position, however, is that the time is not right for any offensive action, and all we ask is for more patience."

Safran began to say something, but Vanek cut him off. "We understand that Israel has been more than patient over the past decade. More patient, perhaps, than anyone should have expected, given Iran's past declarations and deceptions. It is a credit to the great State of Israel that you have exercised such measured restraint, limiting any military action against Iran to the airstikes on its nuclear facilities five years ago. All our president is asking is that Israel continue that restraint for just a little longer while we try to solve this diplomatically."

Safran sighed. "I am a diplomat, Mr. Vanek, and I too hope we can contain Iran through diplomatic means. But if diplomacy fails, you will see me again. Let us hope it is as partners and not as opponents." He stood up and shook Vanek's hand as everyone else in the room took the cue that the meeting was over.

"Let's hope I see you before then, Mr. Ambassador," Vanek said. "And perhaps it will be with cocktails in our hands and under lighter circumstances."

A Marine captain entered the room and escorted the two Israelis out. When the door shut, Vanek turned to Ambrosi. "That went well," he said.

"It did?" Ambrosi asked.

"Well, except for that asshole's comment of us not doing anything over in the sandbox." Vanek pocketed his pen and zipped his note-book shut. "Old Moshe there got an initiation of what its like when you come into the White House without doing your homework, and using day-old talking points." He added, "If you send me your notes, Leo, I'll consolidate them with mine and brief the boss on the meeting when I see him after dinner."

"Sure thing," Ambrosi answered. When Vanek left, he turned to Parker. "Sit down, Scott." Parker flipped the business card Miller slid across the table to him before leaving, put it in his pocket, and did what he was told.

Ambrosi leaned on the table next to Parker. "Do you know why we were invited to this meeting?"

Parker quickly tried to think of a good answer to what he was sure was a trick question. Two seconds. Nothing. He gave up. "No."

"We...or more accurately *I* was invited to give the impression of a confident administration that was looking for realistic ways we could work with Israel on this while at the same time keeping them from going off half-assed and starting another war that, frankly, we're not ready for. I wanted you to come along when I found out there would be two of them. It's always better to have more people on your side of the table to make the other guy a little uncomfortable."

"I figured that much," Parker said.

"What I *didn't* bring you along for was for you to open your god-damn mouth!" Ambrosi wiped spittle from the corner of his mouth. "I know the fucking risk of sharing intelligence with those bastards. And I damn-sure didn't need you to point that out in front of them. You made me look like an idiot in here."

"They know we're not stupid," Parker said. "I didn't tell them anything they don't already know."

"Then you didn't have to say anything at all. Which was exactly what you were supposed to do."

"With all due respect, a quick 'Hey Scott, don't say anything when the Israelis get here' would have done the trick."

"'Hey Scott, don't ever speak in a meeting again unless you are asked a direct question.' How's that? Is that better?"

Parker pursed his lips. "Yes, sir."

"Good."

"Can I go now?"

"Please." As Parker stood up to leave, Ambrosi said, "One more thing." He looked at Parker and waited until the steam stopped coming from his subordinate's ears. "Do you know what operations Safran was talking about continuing? He talked as if COS knew Israel was up to something. Another round of airstrikes, maybe?"

Parker smiled inwardly. "I'm not sure," he lied. *You really are an idiot, aren't you?* he thought. "Maybe it has to do with those Mossad operatives who keep getting killed that the Iranian and Arab media are reporting as failed assassination attempts. I mean, if you want to believe those sources."

Ambrosi thought about that for a few seconds. "Well, if Israel's playing the assassination game, I think we're right to keep out of it—even if it's just giving them intel," he said, subtly acknowledging Parker's earlier comment without saying so.

Parker slid his hands in his pockets and nodded agreement. His fingers brushed Miller's card. "Yeah, I'm not sure we need to give them any more help than we already are."

Chapter 16

Casey paid for their food, and he and Andie sat at an open pub-style table in the back of the Potbelly Sandwich Works on 11th Street NW. Casey placed his shopping bag on the empty chair next to him.

"So you think the Seahawks are gonna repeat this year?" Andie asked after they both finished their first bites.

Casey wiped the grease from the toasted Italian sandwich off his chin. "God, I hope not. I mean, I'm not cheering for New England, necessarily, but I can't stand Richard Sherman."

"That man talks too much," Andie agreed. "Did you see Roddy White's response on ESPN to Sherman's criticism of him and Julio?"

Casey nodded as he tried to swallow another part of his lunch, forgoing the napkin and clearing the grease drippings with the back of his hand, which he then "cleaned" by wiping it on his jeans. "That was awesome," he said. "Roddy is like a college professor when he breaks down Sherman's schoolyard rants."

"Roddy White," Andie said looking off in the distance, obviously focused on a vision that only she could see. "Now that's a man I'd cook grits for every morning."

"I like grits," Casey said with raised eyebrows.

Andie came back to reality and looked at Casey across the table. "There's a Cracker Barrel in Dumfries where your cracker-ass can get all the cheese grits you want," she said and bit into her ham sandwich.

Casey smiled. "I do love cheese grits."

"Speaking of grits, how are you and Susan doing?" Andie asked.

"All right, I guess."

"You don't sound so sure."

Casey washed down the last of his sandwich with a sip of water and said, "We're still getting used to being just friends."

"You mean *you're* just getting used to it," Andie said.

"Is it that obvious?"

"Not so obvious. But I know y'all haven't been dating for a few years, and from what Susan told me, she's got a new man anyway. That means she's used to y'all being just friends, so by deduction, you're the only one in that relationship still getting used to it."

"I guess you're right, but...wait...she told you she has a new boy-friend?"

Andie smiled. "Honey, Susan and I bonded during all that Cog-burn shit in New York. We call each other a few times a year just to touch base. I'm guessing you didn't know that."

"What? No, I didn't know that," Casey said. "If you knew we weren't dating anymore, why'd you ask in the first place?"

Her smile became a laugh. "Damn, I didn't know you were so sensitive about it," she said. "I'm sorry. Really. I just wanted to know how things were going for you. I get to talk to Susan every few months or so, but the first time I hear from you in almost four years, I get held hostage at gunpoint in my own apartment. That gave me the impression that you've been pretty busy since I left."

"So why didn't you just ask how *I* was doing?"

"Because it's usually the reaction to a question that tells the true story, rather than the answer," Andie said. "Susan told me you were getting along fine with her new beau, but your reaction tells me that's not exactly true."

Casey had recovered from the unexpected investigation and analysis of his defunct love life, and he leaned forward with his elbows on the table. "I get along with Dylan just fine. He's a good guy. Hell, I'm even okay with Susan and I being just friends. We haven't dated for forever, so I've adjusted, no problem. You just happened to ask me how we're doing like less than a week after Susan got engaged."

"She got engaged?"

"Yes, ma'am. She and Dylan are actually getting married," Casey said. "I guess that's really the part I'm gonna have to get used to. Going out for a beer with a buddy who happens to be dating someone else is one thing. Going for a drink with someone else's wife is something totally different."

"Only if the husband is an asshole."

"What?"

"If it's a jealous husband who doesn't trust his wife then, sure, there might be problems," Andie said. "But if Dylan's a good guy like you said, and you both get along okay, there's no reason you can't still be Susan's friend. If anything, it sounds like maybe the only problem here is you, Casey."

"Me?"

"Sure. You're just afraid this Dylan character is going to take away what you think is yours, and he's not going to share."

"Look. Susan's her own person. She's not mine. She never was."

"Exactly, Casey. That's why you shouldn't worry about losing Susan as a friend. She's not going to let her marriage take that away. It just changes the routine, not the friendship."

Casey looked at his empty plate and smiled. "That's what Susan told me."

"Well, she's right," Andie said. "And so am I. So what's in the bag?" she asked, ending the impromptu lesson from "Dear Andie."

Casey was thankful for the change of subject and put the Barnes and Noble bag on the table after pushing his plate to the side. He reached in and handed the book to Andie.

She examined the cover. "*Withering on the Vine*. So they actually had it."

"Two more copies left if you want one. Same building as here, just around the corner."

Andie handed the book back. "No, thank you. Are you gonna read it?"

Casey checked the thickness of Raad's book and put it back in the bag. "Maybe later. I just bought it so Raad could autograph it."

"Then you can sell it on eBay?"

"No," Casey laughed. He checked around the room to make sure the lunchtime crowd was too busy with their own conversations and food to be listening. "I'm meeting Raad at 1500 today. I mean, three o'clock. I told him I wanted to have him sign his book before I went back to New York. But Cohen wants me to try and find out as much information about his near-term schedule as I can or any other clues in his office that might lead us to whoever his contact is."

Andie stirred the ice in her sweet tea and looked up at Casey. "And you trust Cohen? You think he's right about Raad?"

"I do now."

"And that's not because he had a gun in your face?" Andie asked.

"That was no different than the first time we met."

"What do you mean?"

"Well, he tried to kill me, but he missed." He thought of Mike Tunney, who wasn't so lucky. "But then he saved my life a week later. So, yeah, I trust him. As much as you can trust any assassin, I suppose."

Chapter 17

Casey knocked on Raad's door at the Jennings Institute after he already had two feet in the room. Raad jumped in his chair and knocked over a glass of thick, syrupy juice from some fruit Casey couldn't identify. Raad quickly grabbed the overturned glass, salvaging half of its contents. "Oh shit! I'm sorry, sir. I didn't mean to startle you," Casey said, looking around for anything to help wipe up the mess that somehow missed two stacks of paper. The desk calendar was another story.

Raad muttered something Casey couldn't understand and pulled a handkerchief from the suit jacket on the back of his chair. "You want me to grab come paper towels from the head?" Casey asked as Raad did his best to sweep the red-brown liquid into a manageable puddle. Casey saw a folded newspaper to Raad's left with yellow highlights marking a few words here and there. A capless marker on the carpet told Casey that Raad was making the notations when the accident happened.

"No, no, it is all right," Raad said, declining Casey's offer.

Casey bent down to pick up the fallen highlighter. When he straightened, Raad took the saturated linen and dropped it in the waste basket behind him. Casey handed Raad the highlighter and saw that the newspaper was no longer there. *Guess that got ruined, too*, he thought.

"You are early," Raad said, inspecting his white oxford shirt for any stray splash marks.

"I know," Casey said. "I thought the metro ride was going to be longer. I hope you don't mind. Well, except for making you spill your drink."

Raad smiled, relaxed after the clean-up job was complete. "Of course not." He let out a long breath and said, "So you are leaving tomorrow?"

"Yes, sir. That's why I wanted to get you to sign your book today," Casey said as he handed Raad the copy of *Withering on the Vine* he purchased a few hour earlier. "I'm driving back early in the morning and knew I wouldn't get a chance to see you again. At least not until the next time you come up to New York."

Raad took the book from Casey and opened it on top of one of the paper piles that was spared the juice attack. "I am glad you came, Casey," he said as he wrote a note on the book's title page. "It is always a pleasure to see you, and I do not know the next time I will be back to New York."

Casey placed the book back in the plastic bag when Raad was done and took a seat in the leather chair in front of the desk. "May I?" he asked, realizing Raad never actually invited him to sit, but wanting to stay and chat. He was there for more than just an autograph, after all.

"Please," Raad said. "There is someting you wish to talk about?"

"Thank you." Casey set the bag on the floor next to the chair. Casey appeared nervous—only partially acting. "Are you still working with Dr. Brackmann?"

"Pardon?"

"Well, back in New York it seemed like you were busy working with him to try and penetrate The Council. When I called Jennings up there, Brackmann said you were lecturing, but he didn't mention anything about The Council or what else you were working on down here. I was just thinking that with you in D.C., maybe I could link up with Dr. Brackmann at the New York office, and if you *are* still working with him, I could help y'all expose them."

"Casey, we went through this. Now is..."

"I know, 'now is not the time.' I just mean, when the opportunity presents itself, you may want someone who already knows the score to help you bring them down. I could do that. Hell, I'd be happy to do it."

"What do you have in mind?"

"Anything," Casey said, trying not to sound too eager. "I'm right there with Wall Street, the UN. Name it, there's a lot of stuff I could get access to."

Raad chuckled. "We know where you work, Casey. And when the time comes, we will be in touch if there is anything more we need from you, trust me. But right now it is best if we all step back and wait for the right opportunity. We will monitor the situation for when that opportunity presents itself, to be sure, but in the meantime, we must continue to stay busy with our other duties. You have your job with IWG, and I am lecturing. If you must know, I am also helping the NCRI improve its Washington office set-up while I am here, as well. You see, The Council is but one of my personal interests. When the National Council of Resistance of Iran was allowed to operate freely in America two years ago to counter Supreme Leader Khamenei's regime—at least its oppressive policies and rhetoric—the NCRI leadership enlisted my help because of the international contacts I have made through my lecturing and official travel."

Casey made a mental note of Raad's side activities in Washington to pass along to Cohen later, but he wanted Raad to believe he was interested in none of that. "I understand what you're saying, but couldn't we create the opportunity to bring down The Council, instead of just waiting for it to happen?"

"Meaning?"

"Meaning there is a current investigation into a prison suicide that smells a lot like The Council, and if I have a name—any name—that I could connect to the prison system or lawyers or anyone who was in contact with Greg Clawson before he died, I can get concrete evidence of how far The Council reaches, at least in New York."

"And you can find all this out by yourself?"

"I have a contact in the NYPD with access to the investigation."

Raad raised a single eyebrow. "You have a contact in the New York Police Department. Who is it?"

Casey had intended to reveal that piece of information to Raad, but he hadn't anticipated Raad's request for an identity. *Maybe he'll trade*, Casey thought. "Detective Giovanni. Patrick Giovanni. Pat," Casey answered, hoping there wasn't a real "Patrick Giovanni" on the force who now might be on Raad's list of folks to track down.

"I love American names," Raad smiled. "Your detective is Irish *and* Italian? No doubt tormented as a child from both sides."

Casey hoped Raad's interest stopped there. "So do you know anyone we could look into who might connect the murder to The Council?"

"Murder?"

"Clawson. Gior...Giovanni thinks it was a murder made to look like a suicide." Casey could feel his ears turning red at the misstep. The last thing he wanted to do was be caught lying to an Iranian spy.

"Raad shook his head. "I'm sorry, Casey. I do not have a name I can give you. But if you insist on finding more about The Council's reach in New York, as you said, you can start with Wall Street, as you mentioned. Perhaps another set of eyes on the financial activities of the group could prove useful."

Casey accepted the fact that he wasn't going to get a name out of Raad. He looked at his watch and stood up. "Will do," he said. "I'll see what I can put together and then maybe get back with you to compare notes." Casey wanted to leave Raad with the impression that he was eager to take on this new assignment.

"Or bring your findings to Eitan Brackmann," Raad said. "He is the second set of eyes in this now-three-person investigation, and you will not have to put your life in danger on the highways driving back to Washington." He stood and shook hands with Casey as the phone on his desk rang.

"Hello?" he said when he picked up the handset. "Salam. Yek lahzeh." He covered the transmitter. "I'm sorry, Casey. I must take this call. Travel safe, my friend."

"Thank you again, sir." Casey held up the bag as he left the room and shut the door behind him. He made his way to the elevator while he felt for the hotel pen and stationary in his jacket. He began writing down as many details of Raad's office and the meeting as he could before he forgot them. He hoped Cohen could find something useful from the notes.

When he was alone again, Raad opened the safe in the lower cabinet of the bookshelf behind his desk. He removed a small box and set it on the desk, placing the telephone handset facedown into a recessed cradle in the top. He removed another handset connected by a cord to the side of the box and toggled a switch until a small light glowed red, indicating the conversation was now encrypted.

"Clear," Raad said in Farsi.

"The Zionists are on a spy hunt in Washinton. Stay alert and protect your asset," the voice on the other end warned.

"I already have men on it," Raad said. An audible click through the receiver let him know the call was done. He reversed the process to secure the box and locked it in the safe. He hung up the phone and opened the desk drawer to retrieve the newspaper. He checked his watch and went back to work. *Three hours*, he thought.

Chapter 18

The cold wind ripped through Casey's jacket and turned his bones to ice as he hurried to the metro entrance. The escalator underground moved too slow for Casey's liking, but the number of people leaving work as the sun sank lower in the D.C. skyline prevented anyone from moving faster on the left. One or two patrons let their frustrations be known, though their off-color words had no effect on the rate of descent. At the bottom, Casey moved to the side to avoid being run down by people on a schedule.

As Bernoulli's principle played out, there was more space between people, and Casey was more comfortable. The congestion reformed, though at a more manageable level, as the same people lined up to touch or pass cards through the gates to pay for the privilege of riding with the busted heaters, empty cups, and newspapers stuck together by any number of unidentified substances ever-present on big city mass transit. Before Casey reached the gate, he felt a vibration on his rear. He turned quickly and tensed, expecting trouble. A second vibration in the same spot told him the blue-haired octogenarian behind him wasn't just being fresh. When the old woman pushed him aside for holding up the line, Casey obliged and stepped back to an open area and pulled the buzzing cell phone from his pocket.

One more vibration. Casey connected and put the phone to his ear, plugging the other with the forefinger of his free hand. "Hello?"

"Hello?"

"Hello?" Casey asked again, louder.

"Casey? It's Susan. Can you hear me?"

Casey moved further from the crowd. "I can hear you," he said. "I just had to get away from the noise."

"Where are you?" Susan asked.

"Dupont metro station. I was just going back to the hotel. Do you want me to call you back from there in like half an hour?"

"No, no," Susan said. "I need to talk to you now."

"Okay, I'm listening."

"I would've called earlier, but Dylan and I were away this weekend, and I didn't get your message until late last night."

Casey reached back in his memory but couldn't find what he was looking for until Susan prompted him.

"I think I understood what you wanted me to translate, but the sound kept cutting out, and I only got parts of what you were saying," Susan said. "Do you think you can remember it and tell me again?"

"Um, let me think," Casey said. "I think I heard Raad say, 'rapid vra backshnid.' Something like that. I know my pronumciation sucks, but I'm still learning."

There was no response, and Casey checked his phone to make sure he still had reception.

"Casey, what are you getting into down there?" Susan finally asked.

Casey detected a hint of worry in Susan's voice. He didn't want to tell her anything about Cohen's revelations, or even about the man's presence in the States, let alone the fact that Casey was now helping the Israeli. "I'm not getting into anything, why?"

"Because what you just told me is exactly what I thought I understood from your voicemail."

"And?"

"Where did you hear this?" she asked.

"Outside Raad's office. Why? What does it mean?"

More silence.

"You pronunciation wasn't far off, if you heard it correctly," Susan said. "'*v ra pyed va 'v ra bakshnad* translates to 'find him and kill him,' Casey. Who said this? And who were they talking about? You?" Susan's voice was progressively louder with each question.

Casey didn't think long before he answered. "They weren't talking about me."

"How do you know?" Susan asked. "Maybe they were. God, Casey, what are you *doing* there?"

"Calm down, Susan. They weren't talking about me, because they already know where I am. Hell, I was just in Raad's office."

"If they aren't talking about you, who are they talking about finding and killing? And what does Davood Raad have to do with any of this?"

Casey froze and looked at his watch. "Look, I've gotta go, Susan. I'll fill you in when I get back to New York, but I think I know who they're looking for."

"Who? Casey, I don't think you..."

Casey hung up before Susan could finish. He typed a different number in his phone and headed back to the train.

Twenty minutes later Casey was staring at the water of the reflecting pool behind the Capitol building that served both houses of Congress. Casey mused that the watery image was serene—even when rippled by the wind—but it did not capture the majesty of the actual structure that was one of the most recognized landmarks in the country, if not the world, even with the current scaffolding around the dome. He was thankful for the passengers of United Flight 93 on the morning of September 11, 2001, for many reasons, one of which was preventing the al Qa'ida hijackers from destroying this building, which was likely that plane's target.

"Let's walk."

Casey jumped as Cohen walked past. "Fuck! Stop doing that." He caught up and eased to a more liesurely pace, hoping his heart rate would do the same.

"Try to be more aware of your surroundings," Cohen said. "What did you find out from Raad?"

"Nothing specific at his office, but I've got other information you need to hear."

"Such as?" Cohen prompted without looking at Casey, noting the other pedestrians in the area as they made their way north along the water's edge.

Casey was more anxious. "Raad may know you're here."

That got Cohen to turn his head towards Casey, but he continued walking—slower, so the shorter man beside him would not have to work as hard to match stride. "You told him?"

Casey stopped. "No, I didn't tell him!" he said, a bit too loudly as a couple several yards ahead of them turned to see what the outburst was before they turned right at the end of the reflecting pool.

"Keep walking."

Casey caught up. "I didn't tell him shit about you. Not even by accident. But I overheard something Saturday morning that I had a friend translate."

"Friend?"

"Susan Williams, from my office," Casey said. "You met her before in Central Park."

Cohen vaguely remembered the presence of the woman when he stopped two Mossad assassins sent by Eli Gedide to finish the job Cohen was supposed to do in Savannah. "What did you hear?" he asked.

"I heard Raad almost yelling at someone in his office before I got there. I thought maybe I could learn some new Farsi cuss words, so I tried to remember what he was saying, and I called Susan to..."

"What did you hear?" Cohen repeated.

"...translate the...oh. Well, apparently Raad told leather jacket to 'find him and kill him,' which is why I needed to tell you as soon as I found out."

Cohen moved off the concrete walkway as they came to the north-west corner of the pool and stopped under a tree near Pennsylvania Avenue. "What makes you think they know I'm here?"

"Timing, for one," Casey said. "And you *are* here to stop Raad's shenanigans."

"I may not be as nimble as I was twenty years ago, but I'm not that rusty," Cohen said. "The only people who know I'm in this country looking for an Iranian asset are you and Ms. Jackson. It's not likely that Raad and his people are looking for me."

"What about your friend from the Holocaust Museum?"

Cohen was angered by Casey's accusation. His squinted eyes and flexing jaw muscles visibly betrayed that anger, but he kept his voice steady. "Josef Kronfeld is one of the few people in this world I trust with my life. If I questioned his rectitude, I would have never asked for his help."

"Then who would Raad be sending someone out to kill?"

Cohen thought for a moment. "It is possible Raad's concern has nothing to do with Mossad's operations."

"But if it does?"

"Then perhaps we have an unknown ally we should meet."

Chapter 19

"He asked for my opinion, and I gave it," Parker said as he shut the door of the national security advisor's office. "I kept my mouth shut like you asked, and I only spoke up when he asked me a direct question."

Ambrosi removed his jacket and sat behind his desk. "I'm not faulting you for that," he said. "I just wish you would have stuck to the considered opinion of this office—my office—instead of spouting off views that the NSC has debated ad nauseum and rejected."

Parker and Ambrosi had just returned from the President's Daily Briefing, or PDB, in the Oval Office. The president received the consolidated top secret report from the director of National Intelligence on the most pressing or significant issues being followed by the Intelligence Community. Ambrosi was occassionally invited to attend when he was in town, though it was rare that he dragged Parker with him, and only when the president requested.

"Nothing's changed since November, Scott. I think CJCS and his team showed pretty clearly that the sanctions are slowing down Iran's progress to a weapon. But you tell the president we should lift sanctions as a goodwill gesture to have them drop the program?" Ambrosi shook his head. "We saw how well that worked with North Korea."

"I didn't say we should drop all of them," Parker said. "Just some of the economic sanctions that aren't doing shit except making the Iranian people pissed off at us."

"It sounded like you *want* Iran to succeed."

"Hell no. I just think our best bet—and the president does too—is to get the Iranian population on our side to force the regime to stop its pursuit of nuclear weapons. If they see we are looking out for them, we can use that good feeling to grow or strengthen any opposition in the country."

Ambrosi eyed his deputy. He knew Parker well enough after working closely with him for over a year, first as an NSC staffer and now as his deputy, to know the man had something else in mind. "So all the free money they have when sanctions are lifted will be put into infrastructure improvements and agriculture instead of longer-range ICBM production? And the people will thank America for their new fortune? That sounds a little naive, and frankly out of character for you."

"Not really," Parker said. "I just didn't get a chance to explain myself better in there."

"So explain it in here," Ambrosi said. "Because I guarantee COS is going to ask me what you were smoking."

"When we ease sanctions, we officially demonstrate that we care about the Iranian people. When the regime fails to improve the social and economic conditions of the country, instead funneling all of their money and effort into their military—which they will— then we have a reason to do what has to be done."

"I thought last week you said we shouldn't do anything."

"I argued that we let Israel loose to take care of things, but nobody wanted to do that. So let's change the scenario," Parker said. "For years it's been, 'give them a chance.' Let's give them a chance, and when they fail, we hammer them. If we don't want to get our own troops involved when Iran shows they can't be trusted, let Israel do what has to be done—or Saudi Arabia. Either way, the international community can't protest any action against Iran at that point."

Ambrosi sighed and rubbed his forehead. "Well, there's no way the president or Congress will condone an international response in which we aren't heavily involved in some way or another. And then we will be stuck in another war in that shithole part of the world. Iran won't fold at the first sight of U.S. troops across the border like Iraq did, either. And that means a lot more American deaths than the U.S. public is willing to stomach."

"Possibly."

The two men stared across the desk, each trying to read the other's thoughts. Ambrosi broke the silence. "Well, you're not the one making the decision..."

Neither is the president, Parker thought.

"...so we'll see what State and Treasury have to say about it before we think about changing our position," Ambrosi said. "Until then, I want you to keep your opinions to yourself. We'll bring up the issue again at the next principals meeting on Friday. Can you do that? Not stir up anything until we hear from the others?"

"Fine by me," Parker said, nonverbally adding *prick* at the end of his statement. He knew there were others who would take him seriously.

Chapter 20

Inside the Dupont Circle Hotel on New Hampshire Avenue, Davood Raad inserted quarters into a pay phone. Despite the American hysteria of government eavesdropping after the revelations of a contract employee of the National Security Agency, Raad knew that the ability of even the "all-knowing" NSA to monitor and analyze every conversation of every individual was extremely limited, if not impossible. Even with vulnerabilities associated with landline communication, pay phones that were not specifically targeted still provided a reliable means to transmit messages that avoided keywords which alerted monitoring systems to flag the conversation. And they provided anonymity.

"Hello?" the voice on the other end answered.

Raad still took the precaution of keeping his voice low, not to deter the electronic ears, but the living receptors of anyone passing through the hotel lobby. "Trouble is coming," he said, "but we are on it. Do not break routine." He hung up, not waiting for a response, and headed for the front exit.

Chapter 21

Tehran, Iran

The sun slipped below the horizon, though between the buildings and the smog, it had not been visible for over an hour. It would not be long before the street lamps along Behesht provided the only light on the south side of Park e-Shahr. Parang Jaarda and Ehsan Masani walked east on Behesht towards the Tehran Municipal Building. Both in their middle-twenties, the two men found themselves out of work in a city hit hard by economic stagnation as their country was being choked by international sanctions.

While the hard times they found themselves in may have led them to a life of petty crime in any other country, the penalty for theft in Iran was so severe, and the likelihood of being turned in to the authorities by other citizens fearful of being accused as accomplices, drove them to look elsewhere for gainful employment and a sense of purpose. Increasingly, more and more young people their age found that purpose in the mosque or the military. Parang and Ehsan found theirs in the opposition.

Youth in the smaller towns and cities beyond the borders of Tehran were prime targets for jihadist or extremist recruiting. The summer after he finished secondary school in Karaj, while selling bottled water from a cart outside Enghelab stadium, Ehsan struck up a conversation with a thirsty customer on a recruiting tour. Two months later, Ehsan was in a camp in eastern Sistan va Balochistan training with members of Jaysh Muhammad, Mujahideen e-Khalq, and Jondallah. After six months in the southeastern province, he was back in Tehran.

Eshan and Parang were briefed on their mission for what the Americans who funded them called "Turnstile." Neither man knew what the term meant, but they understood what they were expected to do. Not a particularly religious man, Eshan had no desire to become a martyr, and he let the al Furqan leaders know as much from the beginning. He was reassured that he would not be asked to don a bomb vest or drive an explosive-laden vehicle into a building, but he could not be guaranteed that his missions against the Iranian regime would not be considered suicide by many. He was placed under the tutelage of former members of Jondallah, a Baloch resistence group that excelled at more conventional, but limited military attacks on government elements including Iranian army and IRGC personnel. Eshan was given an assignment of smaller scale, but of arguably greater importance.

"Hey, look," Eshan said as he stopped in from of the Sangalaj Theater. "I saw *Macbeth* there at the Fajr Festival two years ago."

Parang stopped and looked up at the front of the building on their right. "You didn't see it here," he said. "Sangalaj only does Iranian plays. Come on." Parang moved on, and Eshan followed.

The two men wore Western-style street clothes that both masked their affiliation with Ansar al Furqan and provided a sort of camouflage, as they looked no different than any other university-aged men in the capital city. Unlike their more fortunate urban contemporaries, however, they were not looking for outlawed gatherings with music, drugs, and women in one of the many apartment high-rises both ruined and defined the Tehran skyline. They were looking for Qalibaf.

Mohammad Baqer Qalibaf was elected mayor of Tehran in 2005, following Mahmoud Ahmadinijad's elevation from mayor of that city to become the country's president. Qalibaf ran for president in 2013 and placed second to Hassan Rouhani in that election. He rode the support he gained on the national stage in that loss to a successful campaign for a third term as mayor and was seen as a front-runner to win the presidency in 2017. While Qalibaf held a Ph.D. in political geography and occasionally lectured at nearby universities, it was not his academic credentials that made him a target of *Turnstile* and al Furqan.

Qalibaf was a secular conservative who had served as a commander in the Islamic Revolutionary Guard Corps and second-in-command of the county's Basij force—a volunteer auxiliary militia organized to augment military units in combat operations against the Iranian homeland. In reality, Basiji served as local enforcers of Iran's myriad moral codes, breaking up demonstrations and punishing violators and dissidents, often with extreme violence. In the eyes of many Western leaders and internal opposition groups, a Qalibaf presidency would all but guarantee another decade of political and social repression, and Iran's march to an operational nuclear weapon would continue unimpeded.

Parang and Eshan slowed their approach to the Tehran Municipal Building where Qalibaf was meeting with members of the city's transportation and infrastructure development boards. The intelligence al Furqan received indicated that Qalibaf would be departing at 5:30 p.m. to attend a strategy session with other members of his political party, the Islamic Society of Engineers, over dinner at Bistango in Tehran's Raamtin Hotel. Al Furqan's leadership sold the operation to Eshan and Parang as a mission in which every measure of support to ensure their safe return would be taken, but both men knew death was a distinct possibility.

"Look. There he is."

Eshan looked up at Parang's prompting. Mayor Qalibaf emerged from the building fifty meters ahead. A black sedan sped past on their left, brake lights illuminating as it slowed to pick up the professor-politician. Parang put his hands in his jacket pockets and the men picked up the pace.

The driver stepped out of the car and hurried to the curbside passenger door. Qalibaf turned to the man who walked out with him and grasped his hand as they exchanged farewells.

Thirty meters.

Parang's hand emerged gripping a silver snub-nose revolver. He let his arm hang down, and he quickly wiped nervous sweat from his forehead. The distinct click of Eshan's opening switchblade knife was masked by the city sounds around them and the pounding of Parang's own heartbeat, increasing with each stride.

Twenty meters.

Eshan broke into a run as Qalibaf moved to enter the waiting vehicle. The driver was behind the car door, holding it open, leaving Qalibaf exposed and unprotected. Eshan angled left to close the remaining distance.

Parang steadied his own weapon and took aim. The pistol kicked up in sync with the loud pop as the driver fell to the ground. His attempt to protect the mayor ended with a flash, followed by complete and permanent darkness as Parang's bullet ripped through his left cheekbone.

Three more shots immediately followed, louder than the first. Parang dropped the revolver and grabbed at the burning sting in his thigh. He saw Eshan twist to the left and collapse, just two meters from the target. The burn was overcome by intense pain as Parang tried to stand. He turned his head toward the trees across the street and lurched forward to make a dash for cover and the waiting car on the other side of the park. A hard rap on the back of the head ended Parang's hope of escape, and he fell to the ground.

Chapter 22

Washington, D.C.

*F*ive-seven, tops. The number came more from a guess to make Casey feel good about his own towering height of five feet seven-and-a-half inches than any real measurement. The dark-haired bartender on the top floor of the Pour House on Pennsylvania Avenue, dressed in black tight-fitting jeans and equally tight black t-shirt, drew Casey's attention away from the droning SportsCenter replay on the TV across the room from the moment he sat down. By the time he finished his Reuben sandwich and half a mug of draft Leinenkugel's, he had gotten the woman's phone number and a promise to show him around D.C. when she got off work.

"Can I take your plate, sir?"

Casey snapped out of his daydream and looked up at the goatee-sporting man with shoulder length blonde hair who eyed him quizzically from a height several inches over five-seven.

"Sure," Casey said. The man was gone in a rush with the empty plate before Casey could say anything else, despite the fact he was the only customer in the place.

Casey turned his attention back to the bartender fifteen feet away. She laughed loudly into her cell phone, caught Casey's stare, and turned her back for more privacy. Ashamed of his voyeurism, Casey downed the last of his beer and stood up to leave.

"Sit back down," a gruff voice commanded.

"What? How the hell'd you know I was here?" Casey asked as he did what he was told.

Lev Cohen ignored the question and sat in the chair next to Casey. "Kronfeld's network has tracked Raad to a building in Rosslyn, Virginia, across the river from Foggy Bottom." He handed Casey a scrap of paper with an address. "Apparently this isn't the first time he's been there, and he's made the trip at least three times in the past two weeks. Josef just learned of this this morning."

"What's there?" Casey asked.

"For one, the new headquarters for the NCRI in this country."

Casey brightened at the comment, feeling for once that he could actually add something to Cohen's investigation. "Raad's helping them set up contacts and stuff. From his lecture tours."

"Why didn't you tell me this yesterday?"

The admonishment made Casey sink slightly. "I forgot."

Cohen did a quick check to re-verify no one was within earshot. "Couldn't he do that in an email? Why would he personally need to go down to their offices?"

Casey didn't have a good answer for that and told Cohen as much.

"Okay," Cohen said. "Whatever his reasons for wanting to meet in person, that doesn't change what I need you to do."

"What's that?"

"I want you to go to the building and see who else occupies it."

"Didn't your friend's 'network' make a note of that when they tracked Raad there in the first place?"

"They noted the NCRI office, then did what I requested and tracked him to that location," Cohen said. "They're not spies."

"Neither am I."

Cohen cautioned Casey to keep his voice down. "I'm aware of that, Mr. Shenk. That's why I'm only asking you to find out the names of the other businesses with offices in that building. I don't expect you to confront or even talk to anyone. Depending on what you find out, there may be a need for that, but I'll handle it when the time comes."

"Then why don't you ask Kronfeld to have his people go back and get the names?"

"There's no time for that," Cohen said. "You're here, and you said you would assist me. We need to find Raad's source before any more operations are compromised."

"What are you going to do?"

"I'm going to see who Raad has been meeting with after hours at a Muslim community center in Vienna."

"Austria?"

"Virginia," Cohen said with a huff. He checked his watch. "I would write it off as more book signings, but Raad's visits have ocurred between nine and ten at night. If the last two weeks indicate a larger pattern, he'll be there tonight."

"And if he's not?"

"Then I'll try to find out what I can." Cohen checked his watch again. "I'll meet you at Ms. Jackson's apartment at eleven-thirty."

"What if she's out?" Casey asked.

"Another beer?"

Casey's head whipped around as the shapely bartender appeared next to him. "Oh, um, no thanks," he said, returning her smile. He looked back to his right, and Cohen was gone. When he turned around, so was the bartender and his empty glass. *What the hell just happened?*

* * *

Casey arrived at the address Cohen gave him just after one in the afternoon. After checking out of his hotel, he drove his car to the building that housed the U.S. headquarters of the National Council of Resistance of Iran, or NCRI, among others. The six-story building looked like any other office building in any other city in the country. Three to six months to clear the trees, lay the pipes, and run the wires—two weeks to erect. Lots of glass, lots of steel, plenty of conformity, and no character. *The difference between the suburbs and the city of monuments*, Casey thought.

The front lobby was spacious and sterile. Casey nodded to the security guard. The tired looking man behind the oversized podium raised his eyes to note the newcomer's presence and returned to monitoring the computer screen in front of him. He never moved his head. Casey took the man's indifference as acceptance, and he moved to the bank of elevators on his right, debating whether or not to snap a photo of the directory on the wall with his cell phone. He looked at the guard again and decided not to press his luck. He thought studying the names of the organizations in the building and trying to remember enough to write down when he left would arouse less suspicion despite the increased chance of missing something.

He started from the top—of the list, not the building. First floor: FedEx, Concessions, Security, Mail Room. Second: National Temps, *Potomac Life* Magazine, Vacant. Casey noted that NCRI had secured the entire fifth floor of the building. The only other organization that didn't share space with a law firm, lobby group, or small tech company was Horus Rhind Security Solutions located on the third floor. He noted the company and tried to create quick word associations to remember the law firms and lobby groups—five in total.

At a U.S. Post Office mailbox fifteen feet from the office building entrance, Casey took a pen and a blank index card from his jacket and wrote down the names from the directory. He looked them over and was satisfied he got them more or less correct. His eyes came back to "Horus Rhind Security Solutions." *Horus*, he thought. *Why does that name sound familiar?*

"I don't fucking care! If he wants to try it, let him. One phone call from me, and he'll wake up with a goddamn horse head in his bed."

Casey watched a man in his early thirties wearing the ubiquitous D.C. black topcoat and gray scarf that was more for fashion than warmth navigate his way through parked cars in the lot adjacent to the building. The man stopped in front of the entrance and ran a bare hand through his hair.

"Okay, fine," he said, several octaves lower than his previous tirade. "We'll try it your way. But if you can't convince that asshole to change his postion, we won't have a choice but to turn up the heat....I'm serious, Pat. This is too important."

"Hey, Scott."

Scott looked up and gave a dismissive wave and nod of his head to a trio of matching young professionals leaving the building, keeping his cell phone to his ear. He checked his watch. "All right," he continued. "Just let me know how it goes....Sure thing....Bye."

Whether out of amusement at the man's outburst, curiosity, or just because, Casey snapped three pictures of the man on his own phone and pocketed it seconds before the man disappeared through the front door. Casey took a deep breath, relieved he hadn't been caught in the act and wondering why he took the risk in the first place. He pondered what might have happened if he *had* been spotted, and he shuddered at the thought of a *Godfather*-like warning in his own bed. *I'm leaving tonight, anyway*, he thought, shaking his head at his juvenile paranoia.

Better get this stuff to Andie so we can talk it through before we pass it on to Cohen. Maybe I can get back to New York before Jim tears me a new one, and I'm out of a job.

Chapter 23

By mid-afternoon, Casey was back in Andie's apartment. Andie told her editor she was going to be out for the rest of the day running down a lead for a story she was working on about the increasing influence of Congressional staffers in steering Pentagon budget priorities. She had just come from a short meeting with a potential source, so she wasn't exactly "lying" to her boss, but she paused her investigation when Casey called and said he needed to see her.

"Okay, give me that name again," Andie said after she set up her laptop on the coffee table in front of the couch. She was still dressed in her matching red skirt and suit jacket, though she had left her heels by the door and unbuttoned the jacket.

"Horus, with a *u*, Rhind—Romeo, Hotel, India, November, Delta."

Andie typed and deftly manipulated the computer's touchpad. She leaned closer to the screen and clicked through pages of the search results. "There. On the fourth page," she said. She clicked on the entry for the Horus Rhind Security Solutions corporate page as Casey took a seat next to her.

"Horus Rhind Security Solutions," she said as Casey scanned the page. She lost him as she quickly moved to different tabs on the website, eventually stopping at the "About" page. "'Providing timely solutions to world problems before they become problems since 1953.' How cute," she commented with just a hint of sarcasm in her voice.

"Problems for who?"

"Whom."

Casey looked at Andie and shook his head. "You're just like Susan. Always correcting my English."

"Maybe we'll eventually fix you someday," Andie smiled.

Andie went to the "Contact" page and a fillable form to email the company popped up. "I hate that," she said. "You send an email and good luck if they ever respond to you. Why don't they have a phone number?"

"Right. So you could leave a voice message," Casey said. "They'd be sure to call you back right away."

"Jackass."

Casey laughed, but only for a second. He leaned forward and touched the top of the screen when Andie went back to the "Home" page. "That," he said. "That's why I knew the name."

Andie saw that Casey was referring to the company's logo. An outline drawing of an eye with a curled line slanting right below the eye's pupil. Now that she looked at it closely, it looked vaguely familiar, though she didn't know where from. "What is it?"

"It's Egyptian," Casey said. "Kind of an 'all-seeing eye' like the Eye of Providence on the one-dollar bill."

"Like the Masons use."

"Yeah. Except this eye, the Eye of Horus, was around a long time before the Masons showed up."

"Are you like a closet Egyptologist, or something?" Andie asked. "Or just a general purpose nerd?"

"The latter. I'm a devout follower of all things Indiana Jones. I even wanted to be an archaeologist when I was younger, after watching *Raiders of the Lost Ark*."

"Why didn't you?"

"No money," Casey said. "I don't mean I got turned off the idea because archaeologists don't make any money, I just didn't have money to stay in school for ten years to get a Ph.D."

"So you filled vending machines."

"No, I joined the Navy. Vending machines came after that."

"That's right," Andie said. "I forgot about that." She turned back to the computer screen. "So what does this Egyptian eye have to do with a security company? Does it mean they 'see everything,' like future problems, as they claim?"

Casey thought about that. "Could be. But the reason I know about the Eye of Horus—I mean, besides my Indy fetish—is because of the Illuminati."

"The Illuminati."

"They were a secret society in the late 18th century that had people in the Bavarian government and other organizations. Their credo was something about stopping injustice by controlling the actions of the government through manipulation rather than straight-up domination. They were exposed and outlawed, but lots of folks thought they just went underground and actually spread to the point that they were responsible for the French Revolution in the early 1800s. Some people think they made their way to America and that they still exist, counting several past presidents among their members even," Casey said. "People say the same thing about the Masons."

"Do you actually believe that crap?" Andie asked.

"Not really, but I'm starting to rethink all that stuff after finding out about The Council. Not that they're the same, or anything—or even related—but if one group exists, who's to say the other ones don't. I mean, the Masons are real. It's only a question of how much influence these groups really have and how much is just myth and conspiracy theory."

"And this Egyptian eye is the symbol of the Illuminati?"

"I don't think it's *the* symbol, but it was one of them," Casey said. "And conspiracy nuts try to associate anything that even looks like it to the Illuminati—like it's proof of their infiltration into today's governments."

"Conspiracy nuts like you?"

"I'm not a conspiracy nut," Casey said. He saw Andie's smile and knew she was trying to get a rise out of him. "Okay," he said, returning the smile. "Maybe I like reading about conspiracies. That doesn't mean I believe all of them. I just think they're interesting. And the ones that stick around for a long time usually have at least some bit of truth to them."

"So is there anything to this security company using the Eye of Horus as their logo?" Andie asked, getting them back on track.

"Maybe they chose that because the founder's name is Horus. If my name was Horus, I'd have a big tattoo of that eye on my chest," Casey said. "You gotta admit, it looks pretty cool."

"What if it's not anyone's first name?"

"Horus Rhind? Sounds like a name to me," Casey said.

"Yeah, but this site came up on the fourth page of the search," Andie said. "Look here. All the links before this one hit on something called the Rhind Mathematical Papyrus." Casey looked closer at the computer screen. "I only searched on 'Horus Rhind,' though, without the 'Security Solutions' part," Andie added. "Otherwise the company would have probably come up first."

"But no actual person named Horus Rhind?"

"Doesn't look like it," Andie said. "If there were, you'd think there would probably be a LinkedIn profile, or something. Especially if he was associated with a company named after him."

"What about that 'Rhind' thing?"

Andie went back to the first page of the search. "Rhind Mathematical Papyrus," she said. She scrolled down and quickly read through the article. "Look at that." She pointed to an image on the screen. "This papyrus they found breaks down that eye symbol into some kind of mathematical formula. Hence the name, I guess."

Casey studied the picture, and after a moment leaned back into the couch. He wrestled with how to articulate what he was thinking. He finally decided there was no way to say it without looking dumb, or without giving evidence to Andie's "conspiracy nut" accusation. "What if Horus Rhind isn't really a security consulting company, but it's actually a front used by The Council?"

"Front for what?" Andie asked.

Casey was relieved that Andie chose not to criticize him. Instead, she was apparently helping him work out the problem. "After the bombings in New York, Paul Giordano ran into a speed bump when he was looking into the identity of the guy who hit Soren's Deli. Turns out a Maryland law firm named Penrose-Klein represented the bomber's family or something like that, and when Giordano talked to one of the partners there named Escher, the conversation went south real quick. Giordano tried to call back, but the number was no longer in service."

"And they were a front for The Council?"

"That's what we found out later," Casey said. "But in that case, they seemed like they had a specific purpose—handling legal problems. The question is: what purpose does Horus Rhind serve?"

Andie watched in silence as the wheels in Casey's head turned. After a minute she asked, "You sure you aren't just trying to find something that not really there?"

"The opposite," he said. "The more I think about it, the more it fits."

"How?"

"Penrose refers to the Penrose Triangle. The 'impossible triangle' that's just an optical illusion. You can draw it on paper, but it can't exist in real life. Even the man's name that Giordano talked to was a ruse—Escher, as in M.C. Escher, the artist."

"And Horus Rhind?"

"Another ruse," Casey said. "The Eye of Horus and the Rhind papyrus."

"Okay. Maybe it's just a clever name. But go back to your other question. What does Horus Rhind actually do?"

"Maybe that part's not a ruse."

Andie stood up, finally took her suit jacket off, and fell back in the couch with an audible sigh. "Now you lost me."

Casey pivoted on the couch to face Andie. "Let's say Horus Rhind actually does provide security solutions. Not for companies, necessarily, but for governments—the U.S. government, specifically. But in this case, the government is an unwitting client."

"How do you mean?"

"You know better than I do how our government can't come together to make a decision that everyone is behind. That's the nature of the system—three branches, two major political parties, elections every two to six years. Add the military folks who rotate regularly, and it's easy to see why we can't agree on any long-term national security policies. But think about this: what if The Council isn't plagued by partisanship and turnover like the rest of Washington? That kind of consistency by itself would make it pretty powerful."

"If people listen to them," Andie said.

"So they stack the deck in their favor."

"By having powerful people from both sides of the aisle," Andie added.

"Exactly."

"But who?"

Casey didn't have an answer for Andie's question. The only people he had actually come into contact with who were associated with The Council were just utility men—people who did the grunt work—at least that was his impression. Andie's question agitated him, whether that was her intention or not. He was once again forced to accept that almost everything he knew about The Council's history, it's activities, and even its membership, was based on what Davood Raad told him. The same Raad that Cohen revealed was, and had been for decades, an Iranian spy. "I don't know."

"No ideas?"

Casey shook his head. "We know Keith Swanson, Senator Cogburn's guy, was somehow involved, but that doesn't mean Cogburn himself is a member of The Council. You would think the big brains in the group would have to be people at least on Cogburn's level though, wouldn't you?"

"I see what you mean," Andie said. She went to the kitchen and pulled two bottles of water from the fridge, handing one to Casey as she resumed her spot on the couch.

"Thanks."

"Did you see anybody today when you were in Rosslyn that maybe you recognized, or someone going into the building that was headed for Horus Rhind?" Andie asked.

"No, nobody…wait." Casey took his cell phone from his jacket and handed it to Andie. "I saw this guy going berserker on the phone with somebody as he was walking from the parking lot." He watched Andie resize to picture to get a closer look. "I only took the picture 'cause I thought it was funny. Like one of those phone tough guys who probably got his ass kicked in high school and takes it out on folks now that he's a D.C. big-shot," Casey added. "I'm just guessing, though. I don't know who he is."

"I do."

"What? For real?" Casey moved closer to reexamine the photo, as if Andie's identification would magically trigger his own recognition of a face he'd never seen before.

"That's Scott Parker," Andie said. "I met him last year when I was working on the White House's response to the Russian annexation of Crimea."

"He works at the White House?"

"Sort of. He's the deputy national security advisor."

"No shit," Casey said. "He looks kinda young for that job."

"Lots of people have said the same thing, but he knows his way around Washington well enough," Andie said. "Plus it helps when the president picks you by name for a job."

"So he's got the president's ear?"

Andie handed the phone back to Casey. "I think the president wants to be challenged, and Parker's not afraid to speak his mind—unlike most of the political 'yes men' that roam the halls of that place."

Casey stared at the picture, and an idea began to take shape in the back room of his mind, looking for light. He glanced at the clock on Andie's wall. Three forty-seven. "If Horus Rhind is connected to The Council, maybe Mr. Parker is connected to them. I would think a deputy national security advisor would be a good candidate for part of the brain trust we were talking about."

"That's assuming he was going up to Horus Rhind in the first place, and that only works if Horus Rhind is The Council."

Casey saw her point. "I'm willing to make that leap," he said. "At least we have a potential lead."

"A lead to The Council, maybe, but didn't your friend ask you to go there to find out what Raad was doing there?" Andie asked.

"Yeah, but Raad already told me he was working with NCRI, who happens to be in that building," Casey said. "Maybe he had other business over there, too."

"So what do you plan on doing?" Andie asked. "Don't give me that look. I can tell you've got something brewing in that head of yours."

"I need to meet Parker," Casey said. "If I can confirm he was going to Horus Rhind on business for The Council, maybe we could find out who is giving Raad his information—if it isn't Parker himself."

"You want to meet Parker."

"Yes, ma'am."

"And what exactly would you say to him when you meet him?"

"I haven't worked that part out yet," Casey admitted. "But if I could get him to tell me what he was doing at the building, maybe I could get him to slip something about The Council. Maybe I'll ask him if he knows Raad."

Andie shook her head. "I don't think that's such a good idea."

"Why not?"

"I heard he's got a bad temper," Andie said. "You probably don't want to say anything that would piss him off."

Casey thought about the overheard phone call that prompted him to take the man's photo in the first place. "Okay, maybe I don't ask him about The Council, or even what he was doing at the office building in Rosslyn. Asking if he knows a famous Iranian scholar won't hurt, though. Anyway, it's more of his reaction than his words that I'd be looking for. Didn't you say that's how you get at the truth faster?"

Andie nodded reluctantly. "That works for reporters, but you're just some white guy off the street as far as he's concerned. Plus, what if he is Raad's source? You mention 'Raad' to him and your night—or your life—could end a lot sooner than you want it to. Why don't we just pass this information to Cohen and let him take care of it?"

"Cohen's checking out another place Raad had been going to regularly," Casey said. "He said he's on a clock, so if I could either confirm or eliminate Parker as someone of interest, that'll save him some time."

"Maybe," Andie said. "But you don't even know how you're going to find Parker, do you? Or were you going to just head back to that office building and hope he's still there?"

"I was thinking I might find a local reporter with connections who might track him down for me."

Andie sighed. "Aren't you supposed to be going back to New York tonight?" she asked as she got up and retrieved her own cell phone from the kitchen counter.

"I am. After Cohen comes over, though."

"Over *here*?"

"Oh, I forgot to tell you. Cohen's gonna meet us here at eleven thirty tonight," Casey said. "I mean, if that's okay with you."

"Do I have a choice?" Andie didn't wait for an answer as she turned her attention to the person on the other end of the call. "Hey, it's Andie…Good, good. Look, I need a favor…."

Casey watched the screensaver on Andie's computer roll through a series of pictures, trying not to look like he was eavesdropping on her conversation—which he was. Atlanta Falcons logo, a dogwood, pictures of people Casey assumed were family members. Smiles, mostly. He knew a little about her background, like she was also from Georgia, a reporter, taller than Casey, and one of the most stunning women he had ever seen. Beyond that, though, he didn't know much. *That's too bad*, he thought.

"Jerry will call back in an hour," Andie said.

"Who? Oh, the guy you just called," Casey said. "PI?"

"Yeah. Well, part-time. He's got a regular day job, but he does some private investigating on the side to help pay alimony on two failed marriages."

"You think he'll find out anything we can use in just an hour?"

"Jerry might be an amateur, but he gets results." Andie smiled. "And for what you're paying, I wouldn't be surprised if he calls back in half that time."

"What *I'm* paying him?"

"My southern hospitality requires that I help a friend in need, but it doesn't mean I'm bankrolling your little adventure," Andie said. "If you want, you can pass the bill to that Israeli assassin you're working for. I'm sure he'd be happy to pay."

Chapter 24

"There he is," Jerry Blocksidge said.

Casey looked through the windshield of the part-time private investigator's thirty-plus-year-old Buick sedan. He watched Scott Parker leaving a low-key Thai restaurant located in one of the countless strip mall-type business set ups invariably anchored by a Safeway or Food Lion grocery store that were found throughout the Virginia and Maryland suburbs of D.C. "Who's that with him?" Casey asked, referring to a dark-haired man in a grey business suit and black overcoat who accompanied the deputy national security advisor.

Blocksidge kept his eyes on the target and said, "Hey pal, I'm doing this as a favor for Andie. She wanted me to track down Parker...there his is."

Casey left it at that. Despite his curt manner, Blocksidge did get results. Andie had asked him to find Parker quick enough to allow Casey to intercept him and ask the man some questions, and in twenty minutes, he found out that Parker was meeting a friend for dinner—including the time and location. When Casey met Blocksidge in the parking lot at half-past seven, he asked the PI how he was able to find that information so quickly, let alone finding out anything at all. "If I told you that, you wouldn't need me, would you?" was his response.

Casey was still impressed, despite the man's superiority complex. When he asked if he could send Blocksidge payment for his service after he returned to New York the next day, Blocksidge laughed. "I told Andie this was a freebie. No charge for something this easy." When he saw the confused look on Casey's face, he understood. "She was busting your balls, wasn't she?"

It was a little after eight when Parker and his friend exited the restaurant and headed toward the parking lot. Casey knew he couldn't afford to blow the opportunity even with the added unknown of the extra man. He thanked Blocksidge for his help and had just shut the passenger side door when the car sped away.

The lights in the parking lot illuminated every third car, and the others remained in relative darkness. Three rows away, yellow lights blinked, and a distinct click told Casey which car the men were headed toward. He picked up his pace and trotted to intercept Parker and his companion.

Casey reconsidered his approach on the drive to meet Blocksidge. He knew Andie was right in one sense. He was supposed to be helping Cohen find out who was helping Raad, but the peculiarity of the shady existence—in his eyes—of Horus Rhind kept drawing him back to The Council. He thought of Giordano and the whole reason he came to D.C. in the first place. Cohen's presence and revelations were unexpected, but they only fueled his desire to break into the mysterious world of The Council. Because Cohen's mission and his own, if not complimentary, were not contradictory, Casey decided to find out if Parker could help them both.

"Mr. Parker!" Casey called from twenty feet away, stopping the two men before they entered their vehicle.

"Do I know you?" Parker asked as his companion moved around

the front of the car to join him on the driver's side.

Casey stopped his trot and glanced at the other man before turning his attention back to Parker. "I don't think so," Casey answered. "I just saw you coming out of the restaurant, and I wanted to ask you a few questions, if you don't mind."

Parker put the car keys back in his pocket. "About what?"

"I was wondering if you knew anything about the recent assassination attempts on Iranian scientists that Mossad has been conducting—specifically, why they've been failing."

Parker looked at his companion who moved a few inches closer to Casey, never taking his eyes off him. "Are you a reporter?" Parker asked.

Casey felt drops of perspiration trickle down his sides, causing him to shiver despite the layers of clothing he wore to fight off the January evening cold. He swallowed hard. He had no intention of lying to Parker, but he was starting to have second thoughts. Casey decided to avoid the question by asking another one. "Have you met with any Iranians lately?" Every muscle in his body tensed in anticipation of Parker's reaction.

"What?" Parker asked with a puzzled look—not the reaction Casey expected. Parker's friend shrugged. "Look," he said before Casey could answer, "I don't know who the fuck you are, but this interview is over." He took the keys back out of his pocket and opened the car door.

Casey used his last bullet. "What can you tell me about The Council?" That question got him the reaction he wanted—or didn't want.

Parker slammed the door shut and closed the distance to Casey to mere inches with a quick step that caused Casey to flinch. He eyes scanned Casey to his shoes and back. "Who the fuck are you?" he asked with a half-grin.

"Casey Shenk."

"And that's supposed to mean something to me?" Parker tilted his head towards his friend who had moved to Parker's side. "Adam, does 'Casey Shenk' mean anything to you?"

Adam Miller kept his eyes on Casey and said, "Nope."

"What do you do exactly, Mr. Shenk?" Parker asked. "And don't lie to me. I'll know if you're lying."

Parker's threatening tone had the reverse effect of what he likely intended. Casey stepped closer, steeled both by Parker's attitude and the man's reaction to mention of The Council. "I pay your salary," Casey said. "That's what I do. Just like every other taxpayer in this country. But instead of working for the people, you and the rest of your Council buddies just work for yourselves, don't you? You think because y'all have a secret handshake, you know what's best for all the rest of us." It was Casey's turn to smile. "Tell me I'm lying."

Parker's smile was gone. He jabbed a finger in Casey's chest, but the IWG analyst didn't move. "You're treading on thin ice, pal," he almost whispered. Miller put his hand on Parker's forearm and slowly brought his friend's hand down.

"We should go, Scott."

Parker's nostrils flared as he forced oxygen into his lungs. "Thin ice," he repeated as he stepped back and pivoted toward the car.

Casey's heart raced, and his head began to pound. He didn't shy away from confrontation, but he didn't like it. He was no longer cold, as the rush of adrenaline had caused every organ and muscle to rapidly prepare for action. The fight or flight response that was essential to animal survival also raised the flag that Casey was too far out of shape for the required actions of either route. He stood motionless, suddenly tired as his body tried to return to a normal state of operation without inducing a heart attack or collapsing a lung. His recovery effort was cut short before Parker and Miller even got in their vehicle.

Five feet away, Casey saw Parker fall violently to the ground. The cause of Parker's collapse was not immediately evident, and before Casey could take in the situation unfolding before him, his knee buckled, and his elbows hit the pavement as he reflexively braced to prevent his head from ending up as a smashed ketchup packet. Casey saw the man who used his leg as a springboard lunge at the one Parker called Adam.

Miller stepped back to avoid Casey's leapfrogger. A twist of his body and a hard chop knocked the pistol from the assailant's hand. The weapon skidded to a stop three feet in front of Casey. He pulled himself forward, dragging his useless right leg with him and grasped the weapon. He crawled as fast as he could to the cover of a nearby station wagon. Peering around the rear of the vehicle, Casey saw Miller parry a thrust from the attacker who had replaced his lost pistol with a large combat knife.

Parker remained motionless on the pavement to Casey's left. Casey noted the tell-tale rise and fall that indicated Parker was at least breathing, though he didn't know if the man was unconscious or just playing possum. He saw Miller cut the mystery attacker down with a strike to the throat as a second figure sprang from the shadows on the opposite side of Parker's car.

A crowbar slammed the top of Miller's left shoulder, instantly paralyzing the Israeli's arm, but sparing his skull from a direct hit that would have likely ended his life. Miller dropped to a crouch and turned. He sprang up as the new opponent came on top of him, launching the man backward and onto the hood of Parker's car. Casey was mesmerized by Miller's speed and violence. He almost missed the re-birth of the body fifteen feet in front of him. The same man who crushed Casey's knee recovered from his smashed windpipe enough to pick up his knife and charge Miller once more. Miller was unaware of the man's rapid approach as he finished off the second attacker.

Casey felt the cold steel in his right hand and took aim at the back of the gun's previous owner.

"Adam!"

The shout to Casey's left startled him, and the reflexive twitch sent a bullet high and off-target. Miller turned just as Casey's head was jarred loose by a size-eleven leather rocket slamming into the side of his face, knocking him unconscious.

Chapter 25

Cohen sat on the couch in Andie's apartment as Andie returned with a glass of water. "Thank you," Cohen said when he took the glass.

Andie lowered herself onto the couch next to Cohen, but as close to the edge and as far away from the Israeli assassin as she could. She tried not to let her nervousness show, and her practiced reporter's voice stayed level as she asked, "So what did you find out?"

Cohen placed the now half-empty glass on the coffee table and said, "Nothing obvious. Raad wasn't there." He pulled a folded piece of paper from his pocket and handed it to Andie. "The management at the Islamic center said Raad has been teaching a class on why the Sunni-Shia divide means nothing in the West and how Muslims in America should take a more active role in promoting that example of tolerance across the Middle East and beyond."

"You just asked them point blank what Raad's business there was?"

"I told them I was doing research for a book on the influence of Muslim academics in countering anti-Islamic sentiment after the 9/11 attacks. They were more than happy to talk to me," Cohen said.

"And this?" Andie asked after she unfolded the paper.

"A list of other influential Muslims who have visited the center."

Andie looked over the list of names handwritten on letterhead of the Islamic Heritage Center in Vienna, Virginia. There were only eight names, a few authors Andie recognized, and one that made her pause. "Looks like they gave you some good points of contact to help you write your book…"

"I'm not writing a book."

"…and one that's not an academic," Andie said. "This one here, Cyrus Shirazi," she pointed to the name. "He's a U.S. congressman." She handed the paper back to Cohen.

"Congressman?"

"From California," Andie said. "The first Iranian-American elected to Congress."

Cohen looked at the name. He was surprised that America, the "Great Melting Pot," had never had an elected official in the U.S. legislature who was of Iranian origin. Despite the outward façade of universal acceptance, he knew at its heart, America was no more immune from racism and discrimination than the rest of the world, his own country included. "What business would Shirazi have at the center?"

"Role model speaking to other Muslims?" Andie offered. "I don't know much about Shirazi except that it was a big deal when he was first elected. What was it…five years ago?"

Cohen thought for a second. It was probably nothing more than what Andie said, but he didn't want to just brush it off. "Is there a way you could find out more about this congressman?" he asked.

"Sure," Andie said. "How fast do you need it?"

Cohen checked the time. It was eleven fifty. "As soon as you can get it," he said. "Did Mr. Shenk say he was going to be this late?"

Andie brought her laptop to the coffee table. "He didn't tell me anything about being late. I thought he might have called you earlier," she said. "He was going to meet Scott Parker, the deputy national security advisor."

"What?" Cohen straightened up at the news.

Andie relayed what Casey found out at the Rosslyn office building and about his plans to confront Parker. Cohen rubbed his temples, contemplating all of the possible outcomes from Casey's impulsive actions. He couldn't think of any that wouldn't end badly for his own efforts to find and silence Raad's source. He also concluded that there was nothing he could do but wait for Casey to check in and deal with the consequences. If things went sideways after Casey Shenk's amateur sleuthing, he would have to adjust, but the mission remained the same.

"All right," Cohen finally said. "Let's see what we can find out about Congressman Shirazi."

Chapter 26

It was after one o'clock when Casey woke up. He only knew that because the ticking of the second hand on a utilitarian wall clock was off-sequence from the deeper pounding of tribal drums in his head, drawing his attention. He compared the time to that of his watch and noted the date had flipped to "21." One o'clock on Wednesday the 21st. One in the morning or afternoon? There were no windows in the sterile white concrete room to tell him if it was still dark outside.

Two of the six overhead fluorescent lights flickered erratically, only adding to his confusion and growing anxiety. He was seated at a worn metal table where he had rested his head, as evidenced by the small puddle of drool. Casey wiped his mouth with the back of his hand, and he realized that he was no longer wearing his jacket—and he was cold. He saw his coat on the back of another chair across the room next to one of two closed doors on opposite walls. He stood and collapsed to the ground, taking the chair with him, as soon as he put weight on his right leg. Lights flashed in the back of Casey's eyes as the pain reminded him that his knee had recently been used as a stepping stone. *He wasn't after me,* Casey told himself. *He was after Parker.*

Casey looked around as if expecting to see Parker, but he was still the only one in the room. He tried to right the chair and pull himself up when he realized his left ankle was zip-tied to the leg and lower crossbar of the metal chair. *What the fuck?* he thought. He examined his captor's handiwork and shook his head grinning. Whoever did this to him wasn't worried about his escaping, because he could twist the chair a few times and the tie would pop. It wouldn't feel good as it cut off the blood flow to his foot and dug deep into his skin, but he would be free. No. They didn't need to worry about Casey breaking his plastic shackle and making a run for it, they just needed any escape attempt to be loud enough or slow enough for them to come in the room and stop him.

As if someone was following Casey's mental reasoning while he pulled himself back into the chair, the door on his left opened, flooding the room with a rush of not-as-stale air. "So, you're awake," Parker said as he shut the door behind him. The screeching of metal chair on concrete floor as Parker took a seat across the table exacerbated the pain of Casey's throbbing headache.

Parker was no longer wearing the full business attire of a government power broker that he wore when Casey saw him last. Instead, Parker had traded his overcoat, scarf, and jacket, for the more casual "I-took-a-bullet-in-my-torso-that-just-missed-my-ribs-and-any-vital-organs" bandages more common in an army field hospital than the nation's capital—or not. Casey winced as he bent his damaged knee and felt no sympathy for the man in front of him. "What the fuck am I doing here?" Casey asked.

"The good news is, it only appears that your knee is sprained," Parker said. "The bad news is, until we establish how you just *happened* to be in that parking lot when a pair of assassins tried to kill me and my friend, you're in for a lot more than just a sprain."

The other door into the room opened before Casey could say

anything, and a man in jeans and a blood-stained t-shirt entered, removing thick black gloves that glistened with what Casey surmised from watching five seasons of *24* was probably the same blood that decorated the shirt. "He's Qods," the man said to Parker, not even glancing at Casey.

Parker nodded. "Thanks, Alex," he said as the man passed through the room and out the other door, never once breaking stride.

A loud pop startled Casey, and he looked to his right as Miller entered the room and shut the door behind him. He snapped a pistol into a removable belt holster and handed it to Parker. "He won't be needing this again."

Parker clipped the holster to his belt. "Any idea who tipped them off?"

"Who knows," Miller said, still standing. "Lebanese Hizballah's got sympathizers all over. After 2006, that number grew exponentially. Any one of them could have found out and got word up the chain."

"That's Hizballah, though. How did Qods Force soldiers even get into the country?"

"That is a problem, isn't it," Miller said. "I thought Homeland Security was stood up to prevent that." He grinned.

"Yeah, well..." Parker started. A chop of steel on wood as loud as the sound of the handgun came from the other side of the door Miller came in from. A blood-curdling scream followed less than a second later. "Maybe he'll be more help."

"More help than the guy you just shot?" Casey couldn't believe the exchange he was witnessing. The two men in front of him were talking more like two guys discussing off-season baseball trades than people who had just escaped an assassination attempt, killed one man, and—from the sound of it—were torturing another. The scream from the adjoining room had turned to labored sobbing. "Who the hell *are* you people?"

Parker turned his attention to Casey. "Why don't you tell me who you think we are, Mr. Shenk. You seemed to have a pretty good idea outside the restaurant. Or was that just some bullshit show to distract us while your two friends attacked us?"

Another loud chop. More screaming.

Casey started to sweat despite the cold. His eyes darted between the two men waiting stoically for his response. "I...I don't know who those guys were...are," he stammered.

"You seem nervous," Parker said. "You still want to stick to that 'taxpayer' line, or are you going to tell me who you really are?"

The screaming stopped. It was replaced by yelling, followed by a heavy crash against the wall.

Casey's head turned in the direction of the noise from the other room. He looked back at Parker.

"You can talk to us, or you can be next," Parker said, waving a thumb at the door.

Casey clenched his jaw and swallowed hard. "I'm an analyst at the Intelligence Watch Group in New York," he said.

"Okay."

Casey waited for another question, but Parker and the other man remained silent, apparently not satisfied with the simple answer and waiting for Casey to continue. Casey couldn't think of anything else to say that would make the situation he was in any better, and he knew lying would likely make it worse. "I know about Israel's failed operations to kill Iranian scientists, and I have a good idea who's tipping the Iranians off. I just don't know who's giving him the details."

Parker and Miller exchanged looks, and Miller turned a chair around, sitting for the first time since he entered the room. He straddled the seat and folded his arms on the chair back. "Who is it?" he asked.

"Davood Raad," Casey said.

Miller straightened. Casey thought the man stopped breathing until he asked, "Raad?"

"I mean, I think it's him. But I don't have any proof." Casey purposely left Cohen's name out of the discussion. He thought he could sell the story as an investigation he was doing as part of his work at IWG.

"Then what 'not-proof' led you to that conclusion?" Miller asked.

Casey looked at Parker and answered, "He has a contact in The Council."

"Isn't The Council just an urban myth?" Miller asked.

Casey wondered how far to go after Parker's earlier warning that he was "treading on thin ice." He decided that keeping the conversation going was a better option than a beating, or worse, so he went all-in. "They want you to think that."

"But you know for a fact The Council is real," Parker said.

"Yes."

"And how do you know that?"

"They almost killed me," Casey said. "Twice."

Parker leaned forward. "Now why would they do that, Mr. Shenk?"

"Because I found out who they were and what they were doing," Casey said. "Remember the Manhattan bombings in 2011? I was in Soren's Deli that morning."

Parker stood up and turned his back to Casey, looking high along the back wall. "And you think The Council was responsible for that?"

"Yes."

Parker turned around. "What made you come to that conclusion?"

Casey quickly flipped through the mental slide deck of memories from July 2011. Mari. Giordano. Prince. Cogburn. Swanson. Clawson. Evans. Penrose. There was one image that brought it all together. One piece that pointed Casey to the truth...even if that piece itself was a lie. He took a deep breath. "Davood Raad."

"The same guy you just said is responsible for telling the Iranians about our alleged operations?" Miller asked.

Casey's eyes narrowed. "*Our* operations?"

"Mr. Miller is an Israeli diplomat," Parker explained. "He meant Israel's operations." Miller shot his friend a warning glance.

"And he's with The Council, too?" Casey asked Parker.

"What is your fixation with The Council?" Parker barked. "We're not talking about The Council, we're talking about a man you claim is giving information to Iran about the clandestine operations of America's greatest ally. Is he the same man who tried to have me killed tonight? Because if you don't start explaining yourself, we can move you to the next room and try a different method to get the answers we want."

"We're not there yet, Scott," Miller said, trying to keep his friend's temper in check. "Assuming, for argument's sake, The Council is real, and it was behind the Manhattan bombings...you came to that conclusion because Raad told you it was true?"

"No," Casey said. He hesitated and added, "Raad just suggested it might be them. I went to see him to ask if he knew—since he was Iranian and traveled freely to and from that country—to ask him if Natanz was out of commission after Israel bombed it. He heard about my blog post on the 'Complicity Doctrine' where I said the U.S. may have let the bombings in New York happen to justify attacking Iran's Houthi proxies in Yemen. He told me it might have actually been The

Council manipulating the goverment. He asked me to see if I could find out more about The Council to help him in his own research into the group. After that, things happened that made me see Raad was right."

"What things?"

"For one, they tried to kill me and one of my co-workers in my own apartment."

"Right," Parker said with a smirk.

"It's true," Casey said, looking up at Parker. "A lawyer for Penrose-Klein whose name may or may not have been Mitchell Evans. He might have succeeded if his head didn't catch a sniper's bullet from the building next door." Parker didn't answer, but his silence told Casey everything he needed to know. "Friend of yours?"

The pistol clipped to Parker's belt came out before Casey knew what was happening. His eyes widened and he tried to drop below the table for cover, taking the chair tied to his ankle with him. The shot never came, and from his vantage point on the floor, he saw why. The handgun skidded into the corner and Parker crashed to his knees with a scream. Casey watched the man hug himself as the white bandages on his side turned dark red with an influx of fresh blood from the re-opened wound.

Casey cautiously peered over the table as he awkwardly got his chair up for the second time. Miller helped Parker off the floor and into a chair.

"Fuck, man. I wasn't going to shoot him," Parker said. "Damn it, that hurt." He looked at the blood that covered his hand and wiped it on his shirt.

"Good," Miller said. "Why don't you let me handle the interrogation, and you just stick to…whatever it is you're actually trained to do. I want to hear what else Mr. Shenk has to say."

"Everything okay in here?"

Miller and Casey looked up at a man in a dark blue track suit who entered from the adjoining space where the Qods Force operatives were "interrogated." Track suit pointed to Parker, who continued to focus on stopping the bleeding. "That come open again?"

"It's all right," Parker said. He looked at Miller. "Just fell, that's all. I think it's done bleeding."

"How about the other one?" Miller asked, nodding his head toward the open door.

Track suit shook his head. "Didn't make it."

"Any new information?"

"He gave us this." He handed Miller a piece of paper, who looked it over before handing it to Parker. Casey tried to see what was written on the paper, but he lowered his eyes when he saw track suit staring at him.

"Thanks," Parker said. He handed the paper back to Miller, who quickly pocketed it.

"Just give us about ten more minutes," Miller said to track suit, "and then he's all yours."

"Roger," the man acknowledged and left the room, closing the door behind him.

Casey's eyes darted between Miller, Parker, and the closed door. His mouth went dry, and his leg involuntarily pulled on the zip tie at his ankle. "What…what else do you want from me?"

"Answers, Mr. Shenk. Answers," Miller said. "First, what do you know about Davood Raad?"

"Not much," Casey said. "I know he writes books, lectures, used to work for Mir Hossein Mousavi, and he's an Iranian spy." He hoped that last part might keep him out of the torture room.

Parker and Miller exchanged looks. "Sounds like you know more than 'not much,' Mr. Shenk," Miller said.

"So you weren't just helping some academic, you knew you were helping a spy," Parker said.

"Scott, please," Miller said. "We can get to whether you believed Dr. Raad was a spy before you agreed to help him in just a moment. Right now I'm interested in *how* you learned that information."

Casey's heartbeat quickened. Miller's inquiry told Casey that the Israeli knew who Raad was. He knew Raad had a doctorate, and he seemed know that Raad was a spy. The chance that Casey could offer any information this man didn't already have had left the room, and Casey's sense of self-preservation crowded out any other feeling in his body. "Lev Cohen told me."

Miller's face turned to stone. His eyes, unmoving, seemed to look through Casey's, focused on the wall behind. Silence. After a moment, he blinked. "When?"

"Three days ago. I mean, four days ago. Saturday."

"You saw him here? In Washington?" Miller asked.

"Yes."

"Who is Lev Cohen?" Parker asked.

Miller ignored him. "And he personally told you this?"

"Yes, sir."

"Why?"

"He wanted my help," Casey said. He saw his response was not well-received. Miller looked skeptical, and Casey knew he had to convince the man he was telling the truth. "Cohen thought I might have been Raad's source, and when he decided I wasn't, he asked me to use my relationship with Raad to find out who was giving him the information."

"And you thought Mr. Parker here might be that source?"

"That's bullshit!" Parker said. He tried to stand but the pain from his wound ended that idea, and he dropped hard back into his chair.

Casey thought he was safe enough from the hobbled deputy national security advisor to speak freely to the Israeli in front of him. "I think Raad's source is someone in The Council. Cohen wanted me to see what was so interesting at a building in Rosslyn that Raad kept going back to, and I found that NCRI has an office there. Raad already told me he was helping them get established here, but a security company called Horus Rhind is also in the building, and that got my attention."

Miller said nothing, waiting for Casey to continue. But Casey now had Parker's full attention, as well. "I think Horus Rhind might be a front for The Council, just like Penrose-Klein is, or was. And I saw Mr. Parker going into the building yesterday, so I thought he might be part of The Council. I didn't know who he was right then, only after the fact."

Parker said nothing. Miller glanced at his friend and looked back at Casey. "Why do you think Raad's source is in The Council?"

Casey knew the answer to Miller's question would not sound good, no matter how he delivered it. "Raad told me the information I gave him about The Council from my investigation after the Manhattan bombings helped him find a contact there."

"You gave him a name?"

"Well, yes," Casey said. "But the name only helped him find a contact. It wasn't the guy who's acting as Raad's source."

"How do you know?" Parker asked.

"He told me."

"Who told you? Raad?" Miller asked.

"Yes. He said I helped him find a contact within The Council to help him with his research, but he wouldn't tell me who it was," Casey said, wincing at how weak his answer sounded even to him.

"And Cohen knows all of this?" Miller asked.

"Yes."

"I'm surprised you're still alive."

"Who the fuck is Cohen?" Parker asked for the second time, visibly uncomfortable with being the only one in the room who was in the dark.

"We have a history," Casey said. "It's a long story."

The door to Casey's right opened. He saw track suit enter, and with wide, pleading eyes, Casey looked to Miller for a reprieve, a stay of execution, anything.

"Well, I see our time is up, Mr. Shenk." He glanced above Casey's head and nodded.

Casey felt the sting in the side of his neck before he knew track suit was behind him. A second later, the darkness closed in. *Not again*, he thought as he slipped once more into unconsciousness.

Chapter 27

Except for their height, Andie Jackson and Lev Cohen seemed an unlikely pair. It wasn't so much the color of their skin, as bi-racial couples were not uncommon in the Washington area—at least not so odd as to draw stares from any but the most bigoted or sheltered pedestrians. It wasn't even their age difference. What stood out most was the contrast of Andie's natural elegance in both physical appearance and outward demeanor with Cohen's rugged, worn complexion and aura of suspicious caution born from years in deserts and mountains fighting wars even history had forgotten. It was easier for Andie to dress down in jeans, Uggs, and a parka, than for Cohen to go shopping for a suit to match Andie's normally professional work attire. Their wardrobes fit their cover. It was early morning on a cold January Wednesday, and the tourist crowds were non-existent, making the cover less than ideal. But Andie was able to get a rudimentary itinerary for Congressman Shirazi using her reporter's credentials, and the pair had little time to come up with anything better.

They stood by a tree in a landscaped corner by the barricaded driveway to the Library of Congress. From that vantage point, they could monitor both the LOC and the wide brick-and-tree-lined walkway that led to the front entrance of the U.S. Capitol building across the street. Andie checked her watch. "Should be coming out soon."

Cohen looked up from the map he was "studying" and glanced toward the building across 1st Street SE. Shirazi had an early appointment at the Library of Congress before a scheduled hearing of the Joint Economic Committee. They had not heard from Casey since he left to confront Scott Parker, and Cohen suggested they could use the time until he did contact them to observe Cyrus Shirazi in person.

Cohen became more interested in the congressman after Andie dug deeper into the man's biography. Ali Shirazi immigrated to the United States from Iran in 1978 with his wife six months before the fall of Shah Mohammad Reza Pahlavi. By February 1980, the couple settled into a modest home in Los Angeles, and Cyrus Shirazi was born. With his training in systems engineering, the elder Shirazi was hired by an established logistics company's research and development department. When the company expanded to transshipment operations in the Mediterranean in 1991, Ali Shirazi was selected to head the technical operation of a new hub in Tangier, Morocco. His fluency in Arabic, as well as English and his native Farsi, helped move Ali Shirazi up the ladder of responsibility and pay, and Ali moved his family once more.

While in Morocco, Cyrus Shirazi was exposed early to the world of international commerce and foreign economics thanks to his father. The young Persian-American also learned about rising above racial discrimination courtesy of young Arab and Berber bullies around his home in Tangier. Cyrus concentrated on his studies, and by the time he was eighteen, his grades and unique childhood earned him a trip back to the U.S., where he went on to earn a Bachelor's degree in economics from the University of California, San Diego, in 2002 and an MBA from the same institution two years later.

Rather than return to Morocco, where his parents and younger sister still lived, Cyrus Shirazi remained in California. After his studies, Shirazi was hired as a commodities broker for Peregrine Financial where he quickly made a name for himself as a shrewd, knowledgeable businessman destined for huge success. By 2008, Shirazi stepped away from the financial business despite being recently married, and he was elected to the U.S. House of Representatives by voters in California's 42nd congressional district.

Shirazi's biography and rise to a history-making political position in the U.S. government was well-known. It was the man's family connections and his time in Morocco, however, that prompted Lev Cohen's urging for Andie to help him dig deeper. Cohen and Andie found that Shirazi's maternal uncle lived in Algeria from 1984 to 2007. During that time, Payam Khadem was suspected of facilitating the movement of arms to Islamist fighters in North Africa and other terrorist organizations in Europe from his business operations in Oran on Algeria's Mediterranean coast. While Khadem was not on any American watchlists, Israel was well-aware of his activities, including his help in supplying arms to Hamas in Gaza.

If Shirazi spent any time with his uncle between 1991 and 1998, Cohen argued, the younger man could have been exposed to some of the more active elements of the entrenched Islamist faction in the country—including al Qa'ida—who would consider an intelligent, multilingual son of a successful Muslim engineer a prized recruit. More likely, however, Khadem could have influenced his nephew by selling him the ideals of the Iranian revolution of which Shirazi's uncle was an ardent supporter and veteran. Andie thought the chances of such a transformation escaping media scrutiny of a candidate running for political office in America was slim, and she let Cohen know as much.

"And frankly," she had said, "your suspicion of Congressman Shirazi smacks of racism, if you want to know the truth."

"Racism? Because he's Persian?"

"Exactly," Andie said. "If Shirazi were white, or Jewish for that matter, you wouldn't be so quick to accuse him of being a criminal just because his uncle robs banks."

"Payam Khadem does not rob banks. He is a dedicated Khomeinist who has worked for years to arm the enemies of Israel," Cohen said. "If there is even a one-percent chance your congressman was influenced by his uncle during his youth, I cannot ignore the possibility that he too is working for Iran's interests."

"The 'one-percent doctrine.' I've heard that before," Andie said. "I didn't buy Dick Cheney's fear mongering then, and I'm not sure I buy that weak argument now."

Cohen had not been in the mood to argue, and because she was in no way obligated, he took a more pleading approach to eventually convince Andie to help him tail Shirazi anyway. Andie felt there wasn't any harm in watching the congressman walk from one building to another, and though she was convinced nothing would come of the surveillance, her reporter's mind secretly hoped they *would* catch Shirazi in some incriminating act.

So they stood in the cold, biting wind of early morning, waiting for something to happen. The city sounds of construction, buses, and taxis, would have seemed out of place to real tourists in front of the majestic Capitol building, despite the unsightly scaffolding on the dome. For Andie, the noise had long since moved to background, and she decided to break the silence.

"You used to work for Israeli intelligence," she said without looking at Cohen. "But you told Casey you don't work for them anymore."

"That's right."

"So what do you do now?"

"You could say I'm in private practice now," Cohen said after a quick visual scan of the immediate area.

Andie looked at Cohen with the composed countenance of a seasoned reporter or successful poker player. "Mercenary?"

Cohen lowered the map he wasn't looking at anyway. "Hardly," he said. "I think in America you would call me a contractor. Except I work alone—not for a corporation—and you won't find any contracts with my signature on them."

"But you do this work for the government."

"In a way."

Andie wasn't sure what he meant.

"There," Cohen said before the reporter could ask him to elaborate. He nodded toward the Library of Congress building and pointed at the map in his hand to keep up the tourist guise while alerting Andie to the figure of Shirazi walking toward them. Andie wasn't sure what they could learn by tailing Shirazi between meetings—meetings they wouldn't be privy to in the first place—but Cohen argued that anything was better than doing nothing, which was exactly what he felt like he was doing back at Andie's place.

Casey had taken it upon himself to look into the Parker-Horus Rhind "lead," and in the interest of time he did not have, Cohen wanted to see what he could discover on the Shirazi front. Decades of scouting targets had taught him that you could learn more from direct observation than from just reading reports. More often than not, a target who was up to no good would act in ways that unwittingly signaled their guilt. Nervous, erratic movement, stuttering or hesitant conversation, and even an almost imperceptible clumsiness that caused minor breaks in their normal stride, were all indicators Cohen had learned to be suspicious of when he saw them. As Shirazi passed Andie and Cohen, talking into a cell phone with a folded newspaper under his arm and a briefcase in his other hand, he exhibited none of those signs. When he crossed the street towards the Capitol, he didn't head down the walkway to the legislative building, instead turning left to a nearby bench.

"Do we follow him?" Andie asked.

Cohen looked left and right before stepping into the crosswalk. "Come on," he said. "Let's hear what he's saying." They crossed to the Capitol side of the street and stopped at an information kiosk, peering at the brochures and maps taped to the inside of the glass windows. Cohen watched Shirazi's reflection and tried to listen in on the congressman's conversation twenty feet away.

Cohen expected to hear English from the U.S. congressman, but what he heard was something different. He closed his eyes to concentrate, as a brisk wind from the north pushed Shirazi's words away from him. Farsi would make sense because Shirazi was Iranian by birth and upbringing, but the words he *could* hear were Arabic. Cohen knew very little Persian, but he was fluent in Arabic—enough so that he recognized the dialect as North African. Not Egyptian. Further west. There were not enough consecutive audible words for him to discern the nature of the conversation, but given Shirazi's animated expressions, he figured it was more than routine business. Cohen decided it was more frustration than anger that colored the congressman's words. Cohen saw Shirazi pocket the cell phone, and the reflection grew larger. He turned to Andie so he wasn't staring but could still see Shirazi in his peripheral vision. Andie faced the congressman, looking beyond him down the street.

"Asshole," Andie said after Shirazi was past them. "Just left his paper on the bench."

Cohen looked over his shoulder at Shirazi's back then quickly turned to Andie. "What?"

"I hate when people just leave their trash wherever they damn well please," Andie said. "He even walked right past a trashcan. Oh, and look, there's a recycling bin right next to that."

"I don't care if the man dumps paint in the river," Cohen said. "We need to move, or he's going to get out of reach."

"What were you planning on doing?" Andie asked. "He's a U.S. congressman. You can't just grab him and rough him up 'til he tells you what you want to know."

"I don't care who he is. If he knows anything about the leaked operations, I need to find out." Cohen started to move after Shirazi.

"Good, somebody picked up the paper," Andie said. "At least there's some decent folks left in this town. He's even taking it with him."

Cohen stopped suddenly and turned around, grabbing Andie as she crashed into him. He held her arms to keep her from falling and looked over her shoulder. "Where?" he asked.

Andie turned, coming loose from Cohen's grip. She quickly looked around. "He was right there," she said with the uncertainty of a child who knew she was about to be accused of lying even though she was telling the truth. "He was by the bench, heading away from us."

Cohen turned in a full circle. He only saw cars passing on the street and Shirazi moving further away—too far away to pursue him without drawing suspicion. He cursed under his breath and pulled Andie further away from the information booth. "What did he look like?"

"Short. Tan trench coat. Fedora," Andie said. "I think he had a beard. It might have been gray. Or not. I don't know. Like I said, he was walking away from us, so I didn't get a good look. I just know he took the paper. Why?"

Cohen turned his head to find that Shirazi was gone. "The paper," he said, turning back to Andie. "It might have been a dead drop. An emergent one, most likely."

"What?"

"To pass messages," Cohen said. "The drop-off and pick-up were too close together. Plus the device—a newspaper left on a park bench—this had to be coordinated quickly so there was no chance of the wrong person intercepting the message."

"You're assuming the newspaper had a message," Andie said. "It's possible the man walking by just saw a newspaper lying around and thought, 'Hey, a free paper,' and scooped it up to read later."

"And if the man you saw was Davood Raad?"

"You think that was Raad?" Andie asked. "Remember, we're only here because of a feeling you had about Shirazi, not because we had anything concrete that said he was Raad's guy."

Cohen's look told Andie exactly what he thought of her comment.

"Never mind." Andie held up her hands in surrender. "You're the spy."

Chapter 28

Davood Raad returned to his office at ten thirty. He nodded silently to the guard as he passed through the lobby to the elevator. Raad pulled the key chain out of a jacket pocket when he reached his office, but he stopped short of inserting the key in the lock. The door was already open.

He pushed the door slowly, knowing that anyone inside would be alerted to his presence by the squeaking hinges—not that there was any place to hide in the one-room office.

"Salam."

Raad shut the door behind him and dropped his keys and paper on the desk. "Salam," he replied to the man sitting in one of the two high-back chairs. He hung his coat and hat on the corner rack and took his own seat behind the desk. Despite the uncharacteristic beard that covered much of the man's face, Raad knew who he was. The cold, piercing eyes gave him away. "How did you get in here?" Raad asked the man in Farsi.

The uninvited guest smiled. "You should be asking *why* I am here."

"Very well. Why are you here, General?"

Though he was no longer in the ranks of the Islamic Revolutionary Guard Corps, Teymoor Khalaji was customarily addressed by his former title. His role as an intelligence chief in the IRGC made him the perfect match to lead the liaison office within the Ministry of Intelligence and Security that coordinated MOIS operational intel-sharing with the IRGC's overseas arm—the Qods Force. Khalaji's position and pedigree kept him in Tehran, so his presence in Raad's office in the United States was an unusual, and risky, venture. It also did not bode well for the academic. "Consider this a courtesy visit."

"Then forgive me for not having any tea prepared," Raad said.

Khalaji sensed the animosity in Raad's flat comment but let it slide. "I want to personally congratulate you on the work you've done here the past two years. As you are aware, the information you have obtained has saved Iranian lives and is directly responsible for the continued success of the Islamic Republic's nuclear program and the major milestone that was reached earlier this month."

Raad nodded, silently acknowledging the compliment and offering his thanks at the same time. He knew the difficulty involved with Khalaji's trip to the United States, not only with facilitating his physical entry, but with the measures that had to be in place to ensure he wasn't discovered. He also knew that such risks would not be taken just to deliver a semi-official "thank you," and there must be another reason for the visit. "But…," Raad prompted.

Khalaji smiled. "But something has changed."

"How? Do you mean with the intelligence we are getting?"

"In a way," Khalaji said. "The time and target information has continued to be accurate, but the elements conducting those operations have evolved."

"What do you mean?"

"We were able to stop the attempt on Qalibaf with the intelligence you provided, but just barely. The identities of the attackers were not what we expected, and the mayor was almost killed because of it," Khalaji said.

"I am never able to provide identities, only the dates and estimated times of the attacks," Raad said. "Since when does Tehran require the specific names of Mossad assassins before they are terminated?"

"These men were not Mossad," Khalaji said. "They were Iranian. We anticipated Israelis, and our people were not looking for locals. Qalibaf's driver was shot before the attack was stopped."

"Mujahid?"

"Not that we could surmise, though they may have received training from that group." Khalaji shook his head. "No, from what we have found, it appears their mission was sourced through Ansar al-Furqan."

Raad stood and moved to the single office window. He pushed up a few slats on the blinds and looked at the back alley. "No ties to Israel at all?"

"We are still looking into the matter, but it does not appear so." Khalaji watched as Raad sat on the front of the desk and squeezed the bridge of his nose. "That bothers you?"

"It concerns me," Raad said.

"How?"

"Every attack before this was Mossad. Joint operations between the Americans and Israel, coordinated by The Council and executed by Mossad, so the American president and his government could maintain the falsehood of no longer conducting assassinations," Raad said.

"Assassinations that don't involve drones," Khalaji commented.

"The world knows Israel was responsible for the previous attacks. Israel is even investigating the possibility of a leak from its own people," Raad said. "But if Mossad was not involved in this attack, then questions will be asked that draw suspicion away from Israel."

Khalaji shifted in his chair and studied his colleague. Raad had been in America for a few years and in the West in general for longer than that. Khalaji did not know Raad well enough to determine if his familiarity with the American way of life—valued as that knowledge was—had also led to a complacency of thought that caused him to miss the change in the American-Israeli operations from Mossad to internal Iranian opposition forces carrying out the assassination attempts. But he needed to find out if Raad fully understood the implications of that change and the danger it posed to Iran's own efforts in America and the unprecedented access it currently enjoyed.

"That is not our problem," Khalaji said. "IRIB will figure out a way to tie Israel to al-Furqan. Trust me, the Zionists will still be blamed," he added, challenging Raad to take his previous thoughts to conclusion.

Raad shook his head. "Both Israel and al-Furqan will deny that accusation," he said, becoming louder and more agitated as he continued. "Neither will admit working together, if that's the case, and I doubt al-Furqan would take credit for a failed operation in the first place. On top of that, the rest of the world knows Iran Broadcasting is the government's propaganda machine. If we say al-Furqan did it, the West will first ask, 'who is al-Furqan,' and they will not believe the Zionist connection because of where the information came from. The Americans will stand by the Jews, condemn the accusations, and defend al-Furqan's position while decrying its methods. The right-wing media in the U.S. will no-doubt raise the possibility that their left-wing government is supporting the Ansar al-Furqan terrorist group. And there will be increased scrutiny to determine exactly what that support entails."

"How can you be sure?"

"The media in this country is politically polarized—especially with the upcoming presidential election—anything that can be construed as a liability in the eyes of voters will be exploited. And the American people are sheep," Raad said. "They do not think for themselves, but merely adopt the stance of the loudest voice on television as their own."

"So they brand the American president as a supporter of terrorists," Khalaji said. "That is what is bothering you?"

"No! It's the investigation that will lead to that branding that bothers me," Raad fumed. "The more aggressive reporters and congressmen won't give up until they find that one damning piece of evidence, or some connection, that will ruin any chance of the incumbent political party winning the presidency in 2016. And there are countless people in Washington who would gladly speak to the press about anything. It is like a disease with these people. My concern, General, is that one of them may say the wrong thing and expose The Council...and our asset."

Khalaji smiled. "Good."

"Good? That is anything *but* good."

"Easy, my friend. I only meant that it is good you understand the significance of the problem."

Raad stared unblinking at his visitor. "You came almost halfway around the globe to make sure I knew how to do my job?"

"Things are different now."

"Of course they're different," Raad shouted. He instinctively looked to the door and lowered his voice. "Of course they're different. I recruited the most valuable asset Iran has ever had in America, and I've protected him ever since."

"You have," Khalaji nodded. "And you've done well. But now Mossad is in the country hunting our asset."

"And we are hunting Mossad," Raad shot back. "I have people tracking a Kidon assassin as we speak."

"You do?"

"Yes," Raad said. "We know who the assassin is, and we are close to eliminating him." Raad dabbed sweat from his forehead. "It is possible he is dead already."

"*Possible*?"

Raad swallowed hard, wishing he had a bottle of water. "My men were to intercept the Israeli last night, but I have not heard from them yet."

Khalaji's eyes grew wide. "You have not heard from them?"

Raad looked at his watch. "It is early, yet," he said without much conviction. "They likely hit the target after midnight and are just following protocol—keeping low until they are sure no one is looking for them."

"Is someone looking for them?"

"There was no news this morning of any bodies being found in the area where the hit was to take place."

"No idea if the police are looking for anyone for anything else?" Khalaji asked.

"No."

Khaliji stood. "Then it appears your men are at least alive. Or they were killed somewhere else."

Raad clenched his jaw. "You assume the operation failed. Perhaps they took the target to a more private location and disposed of the body."

Khalaji laughed. "Like an American crime drama on television." He shook his head. "Your men were not going after a cheating husband or an amateur drug dealer, Dr. Raad."

"My men are trained killers, as well," Raad shot back.

When he reached the door, Khalaji turned. "My money is on the

Israeli," he smiled. The smile quickly vanished, and with a stern face and a tone of voice more characteristic of a superior addressing his subordinate, he added, "Please inform us when your men report in. I will be leaving tonight, and I will talk to headquarters when I get back about possibly instituting other measures to address the problem."

"What other measures?"

"All you need to concern yourself with is protecting the identity of the asset," Khalaji said. "You have done well so far, but you do not have the experience to handle this new threat. There are others in our organization who will deal with the Zionist spy."

Khalaji nodded his goodbye and was gone. Raad knew he would not be seeing the general again. He resented Khalaji's assessment of his inability to take care of the Mossad threat, but he also knew the man was right. Raad had never been an operator—not the same way others lived in the violent, life-or-death world of clandestine operations where the players don't even have names. Raad's world of spycraft was different. He was effective precisely because his name *was* known.

Raad moved to his desk chair and rubbed his eyes. His hands fell on the folded newspaper in front of him. He put on his reading glasses and turned to the editorial page.

Chapter 29

Casey tried the buzzer to Andie's apartment again. *Five.* He pushed it again, this time holding it in for a continuous ten seconds before he let go. *Six.* The speaker crackled, and Casey grabbed the box with an urgency that might have seemed obscene to people passing by if there were any.

"She's not fucking home!"

A man's voice. Strained by too much booze and too many cigarettes. "S-s-sorry," Casey said, his tongue too frozen to speak clearly. It took all of his energy and concentration to say, "I wath looking for A-a-ndie Jacks-Jackson." Without his jacket, Casey knew he couldn't stay still for much longer, or he would be in danger of going into shock or collapsing from hypothermia exhaustion.

"No shit," the voice said. "I hear it through the fucking walls. She ain't home, and some of us work night shift, so beat it, pal."

Casey got the message. He stumbled down the short flight of concrete steps to the parking lot and sat on the curb. He began shivering immediately despite his best efforts to generate warmth through friction by rubbing his arms. When he lost feeling in his hands, he tucked them in his armpits to defrost until he could start the friction therapy again.

This fucking sucks, he thought, his diction apparently still intact when he didn't have to open his mouth. After five more minutes, he moved closer to a trio of bushes near the walkway and curled into a ball to preserve as much body heat as possible. Casey closed his eyes, and though his body continued to shiver uncontrollably, fatigue proved the more powerful influencer, and he was soon fast asleep.

"Casey!" a familiar voice called from the darkness. Casey opened his eyes and looked up just as Andie got to him.

"What happened?" she asked. "And where the hell is your jacket?"

"Never mind. Let's get him inside." Cohen helped Casey to his feet while Andie unlocked the front door.

When Casey was seated on the couch with a heavy blanket wrapped around him, the chattering and quaking began to subside. Andie brought him a cup of warm coffee and a granola bar to help the internal warming process.

"You're lucky we came back when we did," Andie said as she sat down next to Casey. "Another hour and that 'mild hypothermia' wouldn't be so mild." She watched as Casey devoured the granola and downed the coffee. "Do you think you're okay enough now to tell us what the hell happened to you?"

Casey set down the empty mug and nodded. He stopped short of wiping his mouth on the blanket when Andie shoved a napkin in his face with the speed of a Bruce Lee counterpunch.

"What? Your manners froze out there, too?"

"Sorry," Casey replied. He balled the used napkin up and put it in the mug. He fell back into the leather sofa and pulled the blanket around him again. "Where do I start?" he asked, more to himself than either of the other two people in the room.

"How about the confrontation with Scott Parker," Cohen said from the chair beside the couch.

"It wasn't exactly like I planned," Casey said. He recounted the entire episode from first approaching Parker and his friend, to the attack by the two Qods men, to his abduction and interrogation. Andie and Cohen listened intently, never once interrupting the narrative. When Casey was finished, he looked expectantly at his audience until Cohen spoke up.

"These Iranians were after Parker?"

"Yes," Casey said. "That was the impression I got."

"And the other man that was with Parker, the one you said seemed to take over the interrogation, what was his name?"

"We weren't properly introduced, but Parker called him Alan, or Aaron—no, Adam. His first name was Adam," Casey said. "Parker said he was an Israeli diplomat."

"A diplomat," Andie said with a pensive look.

"From Israel," Casey said, nodding. "That's what Parker said, anyway. I didn't ask to see his credentials."

Andie looked at Cohen. "You know any diplomats named Adam?"

Cohen shook his head. "Well, it should be easy enough to check out."

"He knew who you were."

Cohen turned and caught Casey's gaze. "How do you know that?"

Casey almost wished he hadn't said anything after the look Cohen gave him. "I sort of mentioned that you were the one who told me Raad was a spy."

Cohen pursed his lips and leaned forward. "Did you mention that Raad was a spy first, or did they already know?"

"I mentioned it first," Casey said. "But they already knew. At least that Adam guy did. I don't think Parker cared one way or the other."

"He didn't care there's a known Iranian spy on American soil?" Andie asked.

"I'm sure he cared," Casey said, "but he seemed more interested in what I had to do with those Qods thugs trying to kill him."

"But you didn't have anything to do with that," Andie said.

"I know that. You don't think I told them that?" Casey looked directly at Cohen. "I told them about Raad's source in The Council, but that only seemed to make Parker angry. That's when Adam took over."

"Why did they let you go?"

Casey lowered the blanket off his shoulders. "I don't know. They were being nice?"

"They left you in a parking lot without a jacket," Andie said.

"Yeah, but they put my wallet and keys back in my pants before they dropped me off," Casey smiled.

"Gimme a break, Casey. They almost killed you."

"But they didn't."

"He's right," Cohen said. "They could have killed him, but they didn't."

"They didn't know he wouldn't freeze to death," Andie protested.

Cohen shrugged.

"It's okay, Andie. If they wanted me dead, I would have died right in that room. But they dumped me at a metro station with money for a fare card. I only almost froze to death because I'm a moron."

Andie shook her head, giving up the argument. "You said Parker became more agitated whenever you mentioned The Council," she said. "Was that because he didn't want to talk about it, or because you knew too much about it?"

"Both, I think. Parker is definitely a member, but he's not the guy telling Raad about the operations. So we can scratch him off the list."

"That was your list," Andie said. "Your boy here has a different list."

Casey looked at Cohen. "What list?"

"Not a list, a suspect."

"Who?"

"Your Congressman Shirazi."

Casey smiled and looked wide-eyed at Andie. "For real? You mean Cyrus Shirazi? From California?"

Andie nodded.

"Because he's Iranian? Man, that's kinda racist, don't you think?" Casey shook his head. "After our trip to the Holocaust Museum and everything."

"His travels and family contacts make him suspect more so than his birthplace. I am not so quick to eliminate a possible target until I am sure he is innocent," Cohen said. "On the other hand, you sound quite sure that Parker is *not* Raad's source. Why?"

Casey paused to get his thoughts in order. "I was going to say it's because he never denied the accusation when I said Raad was a spy, and he was more interested in finding how I knew about The Council. But that's missing the whole point of me being tied to that chair in the first place."

"Qods," Cohen said.

"Exactly. Why would the Iranians try to kill their source?"

"Maybe they weren't after Parker."

Both men looked at Andie.

"Maybe Parker wasn't their target," Andie repeated, her reporter's mind filling in where the analyst's and assassin's failed. "Maybe they were sent to kill Parker's friend?"

Chapter 30

The room was deserted. Andie assured Casey and Cohen it would stay that way while they were there. Very few people visited the "Archives and Research" space in the basement of the *Washington Times* building on New York Ave NE, and certainly not outside of normal business hours.

"I didn't think people used desktop computers anymore," Casey said, surveying the rows of stations that filled the center of the room.

"They don't," Andie said. "That's why this place is always empty. This stuff cost money, though, so management isn't ready to just toss them. They still work, and they're reasonably fast. This way, though, we can all work at the same time instead of you two looking over my shoulder backseat driving my laptop at home." She pointed to a laminated paper taped to the desk where Casey sat down. "All the database sites the *Times* subscribes to and the passwords are right there."

Casey sat in front of one of the computers and scanned the list front and back. He recognized some of the sites as ones he used in his work at IWG, but there were many that were more useful to newspaper reporters than geopolitical forecasters. Andie and Cohen were setting up camp across the table as Casey asked, "So what are y'all looking into? I mean, so we don't waste time searching for the same stuff?"

"Lev is going to try and find any connection between Shirazi and Raad that we may have overlooked earlier," Andie said. "And I'm going to look for anything on Israeli diplomats visiting or assigned to the U.S. in the past five years."

"Why five years?"

"A place to start," Andie said. "If this guy, 'Adam,' is really a diplomat, he probably hasn't been in the country more than five years. Diplomatic assignments for most countries generally aren't longer than three or four. And if he is visiting, I should be able to find a record of his having entered the country through the TSA or State Department records."

"Because of his passport."

"Exactly."

"Okay. Then what am I looking for?"

"Think of anything you may have picked up during your interrogation that didn't make sense or that you questioned," Cohen said.

"You mean besides why was I kidnapped, tied to a chair, and about to die?"

"Unless you believe the answer to that question is important to our investigation," Cohen said. "We already know your detention had to do with your presence at the location of the attack, but why were your interrogators so quick to accuse you of collusion with the attackers? What made them let you go? What did you say that changed their minds about your involvement? We talked about this briefly, but we need to find something that may answer those questions beyond mere conjecture." He raised his eyebrows and tilted his head, still focused on Casey. "And keep your emotions out of it."

Casey sat in silence and blinked several times. "You sound like Yoda."

Andie stopped typing and looked up, smiling. Cohen wasn't in the mood.

"I'm serious, Casey."

"I know. I'm sorry," Casey said, also smiling. "Alright. I'll see what I can think of." He looked at Andie. "May the Force be with me."

Cohen ignored the quip and focused on the montor in front of him. Andie went back to her own search, and Casey picked up the list of web addresses and passwords again.

Casey looked at the monitor and keyboard with a blank stare. He brightened when he found a yellow legal pad and sort-of sharp pencil near the end of the table. He dragged the treasure over and picked up the pencil. *Start with assumptions, I guess*, he thought and began writing.

ASSUMPTION: Iran wants Parker dead.

WHY?: He's the deputy national security advisor and Iran hates
America

*WHY?? Why Parker? (too risky)

—because he's part of The Council (true, but...)

We already covered that, he thought. *If Parker is Raad's source in The Council, it doesn't make sense for them to burn their own guy.* He wiggled the pencil with his thumb and forefinger and let the words on the page in front of him blur. *So, Parker isn't Raad's source, but he knows someone on The Council is, and the Qods hitmen were trying to keep him from finding out who.* Casey smiled, thinking that might be the answer, but when he focused again on what he'd already written, two words stopped him from putting graphite to paper.

too risky

Casey thought about that. Too risky because he's a government official? *That's not it. People are killed in D.C. just like any other major city in the country. For stupid shit. This city just happens to have a large population of government folks, so the chance some fed gets mugged is greater than in most places. That's just math.* Casey poked the eraser of the pencil repeatedly on his forehead, as if the gesture would free the answer from his tired brain.

Something came loose.

Andie was right. Those guys weren't after Parker, they were after the other guy. They came through me and Parker like they were blitzing the quarterback and we were the offensive line. We were just in the way of the real target. Okay. So who is Adam? And what's so important about him that a Qods hit squad was dispatched to take him out?

Casey knew Andie was working on that piece. She was searching based on information he had given her, though neither of them knew how accurate it was. But what was Adam's connection to Scott Parker? *Andie's PI friend said Parker was having dinner with "a friend,"* he thought. *It could be they became friends through work, but I don't think members of the National Security Council routinely have friends who are foreign nationals. I guess they could, but it seems like it would be a security risk someone in Parker's position would shy away from.*

The wheels in Casey's head were turning as he tried to picture every interaction between the two that he had witnessed from leaving the restaurant, during the attack, and while he was being interrogated. Friends. *Friends enough that Parker didn't fight back when Adam dropped him for pointing a gun at me. That's definitely more leeway than he would give a mere acquaintance.* He thought of the conversation he overheard outside the office building in Rosslyn when he first saw Parker. From that intitial observation, he concluded that Parker had a short fuse and a violent temper, but he let Adam get away with knocking him to the floor. Friends.

Casey knew that until they actually figured out who Adam was, they wouldn't be able to piece together a bio. But Parker was a known entity. His curriculum vitae should be public knowledge. Despite the *Washington Times*-provided resources, Casey went first to a simple Google search. The Wikipedia article for Parker was as good a place to start as any, and on the right side of the screen he found his first entry point into the deputy national security advisor's past.

Now Casey needed the newspaper's paid help. He read through the list of databases and found what he wanted. In less than three minutes, Casey was staring at the senior-year picture of Scott Parker in a yearbook from Northwestern University. There was nothing spectacular or unusual about the photo. Parker looked as normal as the next guy. Under the picture was a list of activities Parker had been involved in during his undergraduate stint at the university. Student government. Not surprising. Opinion editor of the campus newspaper, *The Daily Northwestern*. Okay. Varsity lacrosse. Mildly interesting. Model United Nations.

Casey scrolled to the index of the digital yearbook copy and found the page for Northwestern's model UN club. There was information about the spring conference the organization hosted that year. Two pictures of students doing...model UN stuff. And a group picture of everyone in the club. The number of people required the photographer to take the shot from some distance away, and as a result, individual faces were hard to make out. Even with the list of names below the picture corresponding to each individual's location in the photo, Casey found it hard to positively identify Parker. Zooming in only made things out of focus.

Before he left the page, Casey leaned closer to the monitor and ran a finger across the list of names. Nothing. Until he reached the last line after the words "not pictured." Sarah Folsom. Adam Miller. Edward Wilson. *Adam Miller*, Casey thought, silently mouthing the name. He moved through the pages quickly, looking for the individual photos again. He slowed when he reached the M's. On the second page, his eyes grew wide. "Adam Miller!" he shouted.

Andie and Cohen looked up from their own monitors. "What?" Andie asked.

"Adam Miller! That's the guy's name. The Israeli diplomat. Come here. Look. There's his picture right there," he said, tapping the screen.

Andie and Cohen left their stations and came around the table to where Casey was sitting.

"This was like seventeen years ago, or something, but that's him. That's the guy who interrogated me with Parker."

"Are you sure?" Cohen asked.

"What? Of course I'm sure."

"What is this? A yearbook?" Andie asked.

"Yeah, from Northwestern University," Casey said. "Miller and Parker were classmates."

"Adam Miller," Andie said pensively. "I haven't come across that name, but I'm still in the middle of checking State's list of foreign diplomat assignments."

"You won't find him that way," Cohen said.

"Thanks for the vote of confidence, Mr. Negative."

"You won't find him in a search for diplomats, because this man is not a diplomat."

Casey looked at Cohen who was still staring at the picture. "You know him."

"Yes." Cohen stepped back. "His name *is* Adam Miller, but he's not a diplomat. He is Mossad."

Chapter 31

"That's how he knows who you are," Casey said. "Y'all worked together."

Cohen shook his head. "No. I was done with team ops years before Miller's arrival. I only knew him as a recruit. A student in one of my training sessions."

Casey tilted the chair back. "You must have made an impression on him the way he acted when I said you were here in D.C. Almost like you were his idol or something."

"He would do well to find another hero," Cohen said.

Casey didn't ask him why. He knew nothing of Cohen's past actions that didn't involve him directly, and he wasn't sure he wanted to. Despite their current cooperation, Casey could never forget that Cohen once tried to kill him. But the Israeli assassin had also saved his life. That was the past, and Casey's world had changed since then. The world had changed. Now they had other issues to deal with.

"So what's the plan now?" Casey asked.

Andie, Cohen, and Casey exchanged looks. "I need to talk to Miller," Cohen said. "I have no doubt that he's the man you overheard Raad talking about. The attack last night is proof of that."

"That doesn't mean they're not looking for you, too," Andie said.

"No, it doesn't," Cohen agreed. "But if the Iranians were targeting Miller, that might mean he's here for the same thing I am."

"To find the leak," Andie said.

"And he must be close since they're already after him," Casey added. "But when we were chatting last night across the table in that cold-ass room with no windows, it seemed like he hadn't made the Raad connection."

"Which is why I need to talk to him," Cohen said. "I think we may be able to help each other and end this quickly."

"How will you find him," Andie asked.

"If he is posing as a diplomat, even if it isn't under official diplomatic cover, I should be able to find him at the embassy."

"You're just going to walk in and ask if there's an 'Adam Miller' working there?"

Cohen peered at Andie with squinting eyes. "No, Ms. Jackson, I'm not. There is no need for anyone else but Miller to know I'm even here."

"That's it," Casey said.

"What's it?" Andie asked.

Casey stood up and walked a few feet away before turning back to the others. "Miller knew who you were, but Parker had no idea. Parker and Miller were friends from their college days. And they both kenw about the leaked operations to kill Iranian scientists."

"Okay," Andie said when Casey paused.

"And I think we all agree that Miller is likely working on finding the leak, same as us. And he's close."

"But you said he hadn't made the connection to Davood Raad yet," Andie said.

Casey waved her off. "Doesn't matter. Raad is just the handler," he said, getting a nod from Cohen. "That means Miller is zeroing in on the leak some other way. He didn't need the Raad-connection to get as far as he did."

"Then how did he get close enough to have an Iranian hit team try to kill him?"

Casey smiled. "Parker!"

"You said Parker wasn't the leak."

"He's not. But he's in The Council. And that's why Miller's using him."

"Not because he's on the NSC?"

"No. That would make Parker a traitor. Giving classified information to a foreign government, even an ally, if it's not an officially sanctioned intel-sharing exchange will land you in jail." Casey looked at Cohen. "That's what got Jonathan Pollard in hot water."

Cohen shrugged.

"So you think the leak is from someone in The Council," Cohen said.

"I've always thought that," Casey said.

"But not Parker," Andie said.

"No, not Parker."

"Then who?" she asked.

Casey raised his eyebrows at Andie's question. "If I had their membership roster, we could start going down the list."

Andie raised her middle finger.

Casey smiled. "Okay. So we still don't know who the leak is, but it's looking more and more like it's coming from The Council, and Miller is working with Parker to find out who it is."

"If we knew who Miller suspected—if he has any suspects—we could try to find a connection between that person and Raad. Establishing that linkage might help confirm the person's role in leaking information to Iran. Then it would be easy to hand it over to the FBI, especially if Parker blows the whistle, and we can get on with our lives," Andie said.

"No FBI," Cohen said. "And no police. If the leak is someone with power inside the U.S. government..."

"Like a member of Congress?" Andie interrupted.

"...the police will hesitate, and he may get away or at least cover his tracks so he will never be prosecuted."

"But isn't that just as good?" Andie asked. "The leak will be stopped if he doesn't want to risk prosecution. Raad's source of information will have dried up."

"Maybe," Casey said. "But only temporarily. Methods can be adjusted. More precautions taken. If Raad's sourse is left unscathed, the same motivation to betray his country in the first place will likely drive him to betray it again."

"Alright, Casey, but let me ask you this: how does killing Raad's source help expose The Council? Isn't that what you came here to do?"

Casey thought about that. Ever since that morning in Soren's Deli, Casey had wanted to bring down The Council, even before he knew of its existence. An FBI arrest in an espionage case would lead to a larger investigation that would garner worldwide media attention and have several positive results. Raad would be detained or deported, his source would be imprisoned, and The Council would be brought to light and possibly dismantled. That was the positive-thinking side. The other side of getting the FBI involved was exactly what Cohen predicted. Raad's source would skirt prosecution, and even if Raad was deported, another Iranian spy would just take his place. And The Council? "What's The Council?" He was still wrestling with the possibilities when Cohen spoke up.

"Your obsession with The Council will have to wait. Right now we must focus on stopping whomever is giving Iran the information that is getting Mossad operatives killed."

"You don't want The Council to fall apart," Casey said, a new understanding coming to mind. "If The Council is actually facilitating these assassination attempts, its demise would mean the operations are halted and Iran continues unimpeded toward a nuclear weapon."

Cohen's jaw muscles flared. "Israel's operation will continue with or without American involvement. Iran must not be allowed to build a nuclear arsenal. Unless you want to see a nuclear arms race between every country in the Middle East, or another war that will have casualties in the millions, they must be stopped. If U.S. intelligence being used in these operations is being provided through this 'Council,' another avenue can be found. Or we will act unilaterally. Either way, I could give a fuck what happens to The Council."

"You *have* been in America too long," Andie said.

"Okay," Casey said. "Forget exposing The Council for now. One thing at a time." He looked at Andie.

She gave a dismissive wave of her hand. "Whatever you say. Just let me know what else I can do to help." She shook her head.

"Thanks, Andie."

"I'm not doing this for you, honey. I'm doing this for him," Andie said, pointing to Cohen. "I don't just read the news every day, I write it. And Lev is right. There are no good scenarios that begin with Iran having a nuclear weapon. Not even for Iran. So if what his people are doing is going to help prevent that from becoming reality, then I'm all for it."

Casey smiled. Andie just reminded him how little he actually knew about her past and what made her tick. But the more he learned, the more he liked Ms. Andrea Jackson. He turned to Cohen. "So what's next? I mean, besides you talking to Miller."

The analyst, reporter, and assassin spent the next half-hour trying to answer that question. After they all agreed on a plan, they powered down their computers and pushed in chairs to leave the room exactly as they found it. When Andie turned off the lights and shut the door, Casey said, "First I need to go back to where the Qods thugs attacked Parker and Miller."

"What the hell for?" Andie asked. Cohen gave Casey an equally puzzled look.

"My car's still in the parking lot."

Chapter 32

Inside a small coffee house around the corner from the Jennings Institute's Washington, D.C. office, things had finally slowed down from the morning rush as the newly caffeine-charged patrons took the noise and bustle with them to their respective work places. Ten o'clock marked the slow time for maybe ninety minutes before the lunchtime marauders invaded. Davood Raad didn't plan on being there for ninety minutes.

Raad sat at a table along the wall, away from the employees restocking pastries and baked goods and brewing more coffee. He sipped on his own cup, watching the front entrance, waiting. The place was small, and no one was assigned to greet guests or help them find a seat. There were no waiters or waitresses as all business was conducted at the counter opposite Raad. In fact, most of the customers simply paid for their drinks and muffins and left.

Raad's "friend" arrived on time. The audible ring of the door opening didn't even garner a reaction from the busy people behind the counter, and the man entered unnoticed. He walked over to where Raad was seated and took his own seat across the table. Raad had never seen him *not* wear that same black leather jacket and jeans. He wondered if the man slept in them.

"Salam," Raad said to the younger man who quickly surveyed the room before acknowledging the greeting.

"Salam."

The two men instinctively kept their voices down, though they conversed in Farsi. There was always a chance someone who overheard their exchange knew the Persian language, though those odds were slim. Time was short, and there was no security guard working the entrance to the coffee shop checking IDs, so Raad suggested they meet there rather than at his office.

"They still have not checked in," the man in the leather jacket said.

"Then we must assume they are dead."

The younger man nodded. "I will take care of Miller myself."

"No. I will get someone else to do it. I need you to deliver a message to our asset." He handed the man a folded envelope and watched it disappear into an inner pocket of the leather jacket.

"After you deliver that," Raad continued, "I need you to keep a watch on him. You are to be his shadow until we are certain that Miller is dead and there is no one else working with him."

"There are more Mossad here?"

Raad finished the last of his coffee. "We do not know that. But for now, we must assume there are. That is why I need you to make sure no one can get to the asset. You are the only one I can trust with this. The less people who know his identity the better."

The younger man nodded and abruptly left.

Raad rolled the empty cup in his hand. "Good luck," he said in English. He figured the cup didn't know Farsi either.

Chapter 33

Casey heard the sound of chains sliding free and locks turning before Andie opened the door to her apartment. He almost knocked her down as he made his way to the living area and dropped the heavy box on the coffee table.

"Easy!"

"Sorry," Casey said as he took a seat on the edge of Andie's couch. He removed the lid from the box and handed her a sheet of paper from inside. They were all the same. Black ink on white paper. Printed on both sides. Three thousand of them. "I got another box in the car."

"You going on a bombing raid?"

Casey looked confused. Then he saw where Andie was looking. "Oh, this," he said, unzipping his jacket. "Pretty cool, isn't it? Picked this up at Goodwill this morning. I can't believe somebody gave this away."

"I can't believe you paid money for that." Andie looked at the box that almost broke her coffee table and saw it was full of paper. She turned over the flyer in her hand and saw it was identical to the contents of the box. "Truth in Hiding," she read aloud.

"When I left last night, I checked back into the hotel, slept for four hours, then woke up at five in the morning and pumped that out," Casey said. He watched Andie's eyes move left and right across the text. "I brought a thumb drive to the Office Depot near my hotel as soon as it opened and had them print out six thousand copies. I figure we can hand them out or leave stacks of them at..."

"Shut up, and let me read it!" Andie ordered.

"Yes, ma'am." Casey sat back in the couch and watched in silence. Andie started over.

TRUTH IN HIDING

An international conspiracy is happening right under our noses. It's not a theory, it's a fact. This is a conspiracy that goes beyond good guys vs. bad guys. It's more complicated than right vs. wrong. It's a situation of life or death. The death of some in exchange for the lives of millions. But who decides who lives and who dies? Whose lives matter more? Is it just a numbers game?

Never mind. Don't answer that. Because YOUR OPINION DOES NOT MATTER.

You have probably heard about the attempted assassinations of some of Iran's leading scientists in recent months. I say "attempted" because you haven't heard about the successful ones. Only the failures. Iran is quick to blame Israel for these operations, and they invariably add the United States to the list of guilty parties for good measure. But who listens to Iran anyway? Well, this time you should.

— B e c a u s e   I r a n   i s   r i g h t . —

Israel *is* conducting operations to assassinate Iranian scientists. Not just any scientists, though. The targets are scientists involved in some way or another with Iran's nuclear weapons program. And we all know what a nuclear-armed Iran means. It means an arms race in the Middle East to establish and maintain some balance of power there. It means a nuclear-armed Hizballah. It means another U.S. war in the region to end Iran's nuclear program once and for all, probably costing trillions of dollars and thousands of American lives. And if Iran or any of its proxies use one of those weapons? Well, let's just say your abacus won't be able to keep up with the body count.

So you decide. Are a few scientists worth the lives of potentially millions of people who will be killed in a nuclear strike (or counterstrike) if Iran continues on its path to becoming a nuclear-armed nation?

"But you said my opinion doesn't matter."

Because it doesn't. Two things are needed to make an effective nuclear weapon along the lines Iran is pursuing. A warhead and a ballistic missile. Iran just tested a warhead, and it already has ballistic missiles. Luckily those weapons don't yet have the range to target America. But they can hit Israel no problem. So now you see why Israel, more than most, has reason to be worried and feels justified in its actions to block Iran's progress?

U. S. of A. — America is helping Israel in its efforts by providing key intelligence to enable these operations. Okay, not directly. That would mean the U.S. is back in the assassination business...which it's not...for the most part. But *indirectly*, yes, we are helping out. Only the information isn't coming from the White House, Congress, CIA, FBI, DoD,...it's coming from a group known as The Council. This group is made up of people from all of those institutions, but they don't represent their individual employers. Instead, these men and women—uniformed officers, elected officials, government civilians, academics, judges, etc.—speak and act on behalf of The Council. They make things happen behind the scenes when partisan bickering in Washington is slowing things down, or when it wouldn't be good for the president, or America for that matter, to have his fingerprints on anything. Like assassinating Iranian scientists. They're doing this "for" America, but without any semblance of official consent. Not the consent of the government, and by inference, not the consent of the American people. It's what THEY think is in the best interests of America, not you. The Council likes to stay in the shadows, so you won't find them in the Yellow Pages. But some of the front companies they operate include the Law Offices of Penrose-Klein and Horus Rhind Security Solutions. Look them up. There may be more.

Here's where things get squirrely. The Council is an organization of people. And just like any organization, you're going to have some (most) that are giving their best every day because they believe in what they're doing. And, just like any organization, you may have a few disgruntled employees who complain about anything and everything and generally just suck the morale out of the room by their mere presence. But every once in a while, there is a bad apple with malicious intentions. That person may not be so easy to detect, but recent examples such as Bradley Manning and Edward Snowden are evidence that these folks do exist.

What if The Council had such a person in its midst? Someone whose loyalty no longer belonged to the organization, but to someone or something outside the organization? What would be the consequences of an insider betrayal of The Council and its off-record support of Israel's assassination operations? Maybe this betrayal comes in the form of providing Iran with operational details of the planned assassinations. Forget "maybe." **This is exactly what's happening**.

Remember the "attempted" assassinations? Those operations failed because someone in The Council (a general, a judge, a congressman?) spilled the beans—to Iran. To Dr. Davood Raad, specifically. You see, Dr. Raad is an Iranian spy. He has been for years. Only, Dr. Raad is hiding behind his academic credentials, bestselling books, and international celebrity. He's been hiding the truth from you, me, everyone…for decades.

"So why hasn't Dr. Raad been arrested for spying on America all these years?"

I never said he was a *good* spy. Maybe he didn't having anything worth arresting him for. But now he has a valuable asset by way of a leak in The Council. And you can see the results on the nightly news. Failed assassinations. Successful nuclear tests. It's not a conspiracy theory, it's a conspiracy fact.

Don't let the truth stay hidden. Speak up, speak out, and **MAKE YOUR OPINION MATTER!**

"You know, you could go to jail for this," Andie said when she was done reading.

"How?"

"You mean besides the obvious libel suit from calling Raad an Iranian spy?"

"Yeah, but it's true," Casey protested.

"Okay, then how about accusing the government of helping facilitate the assassinations of foreign nationals? Or accusing a congressman of treason?"

"I never mentioned Shirazi once in that whole thing!"

"But you said the traitor might be a member of congress."

"So?"

Andie put the paper down and sat next to Casey. "But you have no proof. That's the problem. You made a witty argument with no real proof to back up anything you said. Frankly, it kinda reads like one of your blog posts you used to do."

Casey ground his eyeballs with the heels of his hands and sighed. "Look. We were supposed to put something together that we could distribute at Raad's lecture tonight to help stir the pot."

"Yeah, stir the pot. Not kick the hornet's nest."

"Okay, maybe I was being a little self-absorbed when I wrote this. I saw a chance to put Raad on the defensive and maybe pull back the curtain on The Council at the same time. I don't think there's anything wrong with that."

"Except you also gave away classified information by saying America was giving Israel intel to carry out its assassinations. Don't you think someone's going to want your ass behind bars for that?"

"I don't know if that's true," Casey said. "I just took what Cohen told us and ran with it. I connected the dots and put it down on paper."

"But if it is true, you're in a world of hurt. Talking about it between the three of us is one thing, but printing out...how many copies?"

"Six thousand."

"Six thousand. That's a whole different ball game. If U.S. intelligence is being used to target these Iranian scientists, don't you think that shit would be classified? And you want to tell six thousand people that?" Andie shook her head.

"Well, I'm hoping word of mouth with reach more than just six thousand people."

"You are a piece of work, my friend," Andie said. "Let's forget about getting in trouble with the law, what about getting in trouble with Raad and his people? When those guys attacked Parker and Miller in the parking lot the other night, you were just in the way." She picked up the flyer. "After this, you're going to be next on the list. Hell, you might just jump to the top of that list."

"I'm not too worried about that."

Andie's eyes grew wide. "What?! You better be worried, or you'll likely be dead. Casey, these are professional killers. Just because Raad is a short, out-of-shape, bookworm, doesn't mean his boys are."

"Right. But those 'boys' also know there is a Mossad operative in town whose also a trained killer. I think they'll be busy trying to stop that threat before they shift their sights to a blogger with no proof."

"And if they get to Miller before we start handing out these papers, then they can focus solely on you."

"Man, you're a downer," Casey said. "You don't have a boyfriend, do you?"

Andie stood up and put the top back on the box. "Let's just get this done. We've got four hours before Raad's lecture at George Washington, and since your dumb-ass printed six thousand copies, we've got a lot of paper to spread around."

Casey smiled and adjusted his Atlanta Braves cap. "Where to first?"

Chapter 34

It was almost four when Casey and Andie parked in front of the building that housed the U.S. office of the National Council of Resistance of Iran and Horus Rhind Security Solutions. After handing out flyers around Capitol Hill and the National Mall, leaving stacks near newspaper stands and on benches near monuments and Smithsonian museums, the pair had gone through one whole bax of paper and were deep into the second. With about 2,000 left to distribute, Casey finally convinced Andie to travel across the river to Rosslyn to drop off half of the remaining flyers at The Council's front doorstep.

They sat in the still-running car for a moment, savoring the warmth before venturing back out into the frigid cold outside. A trickle of people exited the building alone or in pairs. Andie figured it would be another half-hour before most of the busniesses in the office building closed for the day, and the parking lot would be flooded with white-collar workers leaving enmasse for the comfort of their suburban dwellings.

"Where do you want to leave these? Or do you want to hand them out individually and risk getting invited to another sit-down discussion?"

"Oh c'mon. That's not gonna happen," Casey said. "It's still daylight, and there's too many people around." He unbuckled his seat belt and looked at Andie in the passenger seat. "Are you getting cold feet?"

"My feet are already cold," she said. "They were frozen by the Lincoln Memorial stop. And no, I'm not getting scared. I'm just cautious."

"Cautious."

"That's probably one of the reasons I don't have a boyfriend."

"I'm sorry, okay? It was a joke."

Andie laughed and Casey smiled, relieved. "You got me," he said. He turned the ignition off and grabbed the door handle. Then he froze. "Holy shit."

"There's Shirazi," Andie said, staring out the front window at the congressman walking out of the building with two other men and a woman.

"What?" Casey glaned at the building entrance and quickly turned back to his left. "No. There!" he said, rapidly swatting Andie's shoulder. "That guy with the black leather jacket walking toward Shirazi. I've seen that guy with Raad twice already." He took his hand off the door as he and Andie watched the two men converge.

Shirazi reached into the side pocket of his coat and removed a cell phone. He thumbed a number in and held the device to his ear.

Leather jacket also put his hand in his coat, pulling something from an inside pocket.

"Oh my god," Andie whispered.

The two men were only five yards apart when the man with the leather jacket dropped his arm to his side.

"What is that?" Casey asked.

Before Andie could answer, Shirazi passed the man and turned into the rows of parked cars. Casey kept his focus and concentration on the leather jacket, until he was startled by the sound of a camera taking multiple shots, one after the other. He glanced to his right and saw Andie busy snapping pictures with her cell phone. He looked back as the man in the leather jacket passed through the other three people and disappeared around the back of the building.

"What the hell just happened?" Casey asked as he turned around in time to see Shirazi duck into a late-model Toyota and drive away.

Andie ignored him. Her face was glued to her phone as her fingers swiped back and forth, manipulating the digital photo cache. "Look," she said as she shoved the phone in Casey's face.

Casey took it from her and looked closely at the screen. The picture was zoomed in, and all Casey could make of it were a bunch of hands, butts, and crotches. "What am I looking for?"

Andie leaned over and pointed. "Right there. The arm in the black jacket. It's your boy holding a piece of paper or an envelope or something."

"It looks like an envelope."

"Okay, now zoom out and go to the next picture."

Casey swiped his finger across the screen and nothing happened. He repeated the move and asked, "How do I zoom out?"

Andie snatched the phone from Casey's hands. She made a pinching gesture on the screen and swiped her finger from right to left. She made a reverse pinch and handed the phone back to Casey. "There. Same arm, no envelope."

"Where did it go?"

"He must have passed it off to someone in that group."

"Shirazi," Casey muttered.

Andie shook her head. "I started taking those pictures *after* Shirazi passed the guy.

Casey imitated Andie's pinch maneuver and looked at a wider shot.

He scrolled back and forth through the photos. Eight in all. The faces of each of the subjects were in varying degrees of focus depending on which picture he looked at. Between the eight shots, though, there was a clear image of all four people. "Do you recognize any of those folks?"

"Not that I could tell."

Casey flipped through the pictures again. "Do you think it's possible he put the envelope back in his jacket? Like in-between a couple of the photos you got?"

"It's possible, but I doubt it." Andie leaned over to see the screen in Casey's hand. "Flip through them again," she said. "See. The envelope guy's hand stays at basically the same height, just below his waist. If he put the envelope back in his jacket, his hand would have moved, and we would have gotten a picture as it either went up or back down, even with the shutter closing and opening like it was."

Casey handed her back the phone. He gripped the steering wheel with both hands, driving his thoughts rather than the motionless car. He finally let go of the wheel and leaned back. "So Shirazi isn't Raad's source," he said.

"Well, we don't know that for sure," Andie commented. "But if that guy in the leather jacket is working with Raad like you implied, then yeah, maybe it was one of those other people."

"So we just have to identify who those people were, and we can narrow the search." Casey looked around the parking. From his vantage point in the car, he couldn't see anybody. "I guess we can't go ask them what their names are now."

"No, but we have their faces," Andie said. "I doubt we'll have any luck, though. Searching for a picture to match a name is a hell of lot easier than the other way around."

They both sat in silence, thinking of their next move.

"Any ideas?" Andie asked after a couple of minutes.

Casey shook his head. "No. I guess we can show the pictures to Cohen when we meet him at the lecture hall. See if he recognizes any of them." He pulled his seat belt around, buckled in, and started the engine.

Andie buckled her own restraint and said in a tone tinged with dejected envy, "I wish we had that damn face-recognition software the feds use. Then we might have a chance of getting some names."

Casey's head came up sharply, Andie's words sparking an idea. he pulled out his own phone and frantically searched his contacts for a number.

"What is it?"

Casey held up a finger as he pressed the phone to his ear. The call connected, and Casey heard a cough before the familiar voice answered.

"Detective Giordano."

Chapter 35

The Embassy of Israel to the United States was located on International Drive in the northwest part of D.C. Home to the embassies of the People's Republic of China, Ghana, Jordan, Pakistan, and others, the aptly name International Drive and the connecting roads of International Place and International Court resembled a gated community along the southwestern boundaries of the University of the District of Columbia. Only, in this community, each compound had its own gates and armed guards, and the neighbors were undoubtedly spying on each other as much they were collecting intelligence on their host.

And there was some diplomacy involved, as well.

But not for Adam Miller. Not officially, anyway. Miller had spent the better part of his Thursday in conferences and attending briefings with the new ambassador, Moshe Safran, fulfilling the duties he was sent to the States for in the first place—at least as far as nearly all the embassy staff knew, including the new ambassador. Outside of those sleep-inducing meetings, Miller was in and out of the "vault"—the embassy's secure meeting place for highly classified discussions—and the communications room where he exchanged encrypted cables with his superiors back in Tel Aviv. It was far from real-time communication, but it let him report back freely on his true assignment.

Tel Aviv sent Miller to the U.S. with a mission to find out if leaks compromising the *Quick Note* operations were coming from the American side. Miller wasn't the only member of Mossad with dual Israeli-American citizenship, having been born in the United States and familiar with the way things worked there, but he was the only one whose college roommate was a deputy national security advisor.

Miller had hoped Parker's position, and their friendship, would help him learn the extent of the U.S. support structure for *Quick Note* from the organizations involved to the numbers, and possibly names, of at least the key individuals with access to the operational plans. It wasn't until after the Qods attack and the interrogation of Casey Shenk, however, that Parker opened up about The Council and his role in that secret club.

That was how Miller thought of it. A secret club where the members were individuals with varying degrees of personal and professional power *within* the system who wanted even greater influence to steer the country in the direction they thought best. They found that influence *outside* the system. In The Council.

Parker's position in The Council was typical of the majority of the group's members. He provided information on current discussions and actions of the National Security Council, and the White House in his case. He was valuable to The Council in this respect, where his opinions were heard and considered by officials outside the NSC who had influence in their own right.

Casey's assertion that Davood Raad was an Iranian spy was not news to Miller. But the revelation that Raad had a source in The Council who was passing him *Quick Note* intel was unexpected. Parker initially refused to believe anyone in The Council would sabotage the group's efforts and betray the very country the organization was formed to guide and defend. *"Manipulate" is more like it*, Miller had thought when Parker explained it to him.

After Mr. Shenk was taken away, Miller had convinced Parker to at least consider the possibility that someone on The Council was talking to Raad. Parker eventually acquiesced, and they parted, agreeing to meet after work on Thursday to discuss what each of them had been able to uncover. Miller couldn't do much from his end without knowing who any of the other members of The Council were. And Parker was not willing to give his friend that information without doing some checking on his own first. It was a "secret" club, after all.

That was where Miller was headed when he left the embassy at ten 'til five that afternoon. He hoped Parker had something worth sharing. Or something he was *willing* to share. It turned out Tel Aviv was vaguely aware of some high-ranking people in the Pentagon who were rumored to be part of a group Aman referred to as "The Society." Assuming the Israeli military intelligence arm's "Society" was actually "The Council," the names were vetted by Mossad headquarters, but with negative results. It was highly unlikely any of the six men and women investigated were Raad's source. Miller wanted Parker's assessment along with any other potential suspects he may have come up with.

Miller walked outside along the south wall of the embassy building, past the ambassador's car and two other vehicles "for official embassy use only." There was no parking to speak of, and the embassy employees came to and from work mostly by foot, bicycle, or metro. Miller was only a transient employee lodged in a nearby hotel, so he walked.

He turned left through the front courtyard and nodded to the guard as he exited the compound. He took the brick sidewalk down

Van Ness Street towards Connecticut Ave. and the Cleveland Park metro station. He looked to his right as he passed behind the sprawling Chinese embassy. Somewhere inside the complex, somone was likely monitoring Miller's progress down the street. They would be watching until he was a block away from the embassy fence and no longer deemed a threat. Miller thought about waving to the camera he couldn't see but decided against it.

Before he turned his head forward again, his peripheral vision picked up something or someone behind him. Not yet on full alert, Miller's senses were nonetheless heightened. Whoever it was still trailed him by fifty yards, and chances were it was nothing of concern. Normally, Miller would make a mental note and check the situation again when he passed a storefront or office window, or when he turned at an intersection. But this wasn't a normal time. Qods soldiers tracked him down and tried to kill him two nights ago. Those two men were dead, but he knew there had to be more. He didn't have time for games.

Miller abruptly stopped and wheeled around, staying on the balls of his feet.

"Turn around and keep walking."

Tension left Miller's body and he did what he was told. In five seconds he was keeping step with a minor Mossad legend.

"We need to talk," Cohen said as he followed Miller southeast onto Connecticut's white cement walkway.

Miller checked his watch. "I'm meeting someone in an hour, so I have to catch the train. But we can talk along the way."

Cohen looked around and saw the pedestrian traffic was still relatively light. "Parker?"

Miller smiled. "So you *are* working with Casey Shenk. I could tell he wasn't lying about you being here, but I wasn't sure about the rest."

"I enlisted his help because of his relationship with Davood Raad. The information about our operations is getting to Tehran through Raad."

"I thought you weren't in government service anymore." Miller shot a glance at Cohen. "Actually, weren't you banished for executing Eli Gedide?"

"I was," Cohen said. "But Gedide had many enemies in Israel. People who he stepped on to get where he was. Many were afraid to cross him, and when I did what they wouldn't, they spoke up in my defense. I am still a son of Israel, and while I may never step foot on my home soil again, there are some who feel my services are still useful."

Miller agreed with Cohen's supporters. The former Kidon assassin had already been useful to him by connecting Raad to the problem he was working. He wanted Cohen on his team, even if the man wasn't acting in any official capacity. Though "official" was open for interpretation. "Will you come with me to meet Scott? If he came up with something, we may have to act quickly. And I could use your help."

The sun had dropped just below the tops of most of the buildings as they neared the entrance to the metro tunnel. Raad's lecture at GWU started at five-thirty, but Cohen was not sure how long it would take Casey and Ms. Jackson. He weighed his options. "I'll go."

Miller nodded as the two men approached the stairs descending into the station below Connecticut Ave. and Porter St. They slowed before the entrance to fall in line with the other travelers who tried to find an opening against the sudden outflow of passengers whose train had just arrived. Cohen didn't like the number of people bumping into each other and jockeying for position, each one with a more important date to keep than the other. The longer it took to move down the stairs, the more impatient people became, and the more anxious Cohen was.

He nudged Miller forward. He knew the younger man was from America and was probably more comfortable with the current situation, but that didn't help Cohen's growing anxiety. It was that little bit of nervous paranoia that had saved his life too many times to ignore it now.

"It's all right," Miller said over his shoulder when they were finally past the newspaper vending machines flanking the entrance. "This is just...ungh...D.C. for you."

Cohen stopped short to keep from being knocked down by a man in a gray parka who broke through the line, causing a sudden pile-up of bodies and creative insults behind him. Cohen watched the man carefully but hurriedly navigate the six lanes of traffic across Connecticut Ave.

"Let's go!" someone prompted.

Cohen turned back in time to catch Miller as he fell to the ground. "What's wrong?" he asked, easing Miller onto his back. Miller's eyes were wide and his face was turning blue. He was trying to speak, but his mouth only moved up and down. And it was getting slower. Cohen ripped open Miller's jacket and tilted the man's head back. He scooped two fingers to clear the open mouth, but there was no obstruction. Miller's face was turning darker by the second.

A crowd had formed around the two, forcing other, less-interested people to go around. Cohen didn't notice. He turned Miller on his side and yelled, "Call the paramedics!" to anyone and no one. He brought his arm back and hit Miller between the shoulder blades with the force of a sledgehammer. He tried two more times before returning Miller to his back. Miller's face was darker and his eyes were bulging from their sockets.

"A pen. A pen!" Cohen shouted.

Cohen searched his own pockets for a pen he knew he didn't have. A black ballpoint held by slender fingers appeared in front of him. He grabbed the pen, unscrewed it, and discarded all but the barrel. With a steady hand that belied the urgency of the situation, Cohen positioned the narrow opening of the plastic tube just below Miller's Adam's apple.

A quick slap of Cohen's hand and a chorus of short screams and groans was followed by a whistle as air escaped Miller's lungs. Cohen lowered his ear to the pen barrel protruding from Miller's neck. He leaned back when he heard a distinct sucking sound followed by another whistle repeated several times in succession.

Miller was breathing.

His chest raised and lowered in time with the audible flow of air. There was an enthusiastic round of applause as Cohen dragged a visibly weak, but improving Miller to the side of the metro entrance. Then the crowd was gone except for a few people who were waiting for the ambulance, and possibly the television crews. Cohen guessed one or all of them had called for the approaching emergency vehicle whose siren could be heard wailing in the distance.

Cohen's thought was broken when he felt a hand squeeze his arm. He looked at Miller. "What is it?" he asked, though he knew Miller couldn't respond at the moment. Not verbally, anyway. But Miller *was* trying to communicate something. The man's bloodshot eyes, now positioned in his skull where they were supposed to be, rolled up. Once. Twice. Three times. Cohen looked over Miller's shoulder. Across Connecticut Avenue. Then he understood. "The man with the gray parka."

Miller closed his eyes and nodded almost imperceptibly.

"I can't just leave you here," Cohen said. "I'll wait until the paramedics arrive."

Miller's eyes opened. He squeezed Cohen's arm again. Harder this time. He repeated the upward eye roll.

Cohen looked at the others waiting nearby. They were busy talking excitedly to each other, occasionally throwing a watchful glance toward the tracheotomy patient and his surgeon. They weren't going anywhere. He faced Miller, whose face seemed to have slackened, drooping slightly. Miller closed his eyes, and Cohen decided there was nothing else he could do there.

"Where are you going?" someone called. "You can't just leave!"

But Cohen was already gone.

Chapter 36

The Lisner Auditorium on the campus of The George Washington University was filling quickly as Casey and Andie made their way to some open seats five rows from the back. Raad's lecture was scheduled to begin in two minutes, but the large influx of "just-in-time" attendees was no surprise. The same scene played out every day at every college in America. There was a good chance a majority of the younger audience members were required to attend as part of one course or another. Casey hoped his message would be welcomed by the students, at least for the entertainment value, but the people he really wanted to reach were in the front of the room—academics, influential alumni, and possibly a few government officials, elected or otherwise—and the star of the show, Davood Raad.

Two men in dark suits and more or less tasteful ties took the steps at stage right. They stopped when they reached the farthest of four chairs at the center of the stage. When they were in position, another pair climbed the steps.

"There's Raad," Casey said in a low voice.

The lead man went directly to the podium and introduced first the other men on the stage and then the guest speaker. Raad moved to the podium and acknowledged the applause with a raised hand.

Andie leaned over and whispered to Casey, "They're reading the flyer."

Casey nodded. He had also noticed. As many as half of the people in the audience were reading the papers he and Andie provided. Most of them were engrossed in the flyer the same way people read programs at a graduation ceremony, more interested in what was in their hands than what the commencement speaker had to say. Raad was talking, but there didn't appear to be many people listening. When several of them started leaning over to their neighbors to point out one thing or another in the "Truth in Hiding" piece, Casey knew the seeds were planted. He just needed a little more time for the words to take root.

"In October of last year, just a few short months ago, Iran executed 26-year-old Reyhaneh Jabbari for killing a man she claimed had raped her," Raad said, providing a recent example of Iranian oppression since 2007, the subject of his newly-published book and the topic of the evening's lecture. "The election of Hassan Rouhani, the man the West hoped would bring moderation and change to Iran, was, as American's like to say, 'a pipe dream.' Iran will not change through the process of democratic elections. Iran is a revolutionary state, and democracy is anathema to the Supreme Leader and is seen as a threat to his rule. Democracy will never be realized in the Western sense of the word as long as corruption in the Iranian government is left unchecked. That is where the change must begin—from inside Iran."

"No wonder no one here ever pegged him for a spy, myself included," Casey said. "That's some smokescreen."

"And if it's your word against his," Andie said, flipping over her own flyer, "I'm not sure you can get people to see through it."

Raad talked for another fifteen minutes before he invited questions from the audience.

"Here we go." Casey stood up and made his way to one of the four microphone stands positioned in the aisles on both sides of the auditorium. He stood behind a student—at least he thought the guy was student—who was quicker on the draw than Casey. Rather than trying to hide behind the taller, much hairier man in front of him, Casey stood slightly to the right, hoping Raad would recognize him when it was the other man's turn to talk. He wanted to see Raad's reaction.

After fielding two softball questions from the front of the room, Raad pointed in Casey's direction. To the sasquatch in front of him. "Yes. In the back."

"Good evening, Dr. Raad. And thank you for speaking to us today."

Raad nodded. But there was no indication that he recognized or even saw Casey.

"Sir, my question is about your arrangements with the Iranian government that allows you to travel back and forth to the Islamic Republic, even though you've made a career out of bashing the regime and its dismal human rights record. Could you tell us how you've managed to stay out of jail or worse everytime you go back?"

I like this guy, Casey thought, looking up at the back of the man's shoulder-length-hair-covered head. A few students in different areas of the auditorium clapped briefly and cautiously before Raad answered.

Raad adjusted the microphone position. "Thank you for your question." He looked around the room as he answered. "It does seem a bit odd that I am able to voice the atrocities of my own government without consequence, but the answer to your question is...a bit embarassing, frankly, and quite contrary to my rather humble nature. But because you asked, the answer is my celebrity. You see, because I am known throughout the world, the regime tolerates my criticism. Any actions to incarcerate, torture, or execute me would be more harmful than helpful for the regime, as the likely backlash would be more economic sanctions and a rise in anti-regime protests within the country. I am lucky in a way, but I do not believe that luck will be with me indefinitely. It is therefore my duty speak the truth of what is going on in Iran as long as the door remains open."

"Thank you," the hairy man said and retreated back to his seat.

"Dr. Raad, I have a follow-up question and comment to your last answer," Casey said as soon as the microphone was available and before Raad could signal to one of the others waiting their turn. "I applaud you for speaking the truth about what goes on in Iran, but isn't there more to the story? Specifically, more to *your* story?"

Raad shielded his eyes from the overhead spotlights and leaned forward to better see his questioner. "I'm sorry. I don't exactly understand..."

Casey cut him off. "I mean, you say a lot of stuff to get people angry at the regime, but you used to work for them. What happened between then and now?"

"You are referring to my time as an advisor to Prime Minister Mousavi. That was decades ago, and it is public knowledge..."

Casey didn't let him finish. "But isn't it true you never left government service? And that the real reason the regime won't kill you or throw you in Evan Prison is because you still work for them? And your celebrity. That's not protection. It's cover. A elaborate cover to mask your real occupation as an Iranian spy. Isn't that the *real* truth?"

A murmur began to spread through the auditorium, growing louder as more people turned to look at the man openly accusing Dr. Raad of espionage and voicing their comments left and right. Casey saw several people holding the flyers he wrote, examining the text closer. Somone hurried behind the row of seats on stage and handed a flyer to the emcee. After a quick scan of the paper, the man jumped to the podium.

Casey removed his ballcap, and Raad straightened with the sudden recognition.

The emcee maneuvered in front of Raad and signaled the security guards stationed at the lower exits. He set the paper down and pulled the microphone to his lips. "Sir, this is not the time or place for protests and accusations. I must ask that you please leave the auditorium immediately. These men will show you to the exit."

Casey watched the guards move closer up the aisles amidst a smattering of boos. He looked back at the stage and Raad examining the flyer on the podium. Another man came on stage and spoke in Raad's ear while he eyed Casey.

The guards were two rows away when Raad moved back to the podium, smiling. He spoke quickly to the emcee. When the man backed away, Raad repositioned the microphone as the guards reached Casey. "Please. Please," he said. "Everything is all right. Please, let Mr. Shenk speak."

The guards moved away from Casey and took new positions at the back of the room in case their orders changed. Casey verified the guards were no longer interested in throwing him out, at least for the moment, and he moved back to the mic. "Hello, Dr. Raad."

"Hello, Casey." Raad held up the flyer. "I see you have taken your conspiracy blog to print. More baseless accusations, I see. I'm just shocked to see you have turned your sarcastic drivel on me."

Casey was surprised by Raad's reaction. He might have expected it from someone else, given the accusation, but Raad was usually quick with an answer to explain away any objections or questioning attitudes. That was how he handled sasquatch. But this was a different tact. Offense, not defense.

"It's only baseless drivel if it isn't true."

"And what facts do you have? Certainly you have facts that led you to your erroneous conclusion. I would like to hear them, Casey." He made a sweeping gesture with his hand. "We all would."

"I have my sources. Just like you have your source inside The Council." Casey wished Giordano had gotten back to him so he would have a name to throw in Raad's face.

"And when was the last time you talked to your source, Casey?" Raad asked, dodging The Council issue. "If he has the evidence you don't, shouldn't we be hearing from him?"

Casey flinched at the tap on his shoulder. Andie whispered in his ear and nodded to the man who had talked to Raad while he read the flyer. Casey didn't recognize him, but he knew the leather jacket next to him. Both men stood by the exit, scanning the crowd.

Cohen, Casey thought. *Not Cohen. Miller. Raad thinks Miller told me. And Miller's dead. That's why Raad's so confident.* Casey put his cap back on. *But he probably doesn't know about Cohen...possibly.*

"Or perhaps your source doesn't have any evidence. Is that it Casey?" Raad shook his head. "You should think twice about who you trust next time before you get yourself into some real trouble." He gestured to the guards, and Casey was quickly grabbed at the elbows by the uniformed men.

Casey looked around at the faces of the audience as he passed them on his way to the exit. Many were smiling. *Glad y'all had fun,* he thought.

"Thank you all," Raad said to the audience. "This has been a most enjoyable evening." Polite applause echoed in the hall as Raad left the stage and exited on the opposite side from Casey, his two men in-tow.

Chapter 37

Raad conversed rapidly in Persian with the two men next to him as they left the auditorium and descended the short flight of stairs to H Street. "Do not worry about Casey Shenk. He is only a nuisance. No one will listen to his rants."

"But what he wrote was true," the other man besides Raad in a coat and tie said. "If the authorities check out his story, we are finished."

"Settle down, Payam. I know Casey Shenk, and trust me, the only people who will dig deeper into what he said are The Council. And they will not dig far. They will be more concerned with protecting their secret existence than embarking on a mole hunt. I do not think Mr. Shenk has long to live after what he pulled tonight. And not just at the lecture. This flyer," Raad said as he pulled the folded paper from his pocket, "is his suicide note. He will be executed soon, but not by us."

"Jahan," leather jacket said as the group moved to the sidewalk.

Jahan leaned on a polished black sedan twenty yards away. The hood of his gray parka was down as the wind had died with the arrival of darkness. "Salam."

"Salam." They took turns kissing Jahan's cheeks, grateful for his safe return, but more so for his successful extermination of the Zionist spy sent to disrupt their operation.

"We may breathe easy, my friends. But only in this moment," leather jacket said. "Jahan has bought us more time to continue Allah's work despite the efforts of the Zionists and their American dogs, but we still have a job to do."

"Shahin is right," Raad said. "We cannot be blinded by our good fortune this night. We may praise Allah for Jahan's success, but we must not let our guard down. You gave the message to our asset?"

"Yes," Shahin answered.

"Then we must wait," Raad said. "In a week's time we may resume our work here. Until then, we will have no contact. When it is safe, I will send word."

"And if Mossad has planned another operation before then?" Payam asked.

Raad clapped his driver's shoulder. "Tehran will be on their own. And I am sure they can handle whatever situation arises. We know enough of their tactics and methods that, if the leaders of our nuclear program are guarded, I am confident we will prevail."

Payam was still uneasy. "Tehran may be able to handle their end, but what about us? I do not think we can just dismiss Mr. Shenk and the trouble he may stir up."

"Payam is right," Jahan said. "I think Miller was not working alone." The man in the gray parka had everyone's attention. "He could not have killed Amir and Najid and moved their bodies by himself. Do not look at me like that, Shahin. We all know they are dead, and there was no trace of them at the hit location."

"There is something else," Raad prompted.

Jahan nodded. "There was another man with Miller when I killed him."

"You are sure of this?" Raad asked.

"Yes."

"And you let him live?" Shahin almost shouted.

Jahan stepped closer so Shahin could feel the heat of his breath. "You were not there, boozineh. Assassination in the far enemy's country is not like launching rockets into Basra. You are new to Qods, but you will learn. Fast in, fast out. Live to kill again. Understand, pesar?"

There was silence as the two men stared each other down. Content he would hear no more criticism from Shahin, Jahan backed away.

Raad spoke up as the exchange ended. "The other man?" he prodded.

Jahan leaned against the sedan again and fished a cigarette from his jeans. After the first drag he said, "Big. Well, tall. Solid. Miller was speaking to him as they moved in line to the subway." Another drag. "A Jew."

Raad nodded and stroked his beard. "Then Payam may be correct. If Casey Shenk was working with Miller, he may be working with this other man. And that makes Mr. Shenk a bigger threat than I thought." He had the full attention of everyone around him. He sighed. "We cannot wait for The Council to silence him. We must take care of Shenk ourselves."

Everyone nodded agreement.

"And this Jew."

Chapter 38

"This is America, man! Freedom of speech! Freedom of the press! This lady's a reporter, you know."

Andie shoved Casey down the final two steps. "Just go, jackass."

The two guards who escorted Casey out of the auditorium laughed as they retreated back inside. The doors to the building clicked shut as Casey and Andie reached the sidewalk and turned left up 21st Street, strolling north at a snail's pace. They knew when Raad's lecture was over, there would be a crowd of people spilling out the doors they were just thrown out through. At the moment it was quiet.

"So, did that go how you expected?" Andie asked.

"Not exactly. I think we got our message across to Raad, though. And at least some of the folks in there seemed to think it was an interesting revelation, but something was wrong."

"The guy from the office building."

"That's part of it," Casey said. "I could tell whatever Raad was told on the stage couldn't have been good. Not for us, anyway. Good for him maybe, because he was all smiles and wit after that. But when you pointed out the dude in the leather jacket, I started to get worried."

Andie stopped before they reached the end of the building and faced Casey. "Because you thought something happened to Cohen."

Casey looked at her in surprise. The more he worked with Andie, the more he wondered who was rubbing off on who. "That's exactly what I thought at first. But then I realized that probably wasn't it at all."

"What then?"

"I think they killed Adam Miller."

"Miller?"

"It makes sense. The guy in the leather jacket tells the other guy, 'I just took out the Israeli who can blow our whole operation.' That's something you don't keep from the boss. So the other guy, because he's not dressed like a hoodlum, goes on stage and tells Raad the good news," Casey explained.

Andie shook her head. "I don't buy it. These guys have already tried to kill Miller once. You were there. So they probably had orders to keep trying. They wouldn't risk causing a scene just to tell Raad something they could tell him when the lecture was over."

"Okay, then why do you think it had something to do with Cohen?"

"Because they haven't tried to kill *him* yet."

"They don't even know who Cohen is."

"You keep making that assumption, but you don't know that," Andie argued. "Maybe they didn't know about him before, but they probably do now." She held up her hand when she saw Casey's mouth open. "Let me finish. I don't believe either of those guys would interrupt Raad during a public lecture just to tell him Miller was dead. But if they found out about Cohen, and they were able to kill both him and Miller, *that* would be news. 'Hey boss, we found out there were actually two Israeli spies, and we killed them both.'"

Casey followed her logic, but he wasn't sure he was ready to buy it. "Okay, but how did they find out about Cohen in the first place?"

"Cohen was going to meet Miller this afternoon."

Casey's heart skipped a beat. The scenario Andie laid out played in a rapid, repeating loop through Casey's head. The thought of both Cohen and Miller dead left him feeling exposed. And defenseless. Casey's part, and Andie's too, in the plan to expose Raad and flush out his source was to put the Iranian on the defensive with a public accusation that would rattle him and possibly cause him to be careless. If Raad broke protocol and took unusual risks to protect his source because he felt the noose tightening, Cohen believed he and Miller could exploit any misstep and break apart Raad's operation. But even if Raad became careless, without the Mossad brothers, Casey and Andie were on their own. A blogger/analyst and a reporter versus trained professional Iranian killers. He didn't like the odds.

"You see why we should be worried?" Andie asked, as if she were reading Casey's mind.

"Yeah. I do. I'm also thinking we should have come up with a different plan. One that didn't leave such a big red bullseye on my forehead."

"It's too late for second guessing, Casey. We need to think about what we're going to do next. If Cohen and Miller are really dead, I'm not so sure hanging around D.C. is such a good idea."

"You're probably right. At least I shouldn't. You might not be on their radar at the moment, so there's a chance that if you just walk away now that you'd be safe."

"That might be true, but I'm not going to just let you hang in the breeze," Andie said. "And I don't think you should just get in your car and jump on 95, either."

"Then what?"

Andie took her cell phone out of the empty backpack she was carrying as a purse that earlier held the flyers Casey now wished he had never written. "I helped out a guy once by *not* writing a story I was investigating, and I think he can help us."

Casey watched her fingers as she dialed. He could hear the phone ringing as she held it up to her ear, and his gaze followed. But something caught his eye, and his focus shifted farther down the street over Andie's shoulder. Without moving his eyes, he reached out for Andie's arm and pulled the phone away.

"What the fuck?" Andie exclaimed, looking at her empty hand.

"Hello?" the phone now in Casey's hand asked. "Hello?" Casey thumbed it off and pointed.

Casey's behavior worried Andie, and she turned around to see what caused the sudden change.

Passing in and out of the street lights, Andie saw him. Crouched but running. Silent. Deliberate.

"Cohen," she whispered.

Chapter 39

Cohen slowed when he reached the Marvin Center on GWU's Foggy Bottom campus. The building was a kind of all-purpose community center for the university that included several study rooms and an amphitheater. But Cohen neither knew nor cared about any of that. What did interest him was the man in the gray parka who jogged onto a cross street just past the bland structure four minutes earlier.

With only an initial direction to go on, Cohen ran hard through the streets of Washington until he caught sight of the man several kilometers earlier. His aging lungs were doing him no favors, and the cramp developing in his side was a stark reminder that, while his mind was still as sharp as it was in his youth, his body was not. But whether it was Cohen's lifetime of mastering the skill of covert pursuit or just dumb luck, his quarry soon determined—wrongly—that he was not being followed and slowed his flight to a slow jog interrupted with periods of walking. Cohen had welcomed the change of pace as it gave him a chance to both catch his breath and close the distance.

He reached the corner of the building, trying to stay in the shadows as much as the street lamps and building glow would allow. He slowed and peered around the corner, hoping to catch a glimpse of the gray parka moving slowly down the road. He stopped when he saw he didn't need to run anymore. He almost smiled for no longer having to run through the city he started to hate more and more with each knee-jarring, shin-pounding stride. But he didn't smile. He backed further into the building's shadow and planned his next move.

The group of four were arguing. It didn't last long. Cohen knew his best hope was to take the group by surprise while they were still in close proximity to each other. If they spread out and went their separate ways, he would have to choose. Time was almost up, and Raad was priority one, but he wanted the man in the gray parka dead. The man who killed Miller. Or tried to.

Cohen had run his own mental diagnosis as he trailed the man through the streets of Washington, and he concluded the man had stuck Miller with a dagger or some other sharp implement loaded with poison. It was the poison that had closed Miller's windpipe so quickly. The method had been used before. Cohen had used it once himself. But in that case, in a crowded marketplace in Tunis seventeen years ago, his target was dead in less than a minute. Miller was alive when Cohen left him, so he knew whatever the killer used on the younger Mossad operative was not as powerful. But he assumed it was just as effective. Cohen had bought Miller some time, but it was unlikely he survived. Packing tape on a leaky pipe. Temporary. He hardly knew Miller, but he was Mossad. And to Cohen, that meant something.

With a deep breath, Cohen palmed his semi-automatic pistol and let his right arm hang down by his side. He stepped from the shadows and approached the group directly at a steady but casual pace. He wanted their attention to freeze them in place, but he did not want to appear like a threat. Not yet.

*   *   *

Movement across the street caught Shahin's eye. He swung a hand back to get Jahan's attention. "Look."

Jahan turned around and the others saw the man coming at them. "Can we help you?" Raad asked.

Cohen took three more steps before answering. "I hope so," he said, continuing to close the distance between them.

The other three Iranians formed a semi-circle around Raad. A protective barrier for the senior spy.

Cohen was ten feet away.

"What do you want?" Raad asked.

Cohen extended his arm before anyone could react and put two bullets in Jahan's torso. Goose down feathers floated up as the man's body fell to the ground.

Cohen swung his arm to the next target, but the shot sailed high and wide as Shahin crashed into him like a freight train. The two men fell hard. The Iranian's weight and the force of impact knocked the wind from Cohen's lungs and sent the handgun skidding across the pavement.

Casey and Andie watched from the corner of the auditorium. "We gotta do something!"

"Do what? Get killed?" Andie asked.

Casey took a step forward, and Andie yanked hard on the back of his jacket. "Let Cohen handle this," she said.

"Fuck!" Casey said under his breath. His heart raced. His muscles tightened. "We can't just sit here!"

He watched as Cohen kicked the man in the leather jacket off of him. Cohen sprang to his feet, but the Iranian was faster. And he had a knife. Casey hadn't seen that before. But maybe it wasn't there before. The knife flashed with the reflection of a street light as the Iranian swung across to force Cohen back. Then he thrust the blade forward. Cohen caught the man's wrist and twisted. Casey heard a crack and a clang as bone snapped and blade fell. Cohen crouched to grab the knife but was met with a kick to the jaw that put him on his back.

"Casey! Raad's getting away!" Andie shouted.

Casey took his eyes off the brawl and saw the man in the coat and tie ushering Raad into the back seat of a car. Before he could reflect on everything wrong with what he as about to do, Casey bolted from the corner of the building and ran full-out to the black sedan.

The driver's door slammed shut, and engine roared to life.

"Casey!" Andie cried out.

He didn't hear her. The car started to pull out, and the driver slammed on the brakes as Casey landed with a thud on the front hood. The startled driver recovered from the surprise and put the pedal to the floor. Tires squealed. Rubber burned. And Casey grabbed for something to hold onto. The driver hist the brakes hard, and Casey rolled off. He looked at the windshield wiper covered with blood in his shredded palm. That was the extent of his examination.

Tires screeched again, and engine revved high. Casey stared at the fast-approaching headlights for a split-second. Almost too long. He rolled to his left and felt the wind from the passing car on the back of his neck. *Holy shit*, he thought. He opened his eyes and stared at a pistol two inches from his nose. *Cohen's gun*. He grabbed the weapon without a second though and moved clear of the other parked cars along the side of the road. Almost.

Something caught hold of Casey's ankle, and he fell face first into the street. The pistol fell along with him, and he left half of his right cheek on the pavement. Stars obscured his vision when he rolled over. The flashes framed the bright light from a nearby lamp post in a silent fireworks display just for him.

The lamp light faded. Or was it blocked? Casey saw a halo outlining a figure above him. He thought it might be an angel, but then, angels don't wear winter jackets. His eyes widened when his vision, in a brief moment of clarity, revealed the identity of the glowing specter.

Jahan raised the pen needle high and swung the lethal, poison-infused dagger in a long arc toward Casey's heart, falling to his knees to put the force of his own weight behind the strike. But he never connected.

The Iranian's temple exploded. His lifeless body fell on Casey like a sack of rotten fruit.

Casey squirmed out from under the bloody pile of dead flesh and bone. He gagged at the sight of the man's skull, caved in and spilling blood, bone, and brain. He gagged again. And then his stomach emptied into a putrid pool on the bullet-pocked gray parka.

When Casey pushed himself up, he was standing next to Andie. She was silent, almost in shock, staring at the dead man in front of her. And she was bleeding. Only it wasn't her blood. He looked closer and saw the drops falling off the brass knuckles she gripped in her hand.

"Andie?" he said hesitantly. Nothing. He inched closer, wiping the filth from his mouth with the back of his hand. "Andie?" Casey touched her shoulder.

Andie's head whipped violently in Casey's direction. Her blood soaked hand was raised slightly, and her breathing was heavy.

"Andie, it's me. It's Casey."

Andie's eyes blinked rapidly, and she looked around nervously as if she had no idea where she was or how she got there. She looked at her fist, clenched around the brass knuckles. And then she looked at Casey. A spark of recognition was followed by a long exhalation. Then her knees began to buckle. She grabbed Casey's arm for support, and her friend eased her to the ground. Casey followed suit and sat cross-legged across from her.

"Are you all right?" Andie asked.

Casey didn't expect that question. "Me? Yeah, I'm fine."

"Did I...I mean...is he..." She tilted her head in the direction of the red and gray lump beside them, not wanting to look at it. "Is he dead?"

Casey nodded. "He's dead."

Andie removed the brass knuckles and turned them over in her hands. "I never used these before." Her mouth cracked into a half-smile. "Been carryin' these things around since I left for college. Grandaddy gave 'em to me. Said they might help even the odds if I'se ever in trouble."

Casey smiled. He'd never heard Andie speak with with a Georgia accent before. He figured the stress must have dug it up from way in her past. *Like me, when I drink too much.* "Whole lotta trouble tonight," he said.

Andie looked around. She realized how quiet it was. "Sure was."

Casey touched her knee. "Thank you, Andie."

Andie lowered her eyes and smiled.

"We need to get out of here."

Andie and Casey both jumped.

"Now," Cohen urged.

Chapter 40

Casey noticed that a small crowd had started to gather on the corner where he and Andie had taken cover earlier. He figured they were people leaving the lecture, but Cohen's insitence and the sound of sirens whining in the distance ended his guesswork. Andie, Casey, and Cohen turned west on H Street and didn't stop until they hit New Hampshire Avenue. They waited in the Residence Inn parking lot until a friend of Andie's who promised not to ask questions picked up the three bruised, battered, and bloodied people and brought them back to Andie's apartment.

After the door was shut and bolted, Andie handed out wet towels. "Try not to get any of that shit on my furniture." She was agitated more than usual. Both men understood. What this woman had gone through—what she had done—was not something that was just forgotten after a couple of hours. The images of this night would haunt her for a long time. Possibly the rest of her life.

Cohen tossed the used towel by the door and leaned forward toward the others across the coffee table. "We need to find Raad," he said. "He is likely making preparations to leave the country tight now. If he's not already gone."

"You think he could get out that fast?" Casey asked.

"I don't know what kind of organization he has established here, but it is possible."

"Don't you think he will try to come after us?" Andie asked.

"No. Not immediately," Cohen answered. "After tonight, I think Raad has gone on the defensive. And for a man like him, retreat is usually the first option."

Casey's pocket buzzed.

"But if Raad leaves, then it's over for us, right?" Casey stood up and tossed his soiled towel on the pile by the front door.

"Miller was onto something that didn't even involve Raad," Andie reminded them.

"Miller's dead, though," Casey said. His pocket buzzed again.

Cohen sensed the feeling of defeat coming from across the room. "Because we don't know what, if anything, Miller had uncovered, we need Raad to tell us the name of his source."

"He won't just *tell* us who his source is," Andie said.

"I'll make him tell us," Cohen retorted.

"Here we go again." Andie rolled her eyes and unconsciously opened and closed her right hand.

"You're all-in now, sister," Casey said with a nod.

Andie stopped flexing her hand and raised her middle finger.

Casey backed away and pulled the phone from his pocket.

"Before we can move forward, though, we have to find him," Cohen said. "Do we know where he is staying here in Washington?"

"That shouldn't be too hard to find out, but do you think he'd really go back to his place?" Andie asked.

"It might not matter," Casey said.

Andie and Cohen looked at Casey who wiggled the phone in his hand. "What?" Andie asked.

"Paul Giordano came through," Casey said. "We've got the names of two of the three folks leather jacket passed through in Rosslyn."

"Raad's source," Andie said.

"What are you talking about," Cohen asked.

"Oh shit. You don't know."

Casey recounted what he and Andie witnessed at the office building in Rosslyn, Virginia, earlier that day. Andie showed Cohen the series of pictures on her phone and the disappearing envelope as the Iranian in the leather jacket passed through the group of people leaving the building. Cohen was interested, but he was also visibly disappointed that Cyrus Shirazi appeared to have no part in the possible brush pass.

"This is still not conclusive," Cohen said, inviting more discussion.

"Look, we saw this guy pass an envelope to one those people. The same guy you killed tonight. Raad's guy. Who else would he be passing notes to?"

"So which of those people were passed the envelope?"

"That's the best part," Casey said. "We sent the digital photos to Detective Paul Giordano in New York. He was able to use facial recognition software at JTTF, which I assume is tied to some huge federal database...anyway, he was able to ID two of them." Casey sat back down, and Andie read Giordano's email over his shoulder while he summarized the findings.

"No ID on the tall dude with dark hair. The woman is Erica Stanley. A staff photographer for *Potomac Life* magazine. They have an office in the building where we saw all this. The third person, the shorter, balding guy with the trench coat, his name is Walter Korzen. A career State Department employee who works the DSS watch desk."

"DSS?" Cohen asked.

Andie answered, "Diplomatic Security Service."

"I think that's our guy," Casey said.

"Why him?" Cohen asked.

"Why not? If the tall guy didn't show up in Giordano's database, chances are he's a nobody. And what business does State have at that office building?"

"You said NCRI's Washington office is in that building," Cohen offered.

"But what would a DSS watch officer have to do with that? Unless I'm wrong, watch officers—in any agency—just man a desk and watch their computer screens. Hence the term *watch* officer."

"They answer phones, too," Andie said.

"Okay. Point is, I'd bet your paycheck this guy was at Horus Rhind and that he's in The Council," Casey said. "And if he's in The Council, getting notes from Raad, he's gotta be the leak."

They sat in silence. Cohen thinking. Andie and Casey waiting for Cohen to speak.

"So how do we confirm that? We don't have time to surveil him, and if he is our man, and Raad has been in touch with him tonight, it's possible he's gone off the grid by now," Cohen said.

"Parker," Casey said.

"What?"

"Scott Parker. If Korzen's in The Council, I bet Parker knows him. Or at least knows who he is. And if Korzen's the leak, Parker's gonna want to know about it."

"So how do we find Parker?" Cohen asked. "Again, we don't have any time to waste."

"I can get Jerry Blocksidge on it," Andie said. "He found Parker pretty quick last time."

"Whoa. Hold on. I said Parker probably knows the guy, but what makes y'all think he'll talk to us? I was thinking sending the guy an email or something. I got the impression from our last meeting, when I just showed up wanting to talk, that he didn't like me much," Casey said.

"An email? You're not serious, are you?" Andie asked.

"You both have valid points," Cohen said before a debate started. "We need to find another way to get Parker to meet us. Tonight."

"Well, what's *your* idea?" Casey asked with a bit of frustration in his voice.

"Miller," Cohen said.

"What? You said he was dead." Casey turned his palms out, wanting an explanation.

"He was alive when I left him. And yes, there's a good chance he didn't make it. But there is also chance that whatever he was stabbed with didn't kill him before he got to the hospital."

"I don't believe this," Casey said to himself.

"But we don't know if he even made it to a hospital," Andie said.

"Correct. That's what I need you to find out," Cohen said.

"I just ask if there was an 'Adam Miller' admitted this afternoon?"

"He might not even be using that name," Cohen said. "Just ask if they had someone brought in with a pen casing stuck in his neck." He noted Andie's quizzical look and sidestepped it with another request. "And then see if your friend can find Parker for us."

"So we *are* going to see Parker," Casey said, not particularly keen on meeting him face-to-face again, though he had opened the door by bringing up the the man's name in the first place.

"Yes, but after we go see Miller and have him convince Parker to talk to us.

"*If* Miller's alive."

Cohen nodded. "That's why we need to know where Parker is going to be. If Miller is dead, we will have to convince Parker to talk to us on our own."

Chapter 41

It was almost 11:30 p.m. when Casey and Andie arrived at Scott Parker's brick-front townhouse in McLean, Virginia. By all appearances, it was a modest dwelling for the middle-class D.C. suburbs, but Casey knew it cost close to a million dollars, given its proximity to the District proper. *Just like New York*, he thought. The closer you were to where the action was—in this case, running the government of the United States of America—the more it cost to live there.

Andie had used her media credentials and a little white lie of trying to corroborate eyewitness statements to locate the hospital where Adam Miller was taken. Cohen was right, in a way. The nurse she talked to at the MedStar Georgetown University Hospital informed her that a "John Doe" with no identification and a plastic pen tube in his neck was brought in at 5:37 that evening.

"Damnedest thing I ever saw," the nurse said. "I mean, I've read about emergency tracheotomies and even seen pictures of 'em in textbooks, but to see one for real—and one that actually saved that man's life—that was something else."

Andie gave Cohen the good news, and he immediately took a cab to the hospital. He called her an hour later. Miller was alive and recovering. The emergency room doctors were able to stabilize him quick enough to run a battery of tests to determine what had caused the paralysis that closed his airway and nearly suffocated him. A corynebacterium and diptheriae bacteria cocktail with a neurotoxic venom of the kind found in a Mojave rattler had apparently been injected into Miller's abdomen with a large-gauge needle. Cohen commented that the concoction was probably homemade by someone with a rudimentary knowledge of chemistry. Each ingredient, deadly enough in isolation, seemed to work against the other. The result was a slower-acting poison that gave the doctors enough time to administer their own combination of antidotes and life-saving medications.

Miller was groggy and weak, but lucid enough to call Parker from a cell phone Cohen "borrowed" from a purse he commandeered in the female employees' locker room. Miller didn't say what Cohen's friends wanted from Parker. Not over an open cell line. Especially from a phone with unknown pedigree. Parker agreed to meet with Andie and Casey as a favor to Miller, but without any information regarding the nature of the visit, he couldn't guarantee he'd be any help.

Parker answered the door in gray sweatpants and a purple Northwestern University sweatshirt. He led them into the study and motioned for Andie and Casey to sit in a brown leather setee by the wall. Parker turned an armchair in the middle of the room to face them.

"So, Mr. Shenk, what is it you needed to talk to me about?"

Andie fielded the question before Casey could answer. "We were outside the Rosslyn office building where Horus Rhind is located this afternoon, and we believe this man," she handed Parker her phone, "Walter Korzen, is the one compromising Israel's operations against Iranian scientists which The Council is helping facilitate."

"The Council is an urban myth," Parker said, still examining the picture on the phone's screen.

"C'mon, man, just admit it. We know The Council exists. And we know you're part of it," Casey said. "I've been through too much shit and almost been killed on more than one occasion because y'all keep playing this game. So why don't you cut the bullshit."

"Casey, stop it," Andie said.

Parker flipped the phone back to Andie, who caught it with one hand in mid-air. "I think we're done here."

"You can't hide the truth forever. Eventually it will come out, and y'all will be finished."

"Casey!" Andie barked. "Fucking drop it!" She leaned forward and held the phone out to Parker again. "Please," she said softly. "Just take another look. Adam Miller wouldn't have asked for this favor if he didn't believe us. And we really need your help."

Parker looked for sincerity in the woman's eyes. It was there.

"Please."

Parker shot a warning glance to Casey, sitting quietly next to Andie, and took the phone.

"That's Walt Korzen," Parker confirmed. "I don't know who the others are."

"The woman is a magazine photographer," Andie said. "And we don't know who the other man is."

"But the guy in the leather jacket is one of Davood Raad's people," Casey added.

"If you scroll through the pictures, you can see the man in the leather jacket with an envelope in his hand before he walks through the group. And in the last pictures, the envelope is gone. We think he slipped a note to Walter Korzen as they passed each other," Andie said.

Parked swiped back and forth through the pictures, zooming in and out to get different views. After a few minutes, he handed the phone back. "This is hardly conclusive," he said. He held a hand up when he saw Casey about to speak and added, "But...I agree that it's likely this man passed an envelope to one of these people."

"To Korzen," Casey said.

"Okay. To Korzen. He fits the profile."

"The profile?" Andie asked.

"Insider threat. Maybe not everything that would raise flags with his co-workers and supervisors, but he's definitely a disgruntled employee. I wouldn't doubt that he's been counseled for his attitude, but I don't work with the man on a daily basis."

"Just at Council get-togethers," Casey said.

Parker ignored the comment. "How do you know the other man works for Raad?"

"He was with Raad when he was killed tonight," Casey said. He looked at Andie. "Along with the guy who put Miller in the hospital."

Parker noticed the looks exchanged between the two people in front of him. Miller hadn't said much when he called earlier, but he did tell Parker he had been stabbed and poisoned, and that the man responsible was dead. What Casey Shenk was telling him did not contradict Miller's story, and seemed to add substance to events he saw reported on News Channel 8 that evening. Reports with more questions than answers. Ms. Jackson and Mr. Shenk provided plausible, if only partial, answers.

"Okay," he finally said. "I'll help you."

Casey let out a long breath and leaned back in the sofa.

"Thank you," Andie said. She pocketed her phone and folded her hands in her lap. "We think that after what happened tonight, Raad and Korzen may be preparing to disappear, if they haven't already. We might be too late, but we had to try."

Parker shook his head. "Raad might be moving to get out of the country, but he has to land somewhere. I'll make a phone call, and we'll have people at every final destination and connection for every flight leaving the East Coast today and tomorrow. If he is still in the country, he'll be in custody soon enough."

"And Korzen?" Casey asked.

"Korzen's not going anywhere," Parker said.

"You're sure?"

Parker nodded. "Korzen may want to be James Bond, but he's not. If there's one thing I know about Walt Korzen, it's that he is afraid of disruptions to his routine. That's part of what makes him so frustrated with his current position at State. So, no. Walt Korzen's not going anywhere."

"So should we pick him up him up tonight?" Casey asked. "I mean, just in case? If you give us his address, we could go get him. Or Lev Cohen can."

"Cohen. The Mossad guy you and Miller worship?"

"I don't worship..."

"No," Parker interrupted. "I'll take care of Korzen." Parker stood up. The meeting was over.

Parker unlocked the front door when they reached the foyer. Before he opened it, he said, "Thank you for your help in this matter. And I hope I never see or hear from you again." He shook Andie's hand. "It would be best if you forgot about all of this."

Parker took Casey's hand and gripped it hard. He looked him in the eye. "Forget about *all* of it."

Chapter 42

"No. I'll be back tomorrow....Right, later today....I don't blame him. I said I'd be back Wednesday, but some other stuff came up....Look, I'll tell you about it when I get back....I'll tell him at work....Well, he'll just have to wait 'til next week....Okay....Uh-huh.... Goodnight." Casey hit "end" on the phone and set it on the coffee table.

Andie walked in with two glasses of water. She handed one to Casey and sat on the couch next to him. She had changed into pajama pants and a baggy t-shirt while Casey called Susan Williams. Casey received and ignored several emails from Susan over the previous two days. With things in D.C. now out of his hands, and given the ALL CAPS order for Casey to stop blowing her off, he dialed Susan's number as soon as he and Andie got to her apartment.

"How'd it go?" Andie asked.

Casey shrugged. "About like I expected. Susan's disappointed in me for leaving the rest of the office to pick up my slack. Jim wants to fire me, but not really. Susan said everytime my name comes up, Jim rants about 'broken trust,' and how I deserve what I get."

"Is he going to fire you?"

"I don't know. I think he meant I deserve whatever happens to me down here, though." Casey took a sip of water. "He warned me to stay away from Raad and The Council before I left. Guess he figured I'd get myself killed or something."

"Does Jim know Raad's a spy?"

"I doubt it. He would have told me. He just knows Raad was the guy who pointed me to The Council in the first place, and he knows firsthand that if you keep pushing them, and they think you're a threat, The Council will disappear your ass in a heartbeat."

Andie sighed. "From what I've seen this week, I'd say he's right."

"Yeah," Casey said. "Guess I got lucky."

Andie pulled her legs up under her and turned to Casey. "So you're heading back?"

Casey leaned forward and put his elbows on his knees. He let his vision blur as he stared at the center of the coffee table, his mind running through his options. "I'll drive back mid-morning, I guess. Catch a few hours of sleep at the hotel, pack my stuff, grab a stale muffin from the 'continental breakfast,' and face reality again."

Andie put a hand on his shoulder. A gesture of comfort. And friendship. "If things don't work out in New York...." She let the sentence hang.

Casey looked at her and smiled. "You're a good friend, Andie. I'm sorry I brought all this shit to your doorstep."

Andie returned the smile. "Anytime, Casey."

Casey stood and put his phone back in his pocket. Andie stood, and the two friends hugged. Casey put on his coat and opened the door. He turned and faced Andie one more time. "Thanks again for saving my life today. Thanks for everything."

Andie nodded with a smile. "Just do me a favor, and we'll call it even."

"Anything."

"When you get back to New York, shitcan that welfare jacket you're wearin'. World War II was over a long time ago."

Casey laughed and touched the brim of his Braves cap. "Yes, ma'am." He leaned in and kissed her on the cheek. "Later, Ms. Jackson."

The door shut, and Andie stood smiling.

"Later, Mr. Shenk."

Chapter 43

Walter Korzen locked the door to his apartment and plodded down the stairs to his car. He received a message the day before from Davood Raad warning him that the Israeli sent to find whomever was compromising the Jewish state's operations to assassinate Iran's scientists was possibly narrowing his search to members of The Council. Raad admitted he had no hard evidence that this was the case, but whatever clues led him to that conclusion were solid enough for him to send Shahin with a note delivered in broad daylight. In a crowd of people.

He didn't know if Shahin was the man's real name, and frankly, he didn't care. He had met the man two months earlier in a hotel room where he gave Raad information on the planned assassination of a missile engineer in Dubai, and again on two other occasions. So when Walt saw him as he was leaving another meeting of The Council on Thursday, he was ready for the brush pass. Raad told him that method would only be used if he had urgent instructions that couldn't wait for the normal dead drop or signal protocols that invariably had time lags as much as three days before the two could meet face-to-face.

Korzen opened the envelope when he got home. Five one-hundred dollar bills and a handwritten note. Because of the new "threat," Raad wanted Korzen to lay low, and they were to have no contact for a week. He suggested Korzen take some time off from work, and he was adamant about staying away from any Council meetings. The money was a show of good faith, meant to assure Korzen that his services were valuable to Raad, and that the break was only temporary. Korzen had no problem with that. But the note was another confirmation of what Walt already believed—Raad was a pussy.

Korzen didn't question the man's effectiveness. The reports he gave Raad were obviously getting to the right people, and the *Quick Note* program was a failure. Korzen had killed it. But *Turnstile* was different, and he knew next to nothing about it. After Thursday's meeting, he learned that the intelligence he passed to Raad two weeks earlier had thwarted the first *Turnstile* operation, but the discussion around the room led him to conclude that luck may have played a factor.

Tweaks were going to be made in the security surrounding *Turnstile*, and future meetings about those operations were going to be by invitation only. If Korzen stayed away from the office and skipped the open Council meetings, he was sure to be left off that list. The way he saw it, he needed to be more engaged than ever if he was going to be any use to Iran in thwarting Israel's Mossad attacks. Raad was too scared to see that.

But Walt wasn't afraid. He knew before he started that he was taking a huge risk by talking to Raad. Some people—most actually—would consider him a traitor. Those were the people who didn't see things as clearly as he did. Even members of The Council, who were doing what they thought was best for the country, didn't understand they were doing just the opposite by helping Israel.

The world needed a nuclear Iran. If for nothing else than to keep Saudi Arabia and rest of America's "partners" in check. For a long time, Iraq served that purpose, keeping everyone on both sides of the Persian Gulf and in the Levant on their toes. Saddam Hussein had no use for friends, so he found himself surrounded by enemies. And he built one of the most powerful militaries in the region to keep those enemies at bay.

When America removed Saddam in 2003, dismantling Iraq's military and government for good measure, Iran was left as the only real threat to the Arab kings and princes who ruled with a collective boot on the neck of the underpriveleged masses. The Islamic Republic's conventional military might was tempered by the seemingly endless subsidization of everyone else's militaries with American cash and defense exports. As a result, countries like Saudi Arabia and the United Arab Emirates were wasting money on useless construction projects, manipulating the world's oil market, and evicting the very same U.S. troops that provided the protection they needed to continue their free-wheeling, free-spending, devil-may-care lifestyles—spoiled kids with overprotective parents afraid to discipline their children.

Walt Korzen believed a nuclear-armed Iran would force the kids to stand up for themselves. Maybe then America could disengage from the area on its own terms and re-establish its proper role as the world's only superpower, which was not the same thing as being the world's policeman. American armed forces did not need to fight everyone else's fights, particularly when the beneficiaries were ungrateful brats. Let them get bloody and work through their own problems. Then they would beg for America's help, and the U.S. could dictate the terms of any defense agreements. The U.S. government had walked on egg shells around the Middle East's leaders for too long, and Korzen saw a shuffling of the deck as necessary for America to regain the respect it deserved.

The day Raad recruited him to spy on The Council for the Islamic Republic of Iran, Korzen saw an opportunity to personally boost America's prominence on the world stage. He wasn't helping Iran, he was helping the United States of America. He was a patriot, not a traitor. And he was willing to give his life to that end. He would take a bullet from a Mossad assassin if that's what it took. Raad apparently wouldn't. *Pussy.*

Korzen put his briefcase in the backseat of his car and got in the driver's seat. He put the key in the ignition. As soon as he started the engine, two doors opened and slammed shut in the space of two seconds.

"Morning, Walt."

Korzen froze.

Beep. Beep. Beep. Beep.

Scott Parker. Another man he had never seen before was in the backseat behind Korzen with the barrel of a .45 caliber pistol pointed at the back of Walt's head.

Beep. Beep. Beep. Beep.

"Put your seat belt on so that fucking noise stops."

Korzen reached for the key. "I'll just..."

"Leave it on. We're going for a little ride."

Beep. Beep. Beep. Beep.

"Walter...seat belt," Parker said.

Korzen did as he was told.

"Good," Parker said, buckling his own seat belt. "Wanna get some coffee? I can't think clearly without my morning coffee. You know where Caboose Cafe is?"

"Yes," Korzen said softly. Sweat beads popped from the top of his balding scalp.

"Great. Caboose it is. I'm buying."

Click.

Korzen jumped. When he realized he wasn't dead, he turned his head slowly and saw the man behind him smiling behind the pistol still pointed at him.

"Everyone's buckled in," Parker said. "Let's go."

They drove for ten minutes in silence. They only traveled two miles, but for morning rush hour in D.C., they were making good time. Parker figured it would only take them about fifteen minutes to reach the cafe, which is why he chose it as their destination.

"So, how's work, Walt?" Parker asked.

"Okay, I guess." Korzen didn't take his eyes off the road, partly for safety reasons in all of the traffic, but mostly because he was afraid to look at Parker directly. It wasn't that he was afraid of Parker, but every glance in the rearview mirror reminded him that one wrong move could mean a bullet in his skull.

"Just okay? I would think it was better than 'okay.' First line of defense at State, a seat on The Council. You're making a difference, Walt. There are thousands of govies in this town who just punch a clock and collect a paycheck. They might tell theselves what they do is important, but even they know that's bullshit. But not you. You've got access and opportunity. Yes, sir. That's real power."

Korzen turned the car into the parking lot behind Caboose Cafe. Parker directed him toward the back of the lot.

"Leave the car on," Parker said. He unbuckled his seat belt and turned to Korzen. "Tell me something, Walt. What business do you have with Davood Raad?"

"What? The writer?" This time Korzen faced Parker. He saw the gun with his peripheral vision. It was still pointed at him. "I don't have any business with him. I met him after one of his lectures once, but that was months ago." He looked at both of his "guests" in turn. "I haven't even seen the guy except that one time."

"Walt," Parker started, shaking his head. "Don't lie to me, Walt. We know you've been talking to him. I just want to know what you two discuss when you get together."

"Nothing."

"You don't talk about anything?"

"No, I mean I've never talked to him except that one time after the lecture."

"You're doing it again, Walt. You're lying to me."

"I'm not lying. I..."

Pop!

"Oww! Fuck!" Korzen exclamed after the man in the back seat slapped his bald head.

"We have pictures of one of Raad's goons handing you an envelope yesterday, Walt. What was in it? Was it a message? Money? Both? What did the message say?"

"I didn't get any..."

Pop!

"Shit! Stop it!" Korzen was breathing heavy.

"We have pictures, Walt." Parker sighed. "Davood Raad is an Iranian spy. The man who gave you an envelope outside Horus Rhind yesterday was working for Raad. How do you think that looks? I'll tell you. Not good, Walt. Not good at all."

Korzed stared blankly at Parker.

"It's not just the pictures, either, Walt. Raad's messenger...he was killed last night, along with one of his friends when they were meeting with Raad. Now Raad hasn't admitted that you're his agent, but he will," Parker said. A white lie in the guise of certainty. Korzen didn't need to know that Raad was not apprehended yet.

Korzen ran his hand over his stinging skull and wiped the sweat on his pants as he faced forward again. *Raad will give me up*, he thought. *He'll be extradited to Iran. Maybe traded for that Marine of ours they're still holding. And I'll be executed.* He took a deep breath. *Or maybe I'll just be locked up for life.*

A sudden thought occurred to him, and he almost gasped. *Or maybe nothing will happen to me! They can't let this get out. A public trial will expose The Council and America's part in Israel's assassination games. If the trial is classified, that will attract the press like moths to a flame. And the government can't stonewall them forever. Too many bloggers and conspiracy nuts will catch wind of it and turn up the heat. They can't afford that either.*

"Okay," Korzen finally said. "I *was* working with Raad. But when you hear why, you'll understand."

"I'm all ears."

After ten minutes, four muffled bangs rang inside the car. But no one was in the near-empty parking lot to hear them. Two men exited. When parker's companion confirmed there was no visible evidence on the fogged glass of the four slugs that entered Korzen's torso from behind through the driver's seat, he gave Parker the thumbs up. Parker locked the car and shut the door with the engine still running.

"Wanna get some coffee."

Chapter 44

Dasht-e Kavir, Semnan Province, Iran

A solitary bird darted among the wilting shrubs, its nimble legs a blur as it navigated the arid terrain. It was early March, and it would be another four months before the dark-stemmed mugwort that pocked this portion of the Great Salt Desert bloomed, providing some cover to mask the bird's movements. Despite the ground jay's nervous flitting, it was anything but nervous. The only living things around bigger than the bird were two stationary figures five hundred meters from the lone dirt road that dissected the north and south horizons, but the bird discounted them as predators. They had been there for two days, and the bird was still alive.

"Two uniforms. One suit."

"Got 'em."

"Thick dark-rimmed glasses. Salt-and-pepper beard. Burn scars on right cheek."

"That's him." Miller turned the windage adjustment one click and moved his left hand to the rifle butt tucked into his shoulder.

"Meters, six-seven-three."

"Six-seven-three," Miller repeated.

*   *   *

Nouri Behzadi raised a hand to his forehead and peered west down the long dirt road. A rising cloud of dust preceded the intermittent flashes of sun relecting off the truck's windshield. "Here it comes," he announced to the two soldiers who accompanied him outside the underground facility. The two armed men turned in the direction the scientist was facing.

Behzadi was awating delivery of a replacement part for the explosive yield measuring system before Tuesday's scheduled test. If everything went as planned, he would be back in Tehran in time for his youngest son's sixth birthday. He'd been away from his family for much of the previous year, and he felt he was missing his children grow up. His wife was doing an excellent job keeping house and raising the kids, but Behzadi knew from his own experience that children, especially boys, needed their father at home.

The truck was now clearly visible. Behzadi could make out the color of the vehicle—tan, faded to a dirty white. The sound of its rumbling, jolting approach echoed off the craggy outcroppings on either side of the road and shattered the desert silence, drowning out even the chatter from the two soldiers talking just ten feet away.

Behzadi took a handkerchief from his pocket and removed his glasses to wipe the sweat off his face. He never felt the bullet enter his skull just above the left ear. He certainly never felt it exit, taking most of the right side of his head with it. And no one heard the shot. Behzadi's lifeless body crumpled to the ground.

He was not going to make it to his son's birthday party.

"Target down," Cohen confirmed and lowered his spotting scope.

Chapter 45

Savannah, Georgia

The squeaking hinges of the Sunset Tavern's front door announced Casey's arrival.

"Hi, Casey," the co-owner of the establishment called from behind the bar where she was drying glasses before Happy Hour.

"Hey, Maude."

Casey left the Intelligence Watch Group four weeks after he returned to New York. A four-hour car ride and an entire weekend gave him time to think. Time to unwind from the events of the past week. And time to contemplate what was in store for him next. He expected to be dressed down by Jim Shelton, and even Susan, but he wasn't fired. Which surprised him.

Instead, Casey's penance was unpaid overtime with Jim. News broke early Sunday morning of Dr. Davood Raad's apprehension at Dulles International Airport. Clean-shaven and wearing platform shoes that made him two inches taller, Raad was attempting to leave the country on a fake British passport—the reason the news report gave for his arrest. Casey knew better, and Jim wanted to hear all about it. So for a week, Casey sat in Jim's office after working hours and recounted his entire trip to the nation's capital. In painstaking detail. And Casey left nothing out.

The information sessions with Jim were almost like a form of therapy. When Casey answered one question, Jim asked another. Hearing himself narrate the events of the last five years, from Mike Tunney's death and his introduction to Lev Cohen, to the bombing at Soren's Deli, to his interrogation in D.C. and close call with a Qods assassin wielding a poison pen knife, made Casey seriously reconsider his own view of himself and the life he was living.

He wasn't invincible. He knew that before any of this happened, but you'd never guess it by some of the bonehead decisions he made. He was lucky. But someday—probably soon—that luck would run out. He remembered Scott Parker's assessment of Walter Korzen. "He may want to be James Bond, but he's not." And neither was Casey.

Maude popped the cap off a Rolling Rock and set it down as Casey took a seat at the bar.

"Thank you, ma'am." Casey pushed the sweat-stained Braves cap back on his head and looked at the old man three stools to his right. "Anything new, Jas?"

"Not since 9:42 this morning." Jas Filmore didn't look away from the television monitor behind the bar. He sipped his Scotch and kept his eyes on the ticker at the bottom of the screen. That was where the breaking news was posted first, and Jas didn't feel the need to wait for some talking head to tell him with pictures what he could just as easily read for himself. The fact that he was still "watching" the news didn't seem to boththter him.

Casey had only been back in Savannah for just over a week, but it was almost as if he'd never left. He thought of Susan, Jim, George Smithfield, Paul Giordano, Lev Cohen, Andie Jackson, and even Oscar Horstein as he took a long pull of his beer. He would miss them. They had each touched his life in one way or another. And Casey knew that their inclusion in his life, if only briefly, had made him a better person. He hoped. But it had been time for him to leave.

You can only cheat death for so long, and Casey had done his share of dodging the grim reaper over the past half-decade. Next time he might not be so lucky. And that's what it was. Luck. Sort of. It damn sure wasn't his physical prowess or superior intellect and cunning that got him out of those tight spots and near misses. Hell, that's what usually got him into trouble in the first place. No, it was almost always someone else who possessed the qualities he didn't have that pulled his feet from the fire just in the nick of time. And he knew that.

Despite the protests of some, particularly Susan Williams, Casey put in his two weeks notice at IWG and was gone by the end of February. With the ides of March just three days gone, Casey was home. Having a beer in his favorite bar on the Wilmington River in Thunderbolt, the smell of Naugahyde and old lacquer on the furnishings filling his nostrils and flooding his mind with memories. Good and bad.

He was working as a deckhand for a small tugboat company on Hutchinson Island in the Savannah River, just across from the famed River Street. Pushing construction barges up and down the river, occasionally bringing water to the dredges constantly fighting to keep the waterway navigable, was certainly more demanding than filling breakroom vending machines along Abercorn, but it was also more rewarding.

Casey left Georgia out of necessity, or what seemed necessary at the time, and he returned for essentially the same reason. He was through with international conspiracies. Finished with political intrigue. He was done putting his life in danger chasing the truth behind the news. He was back to being a regular guy, with a regular job, living a regular life. And that was just fine with him. Casey even stopped posting to his Middle-Truths blog. He just wasn't interested anymore.

He finished his beer and asked Maude for another.

"Bodies of three Ukraine businessmen were found dead in a shipping container at Gwadar Port in Pakistan," Jas reported.

Casey looked up at the TV and took a drink.

Well...maybe one more blog post.

About the Author

Matthew M. Frick is a retired naval officer who has lived overseas and traveled extensively throughout the Middle East and Europe. His writings have been referenced in journals, theses, and other media in over five different countries, including India, Russia, and Iran (translated into Farsi and located on the official Majlis website). A native of Stone Mountain, Georgia, he currently lives in St. Johns, Florida, with his wife, two children, and a bluetick coonhound.

32533506R00172